For Brenda Thompson,
who founded Moose House Publications
to make adventures like this possible.

Contents

1: That morning

Andrew Wetmore

September 5, 2020

As Rob pulled hard on the lace of his right running shoe, his phone started buzzing like a wasp in his shirt pocket. He jerked backwards, snapping the shoelace, before he had quite realized what the sound was.

He dug the phone out of his pocket. The screen said *Private number*. Nobody he wanted to talk to had their phone number blocked.

Rob held the phone gingerly until the buzzing stopped, then put it back in his pocket. It started ringing again immediately. He put it down on the stump he was sitting on and let it do its thing while he worked on the shoelace.

The stump was beside a trail that used to be a railroad track. No shoelace emporia within handy walking distance. He tried knotting the two sections together, and then had to puzzle how to get the lace back through the eyelets in a way that was functional, if not aesthetically pleasing. The result was a knot that seemed to press down on his instep.

He undid all that work and tried just using the longer section of lace. That would do, as long as he didn't lace the shoe all the way up.

So much for looks. The next question was, could he actually run with the shoe like that? Damned if he was going to let a little bit of lacing change his plans.

With the onset of COVID restrictions, the gyms were closed. Rob soon got a little tired of jogging the too-familiar, too-crowded streets of Wolfville, so he had given himself a little challenge: run the rail trail from Wolfville at least to Weymouth, then maybe see if he could continue all the way to Yarmouth. Why? Just to say he had done it.

He would grab the bus west out of Wolfville, get off where he had stopped running the last time, put in five or ten kilometres, then catch a bus back home. Lots of new sights to see, and no potentially-sick person breathing on him.

The further he got from Wolfville, though, the more time it took to get to where he would run, and get back again. On top of that, the big new project was taking up more and more of his time. It was only 166K from Wolfville to Weymouth, and he was two-thirds there now, but it was September 5 already. He was beginning to wonder if he would make it to the Sissiboo Landing Information Centre before Christmas.

Rob stood up and flexed his foot. Good enough, perhaps. Not like these were race conditions or anything.

He did his stretches, checked his watch, and then started off west along the rail trail, working up slowly toward cruising speed.

He didn't know this part of the trail well. East from Annapolis Royal, all the way to Wolfville, the trail was tended, groomed, sign-posted and ready for anything from a stroller to an ATV. This stretch, heading toward Digby, wasn't getting the same sort of love.

It had its positives, though, like not having to dodge strollers and ATVs. He set a pace that would let him enjoy the scenery but do something good for his heart, lungs, leg muscles.

Along this stretch, the rail bed was far enough in from the shore that it had houses on both sides: to his left, the fascinating backyards of homes facing Route 1; to his right, the muted facades of snazzy newer homes with waterfrontage. Driveways ran down from the highway, across the trail, to each of these waterside residences. Rob wondered if the two sets of residents ever hung out together, shared a joke, borrowed or lent a tool.

The dog with the bared teeth arrived suddenly from one of those newer homes: no warning snarl, just a peripheral flash of body and intent.

Rob jerked sideways, kicked out awkwardly at the dog, cried, "Get off!" and pitched off the trail into a shallow ditch. His ankle landed hard on something and he cried out again.

The dog seemed to be gathering itself for a second attempt when Rob heard a voice shouting commands. The beast threw him a look of regret and then lurched away in the direction from which it had come.

Rob sat up, then tried to stand up. His right ankle would not work at all. He step-hopped out of the ditch and sat on the edge of the trail, dripping forlornly. The shoe with the short lace was gone.

"What do you think you're doing?"

It was a woman's voice. He looked up, and the woman attached to it was standing at the head of a driveway that crossed the trail just ahead of what would have been his route. The dog was nowhere to be seen.

"I thought I was running."

"Nobody runs here."

"Is this private property? This rail trail?"

The woman paused. "The driveways are. Nobody around here runs here. They run on the track at the Y."

"I run there. But it's closed."

She brushed hair out of her eyes. "Well, that's no business of mine. You shouldn't run here."

Rob struggled to his feet. The pain in his ankle was at the same time less sharp and darker, more ominous. "I hurt myself."

"Did he bite you? He only bites people who—"

"No, no. I fell. He surprised me and I just...fell."

They stared at each other across the width of the trail. She looked to him like an actor who used to be in a show he used to watch. A little older than he was, but well out of his league. He was pretty sure he looked like something pulled out of a stopped drain. "I'm Rob."

"Oh," she said. "Allison. How bad is that?"

"I don't think I should walk on it."

She looked each direction along the trail, up the driveway, back at the house she must have come from, a brick-fronted structure that seemed to spread and spread between the treeline and the water. "Crap."

Looking past her, Rob could see a silvery SUV in front of the garage. "I hate to ask, but could you give me a lift? I'll try not to ruin the upholstery."

She met his eyes. "No."

"No?"

"That car—I'm not supposed to use it. It's just for emergencies."

"Hello: I'm your emergency for today."

Allison looked around again, like she was expecting someone. "It can't be that bad. I'm sure you can get to your car and be out of here."

He shook his head. "My car's at home. I came by bus."

She looked blank. "There's a bus?"

"Of course. But the next one is not for–" he glanced at his watch "–-more than an hour."

She put her hands on her hips. "Why would you use a bus if you have a car?"

"I would be happy to explain," Rob said, "while you drive me to the health centre."

"I can't—"

"What's your civic address?"

"Why?"

"My other choice is to call an ambulance. And I need to tell them where I am."

"We can't have official cars coming here."

He was patting his pockets. "Well, you're in luck, then. Because I've lost my phone."

"Where?"

"If I knew that..."

They looked blankly at each other for a bit. Rob was feeling a sort of shiver spreading through him. *Shock*?

Allison was suddenly beside him, a cool hand on his forehead. "Are you going to faint?"

"I don't know."

There was another pause. Then she said, "Crap. Okay. Stay right there. Don't come to the house."

He wanted to say, *Like I have a choice*, but she was gone, running lightly toward her house and that car she was not supposed to use.

~

The coughing was starting again. It seemed to come a bit earlier each morning.

Mona sat at the kitchen table with her hands around her mug of cold coffee, listening. At least Doug had the strength to cough. Sounded like a sea lion, even from this distance.

The toaster finally did its thing. She buttered the toast, put it on a plate and the plate on a tray with the small teapot, his favourite morning mug, the marmalade jar, the glass dish of orange sections, and this week's copy of *The Berenson Bulletin*, four pages this time. She left out dry cereal, eggs in case he felt none-vegan this morning, soy sausages: she could gauge how he was feeling by how much he complained about being starved to death.

The *Bulletin* made her smile, and sometimes him. Their Toronto grandkids wrote it—poems, jokes, cartoons, silly news items—and their mom laid it out on some computer program and sent it off to the olds, still in the family home in Middleton, within whistle sound of where the train station used to be.

Mona picked up the tray, admiring the smoothness of the handles. Doug made it for her birthday, the first year of their marriage, and it was everything a bed tray should be. His first three failed attempts warmed them in the wood stove, but he kept at it until he got it right. Which is why they celebrate her real birthday in March and her tray birthday in the early summer each year.

She climbed the stairs with a heavy tread so as not to startle him by appearing by surprise in the bedroom doorway. He called it his pedal alarm clock.

Sure enough, his eyes were open, narrow slits but open, when she came into the room. He was lying on her side of the bed, with the whole tangle of sheets and quilt thrown to one side. He looked hot.

"Morning, captain," she said. *The next test.*

"Morning, mate." His voice was gravelly, but he made the right response.

She sat the tray on the bureau and fiddled with it with her back to him while he grunted his way into a more upright position, pounding the pillows until they submitted to his idea of what was proper. "There's a new edition of the *Bulletin*," she said to the mirror. "Shall I read it to you while you eat?"

"No, thanks, love." He cleared his throat a few times. "I have to work my way through what they write two or three times to get the full sense of it. The first time is to work out if it's supposed to be funny."

Mona picked up the tray, moved its legs to the open position, then placed it across his thighs. Doug threw her a fleeting smile. "Not sure I can get around all this."

She nodded. "Pick away at it and leave the rest for the birds."

"This is just my summer cold," he said, fixing her with an earnest look. "Every summer. Regular as clockwork."

She nodded again. She didn't say, *You had your summer cold in August, Doug*. Instead, she said, "You could have that pretty young doctor listen to your chest."

He actually blushed. "What, and go sit among all those sick people? Even that little girl is not worth *that*."

"If you change your mind, do it before lunch time."

He poured himself some tea. "This will be gone by tomorrow, with the blessing."

"I'll start the wash, then," Mona said, "and let you get stuck into that massive meal."

She pulled clothes from the hamper in the corner, then paused at the trousers he had left crumpled on the floor. "Can I wash these? They'll be ready later if you need them."

Mouth full of toast, he waved his hand like an emperor's blessing: *do as ye ween.*

The trousers were heavy like a sack of treasure. Mona unloaded each pocket, separating Doug's necessities (a pocket knife, a tiny screwdriver, coins, a complexity of keys) from huge, damp wads of tissues. There were no crumpled receipts, as he hadn't been out of the house for days.

She set the necessities down on the bureau, thinking, *If he hasn't been out for days, then our mailbox must be full*. Then she looked at the key ring, lying splayed on the top of the bureau, and paused.

Why were there two mailbox keys? They only ever had the one box, even when his contractor business was going full-blast.

Keeping her back to the bed, Mona teased the keys apart so she could look at them. One of the keys had a bit of paper taped to it, with what might be the box number written in Doug's scrawly hand. *Not our box number*.

She turned, not sure exactly what to ask him, and Doug was asleep again. Two bites of toast and a sip of tea.

Mona slipped the key ring into her skirt pocket and gently lifted the tray. She abandoned the laundry project for now and walked the tray downstairs.

In the kitchen she checked the clock. *Might be a good time to go collect the mail.*

~

Natasha, secret agent, was on her way to meet a source. She was all in black—turtleneck, short skirt and tights, even her beret—but this was Wolfville, a college town, and she was pretty sure nobody would look at her twice.

If she saw anyone she knew, they would only see her cover identity, which she had been working on almost since her birth nearly twenty years ago. Good old Natalie Mayne, on her way to some humdrum undergraduate task.

The key was to see strangers, watchers, before they saw her.

She would take a different route than she normally took to throw off anyone staking her out; but, again, this was Wolfville, a one-and-a-half horse town. To take a different route she would pretty well have to swim up the river from the Minas Basin.

Not much traffic, so nobody tailing her. Natasha drove into town like any normal person, at just 5k over the speed limit. She would have preferred to walk, but her source might have a package for her that would be awkward to lug home without drawing attention.

She tucked her car into a space that magically appeared on Elm Avenue and was in position ten minutes before the appointed time. There was a white hatchback parked in one of the spots in front of the library, sticking out like a sore thumb because the library was closed.

Natasha checked her notes. 'Cindy. White Juke.' Then she glanced around just to be sure before popping the note into her mouth and swallowing it.

She strolled across the main lot, approaching the white car from behind the driver's left shoulder. The person in the car seemed to be alone. *So far, so good.*

Natasha tapped on the driver's window, and the person behind the wheel jumped as if she had been shot. She whipped around and Natasha had a quick image of red eyes, pale skin, fine jawline and kissable lips before Cindy, if it was she, put both hands up to her face.

"Hi," Natasha said. "I'm, um, Natalie."

Her inner voice was saying, *Kissable lips? Where did that come from?*

The person in the car said something that sounded like 'Cindy', so that was okay. She started scrabbling in her purse.

Natasha glanced around, trying to be casual about it, but there was nobody close enough to worry about.

Cindy produced a mask and started to fumble it into place. Hiding her other features made her eyes stand out even more. For sure she had been crying.

Natasha realized she had forgotten to pack a mask. *We didn't used to have to do this.* She drew up the neck of her turtleneck over her nose and mouth. It would have to do.

Cindy lowered her window halfway. "I didn't expect you yet."

"Well, here I am. Do you have the stuff?"

Cindy nodded. "In the back." She turned away, hauled down her mask, and blew her nose on a tissue.

"Are you, like, okay?"

The mask was back in place, but Natasha could tell Cindy was trying to force a smile. "Sure. Peachy. It's just a, an allergy."

"I'm glad I saw your ad," Natasha said. "I've been looking for these for a long time."

"I'll pop the trunk."

Natasha walked around to the back of the car and lifted the hatchback. It was like a jumble sale inside.

"One of the boxes on the right," Cindy said to her rearview mirror. "Take the box, too."

"Are you leaving town? I mean, is this like a moving sale?"

Cindy's shoulders heaved but she didn't say anything.

The first box had a jumble of computer stuff–keyboards and a tablet and some sort of mystery gizmo from Apple. The second box was books. The third one was the jackpot.

She dropped straight out of Natasha, straight out of her story, into Natalie Mayne. The plates were just exactly like the ones her mom and dad had at the cottage, back when she still had a dad and a cottage.

The complex willow-pattern design gradually revealed itself as you ate your food, and you could almost always find a new detail you didn't remember from the last time you'd studied the plate. The bridge, the tea house, the courting birds, the boatman, the wattle fence that guarded you from the mysterious world beyond the edge of the plate.

Natalie climbed back into Natasha. "These look good. Six, right?"

Cindy nodded.

Natasha lifted the top plate to check for cracks and chips, even though she already knew she had to have them. And then she froze.

The plate was heavier than she expected; thicker. She turned it over and there was no maker's mark. *No way this came from Walmart.*

Cindy was watching her in the mirror. "These are better than I thought."

"Good."

"I mean, maybe I got the price wrong."

"You don't want them?"

"I do. I do want them. But I thought twenty bucks was for the whole six."

"It is."

Natasha shook her head. "You can get way more than that for these. I'm no expert–"

Cindy ran both hands through her hair as if her head was aching. "If you want them, take them."

Natasha looked around quickly. Nobody seemed to be focused on them. *Probably not a trap*. "Okay, I will. I'll put the box over here..."

She sat the box down gently, as if it were the enormous egg, then turned and closed the hatch. She walked up to the driver's door, thinking fast.

Cindy, in her mask, was looking straight ahead.

"Do you want to grab a coffee?" Natasha asked. "There's a place–"

"I have to go." The car engine started up.

"I wish you would tell me about the plates. They're so beautiful. I would love to know their story."

Cindy turned to look at her. Her eyes were lovely where they weren't sorrow-red. "They're yours now. That's their story."

"Are you okay?"

The car moved out of the parking spot quickly and Natasha flinched to one side. Cindy spun the wheel and the car moved off with an un-Wolfville squeal of tires.

Natasha looked down at her hand. She was still holding the twenty.

She peeled down her improvised mask so she could breathe and went to pick up the box. She took a step toward her car and paused. A smile spread over her face. She heard an authoritative voice in her head.

Deliver the money. Find out what's going on. Rescue Cindy. That's your next mission.

2: And on it goes

Pam Calabrese MacLean

As Mona walked to the mailboxes the keys seemed to grow heavier, as did her steps. She knew from experience that some secrets are best kept hidden. She tried to remember if she had ever kept a secret from Doug.

She blushed for not immediately recalling their next-door neighbour, and the almost affair. It was years ago but all the same it was more exciting than most of her life with Doug.

She walked briskly past the mailboxes, made an abrupt, almost military, about face and returned home. She was almost running.

Once in the house she leaned against the door frame, listening for Doug. Her breathing was ragged, which made hearing anything else unlikely.

When her breathing smoothed she crept upstairs to find her husband sound asleep. Downstairs again, she hid the keys, grabbed her purse, yelled to Doug that she was walking to the store for a few things.

She didn't like to drive so much anymore. That was Doug's job. And once again the question of her managing without him flashed in her head. She was sure his coughing was more than a summer cold.

Mona checked her purse for her mask. She disliked being in public but her nephew had tested positive and couldn't bring groceries anymore. Once again she wished she had more family in Middleton.

A man walking toward her said a masked 'Good day.' Mona realized she hadn't talked to anyone except Doug for quite a while.

As if right on cue she spotted her friend Cora in the garden on a brightly multi-coloured chair.

She called to Mona, "Come, take a load off!"

This had been a running joke since they were in school together. Mona had always been feather-light. Cora was the opposite. Mona remembered her own mother describing Cora 'so round, so firm, so fully packed.'

The friends sat apart together.

"I know it's early but I could make short work of one of your famous martinis right now."

"I could produce a couple if you're willing to take the risk."

Mona gave her two thumbs up and let her eyes roam Cora's garden. Mona did not plant one this year. She'd been so tired. Still was.

"Drinks up!" Cora carried two glasses and a frosty pitcher out to the table between the chairs. She set the glasses on the garden table and filled them to the brim.

"Your garden looks amazing. Makes me wish I'd pushed myself."

She took a sip of her drink, "God, I've missed your martinis!"

"And I've missed you, Mona."

"I'm to the point that I even miss people I don't like!"

They sat in the garden for as long as their martinis lasted. Cora saw that her friend was wrestling with something.

She produced two baskets from under the veranda, handed one to her friend. "Let's do a late pick in the garden before martini number two. Maybe you can tell me what's got your knickers in a knot?"

Mona told Cora about the second mailbox. It was niggling her, but instead of feeling better, she became more agitated. She trembled her way back to the chairs and sat for a moment before she started to cry.

Cora sat beside her, filling their glasses. "There has to be more to it than that."

"Exactly! But I don't know what it is!"

"What worries you most?"

"Doug. He's sick. Coughs like he's a two pack a day smoker!"

"Okay. I get that. But what does it have to do with a spare mailbox?"

"Nothing! Makes me hope it's another woman." Mona burst into tears again.

"What's he saying about the cough?'

"Summer cold."

"He could get tested."

"He won't."

"Maybe you should?"

"What good would that do?"

"Well, if Doug was worried about you. Your nephew was positive, right?"

"Maybe. Where is it they test?'

"We could phone the Health Centre. They'll know where you should go."

"I don't have my phone."

"I dropped mine in the washer. I think the rinse cycle did it in! The rice doesn't seem to be working. I'll drive you, Mona. And I can wait for you."

"What? Kill us both? Or are you thinking about getting us arrested? I'll walk. No laws against drinking and walking."

"As far as you know!"

"I love you, girl."

"Back at you! Stop on your way home. You can take some veg."

"I promise."

~

Just as Mona stepped off the curb in Middleton, Doug bumped his way down the stairs to the kitchen at home. He tried to stand. He had not realized how weak he'd become.

He held onto the counter and made his way around the kitchen. He searched every drawer he could reach. When he stopped huffing and puffing he grabbed a kitchen chair so he could sit to reach the lower drawers.

By all that's good and holy, what did I do with those keys?

He wanted to scream. Mona always told him that screaming is a limited salvation.

Thinking about Mona reminded him: pants; wash; pockets and the bowl Mona kept on the table to hold 'laundry treasures'.

In the bowl were coins, his pocket knife, a tiny screwdriver and his mini-flashlight from a previous laundry. No keys!

Doug sank into the chair he'd been pulling around and sat staring at the wall until he became aware of Mona's phone on top of the fridge. He summoned all his strength, stood up, fell back with the phone in hand.

He frantically dialed, drummed his fingers on the table while he waited. As soon as he got voicemail, he hung up and dialed again.

~

Rob regretted not asking the whereabouts of the car she *is* allowed to drive.

Allison drove the SUV back to Rob as if it was blown glass. Rob was supine on the ground.

He sat up as Allison pulled a ginormous black plastic bag with a zipper from head to foot out of the vehicle. His whole car would fit in it!

For a minute he thought she was going to put him in it, but instead she pulled it over the front passenger seat. She had two small bags that Rob put over his feet before he earned the right to get in.

Getting in took all their strength and a good deal of ingenuity. Rob hoped it might forge a bond.

"Does anyone drive this?" And in his hokiest voice, "Cleanest car I ever did see!"

Allison's scowl made him forget all about his foot and scared him. He jumped and hit his bad foot under the dash and that made him remember it!

After what seemed like a decade since his last breath, Rob tried again. "What do you do?"

"I don't."

"I'm guessing you don't want to play twenty questions?"

"Give the boy a prize. I don't do small talk."

"Okay, let's do big talk. Like your *big* house. Who lives with you?"

"No one!"

Rob thought big house, two vehicles and she only gets to drive one. Interesting and suspicious.

"Are you a spy?

"Are you an idiot? Or is this what pain does to you?"

"No I—"

"Shush!"

"Listen, ma'am, I need to relieve myself."

She gave him a killer look.

"I'm serious. I really need to go. Just pull over and I can take care of myself."

"You can get out and back in with no help?"

Her phone rang and for almost a minute she said yes, yes, yes. She hung up and turned down a road he did not know. Maybe a woods road? A shortcut to town? The last place he'd ever see?

She turned to him and smiled, "I'm so sorry I was such a bitch. I'll come around and help you out."

This whole 'friendly' Allison scared him more than anything else she'd done.

"Getting you out was way easier than getting you in! I'll sit in the SUV until, well, until you're done."

Rob rolled down into a ditch. Ditches were becoming a habit! Then he heard the SUV start and beepbeepbeep as she backed out of the road and headed in the direction of her house, if it even was her house.

After a good number of curse words Rob thought he should take stock of his situation. Already he felt he had been on his back plenty long enough, penance for a sin he couldn't remember and a pleasure he was sure he hadn't felt.

Rob had lots of time to reflect on his day so far—broken lace, broken bone (his ankle resembled a tree burl) and he could not think what to think of the woman. He knew he had a fever. Was she really as negative as he thought? He wrestled with that one for a while until his inner voice said, *A fever can not throw you out of a car and dump you like so much garbage!*

With a little wiggling Rob managed a more forgiving piece of ground. Few rocks and no traffic. No traffic meant no rescue. He'd figure something out in a bit. He felt warm and safe, and he dozed off.

Suddenly he was too awake. There was a silver SUV making its way toward him. He realized it wasn't Allison when a bag of muscles got out, grabbed him up and threw him onto the back seat.

"Why don't you answer your effin' phone?"

As he was trying to convince himself that this was Allison's SUV, Rob noticed a fibreglass partition separated the front and back seats. As hard as he wracked his brain he could not place it in Allison's car. But he could also not 'not place' it there.

He slept again and woke as they reached the Health Centre. Two ambulances were just arriving.

"Jeez, Allison, we're going to be here all night." Rob's voice had started to slur.

The booming male voice rattled the partition, "How do you know Allison?"

Rob passed out. He was half-aware of being picked up and placed (gently this time) into a wheelchair.

Waking again to his new friend he asked, 'What's your name?'

"Nothing I'm telling you."

"Okey dokey, smokey," Rob managed to say before he passed out again.

In and out of consciousness had quickly come to be the same thing. Was he talking or was it the guy?

"Why were you phoning? You don't know me."

"I had eyes on since you broke your lace."

"Why?"

"Nobody runs there!"

"I heard that somewhere before. Why are you waiting with me?"

"Now, isn't that just the question on everybody's lips?"

"Why don't you answer me?"

"Need-to-know, and you don't."

"You don't have to wait. I can get a cab home."

"Not on my watch!"

Then the nurse was there to take him away.

The young doctor stood over Rob's bed. Rob struggled to focus. Broken ankle, minor surgery, sign here. So he did. He wondered how they knew him and his address and on and on. He was sure he had told no one.

He woke in a different room. He asked if his jailer was still waiting. The nurse laughed and pointed to the chair beside the bed. Rob closed his eyes, opened them several times before he could see clearly.

"Allison?"

~

Natasha picked up the box and strode to her car. She put the dishes on the passenger seat, scooted around to the driver's side and got in. She had decided that rescuing Cindy needed immediate attention. She thought if she hurried she might catch-up and follow her.

She tore away from the curb in hot pursuit of her latest mission. She wondered what she might be saving Cindy from and if she wanted to save Cindy for her own entertainment.

Natalie, usually quiet in Natasha's presence, asked, *What type of entertainment?* Natalie often let the air out of Natasha's spy life and shook what confidence she had. Not this time. Natasha was focused.

She turned the CD player on and Peter Gunn's theme song filled the car. Natasha cranked it louder. It drew a few stares, but Natasha knew she was invisible in black.

The Nats drove around for an hour before spotting Cindy's car. It was parked outside a century home that had likely been a half-century apartment for half a century.

She drove around the block four times: twice with all left turns and twice with right. Making sure she wasn't being followed.

On the last circuit she parked on the opposite side and four driveways before Cindy's car, and settled down to watch. It was very warm even in the shade of the huge tree so Natasha was reluctant to put on her black hoodie, but it too was part of her camouflage.

She napped and almost missed Cindy, who was taking boxes out of her car and carrying them in the front door of the house.

Natasha didn't waste any time getting to the door. With her face to the wall, she stealthily slid along the hall toward an open door.

Cindy emerged. Her shoulders were hunched forlornly and she'd been crying again.

Natasha melted into Cindy's apartment and sat in a chair that faced away from the door. *I am a shadow. What if I scare her and she never wants to see me ever?*

Natasha did a rewind back to the hall. She stood hidden by the open door.

Cindy arrived with boxes, set them down and closed the door in her face. *Never saw that coming!*

Natasha knocked on the door.

"Hello. Who are you? Oh, the dishes person...no refunds."

"I've been following you to—"

"To rob me?"

"No. I wanted to give you the money for the dishes."

"Very nice of you."

"Then my curiosity got the best of me. The crying, the red eyes, the screeching tires, you know."

"So much for the good Samaritan act. My roommate kicked me out."

"Not so hard to get a new roommate in a university town," Natasha said.

"Can we leave it at that? Will that satisfy you?"

"No. I don't think I can do that."

"What's it to you, anyway?"

"Well, I have another reason for being here."

"Do tell."

"I will if you will."

Cindy frowned. "Will what?"

"I'll question you and you have to answer. Or forfeit. Then you get to question me.""

"Can I trust you with my secret?"

"Yes! And once you know mine you'll understand."

"She was more than a roommate. We were partners."

"Business?"

Cindy gave her a funny look.

"Oh. Not much of a secret these days. So you're bent."

"But I'm not broken."

Cindy sat and waved Natasha to another chair. "So your turn. I've forgotten your name."

"Natasha. I'm a spy."

Cindy guffawed and kept on laughing until tears rolled down her cheeks. Natasha was offended.

"It's true I'm a spy and I'm here to rescue you!"

"Oh, sorry. I get it now: by day a mild-mannered student; by night a raving lunatic!"

Natasha stood up abruptly. The vase that was sitting on top of boxes tumbled. Natasha was able to snatch it from thin air.

"Well, you rescued my mother's vase. I shouldn't have laughed. But I feel like I've been crying forever. Sit down, please. I'll make a pot of coffee. Please."

After the girls had consumed too much coffee Cindy said "I'm anxious to unpack. Thanks to you. I sure didn't feel like that two hours ago."

"I'd love to help, but I have to go to Middleton. Someone wants to buy some of my school books and I need the money so I can buy more books. Yay, university!"

Natasha stood up to go, then paused. "I could come back and help with the unpacking then. I'll only be gone a couple of hours. What do you think?"

"I could whip up some supper."

"I'm a vegan."

"Me, too."

As Natasha was getting in her car, she saw Cindy watching her through the uncurtained window. She lowered Peter Gunn before she started the engine, then pulled out sedately.

None of this was lost on Natalie. *What's up, Tasha?*

Natasha growled. *So glad I decided to save secret you, Natalie, for another time!*

The trip to Middleton flew by. She stopped for gas before she headed home. She pulled out, pleased about the money for books, the willow pattern plates and, most of all, a new friend.

She almost didn't see the woman step off the curb into the street.

She jerked the steering wheel hard and her front tire hit the curb. The car flipped several times, spewing its contents out the open windows. It landed on its roof and slid shrieking towards the woman.

Natasha saw the woman's face as the last of the plates hit the road and shattered.

3: Iceboats

Marie Mossman

At the Middleton hospital, Rob lay in his bed. Now that his eyes worked better, he saw the light blue sky and part of a maple tree through a rectangular window opposite him. A few of its leaves had turned red.

An aide pushed a trolley with a metal basin of water and a face-cloth into the small room. Beside the basin was a short pencil, and a lunch menu.

Allison moved her chair to the far corner and sat there, still and quiet.

The aide positioned a mirror for Rob, and then rushed away. He groaned when he saw his reflection. He was sweaty and his skin more sallow than usual. Had he been drooling?

He wiped his face and combed his short dark hair with his fingers. He stuck the menu under his pillow.

And then he looked, for the tenth time, to the end of the bed where his injured foot lay on top of the thin hospital blanket. His toes peeked from one end of the cast.

The morph must be wearing off. I won't ask for more. I'm tough. I can stand it.

He remembered painted white lines. They hadn't registered in his conscious brain earlier, but now he was certain they existed. One ran on the shore side of the trail, from the shore to the brick structure on Allison's property, and partway up the structure. In his mind it was Allison's property.

Was the brick structure part of the house or not? Doesn't matter. *I was in the ditch long enough to know the building's there.*

It's got two extra white lines going partway up the shore-facing wall. The painting makes most of the wall look like a double garage. Unless you really look, and then you see it's one extra wide, extra high door.

His mind started a list of possible reasons.

Why would they need it for a regular residence? It's not a regular house, dummy. It's posh. Flying in from Toronto for the weekend? Maybe, if they're rich. Gotta be, with a shore-front estate. Okay, they're rich. Maybe they have a disabled child, or granny they want to protect from viruses.

Maybe....No. Not socially acceptable, especially if true. Forget it.

Did any of his legal reasons for the *trompe l'oeil* wall explain Allison—her alternating bitch/helper/abandoning-bitch behaviour?

If they're running drugs, is there any point reporting suspicions?

The young doctor now stood at the doorway of his room. "You're a lucky boy. Your bones were in place. They won't need resetting. End of my shift. Any questions?" She forced a smile and started to turn away.

"Yes, Doctor, please. When will I get more morphine?"

"You didn't have morphine." She rolled her eyes. "We gave you an infusion, so we could get the cast on. You were thrashing like a baby with colic. Buy a painkiller at the pharmacy when you leave." Her tone was not sympathetic.

Sheesh! Just as well I kept my trap shut when she called me 'boy'.

"I've recommended you leave as soon as you can. Better for everyone." She nodded her head toward Allison, who smiled like the helpful angel she wasn't.

"Doctor, please don't go. I need a taxi." His muscles went taut.

"I've been on duty for twenty hours. I fix bones. I don't call taxis. Work it out with your friend." Doc walked away.

Grey clouds moved in, turning the rectangle of sky dark.

There's gotta be a call bell I can push for help.

He pretended to scratch his head, looking and feeling around his pillow for a cord or anything that might lead to a bell.

Allison sat up straighter and looked in his direction.

He settled back, closed his eyes, and faked falling asleep.

When he heard Allison mumbling into her phone, he let his arm knock the basin of water off the trolley. As the basin fell to the floor, he grabbed the pencil.

The crash brought the aide to the room. "Is everything o—Oh! Be right back."

"I need help. Call your supervisor, call anybody. I beg you," Rob said. He was flushed, and fidgeting with the edge of his blanket.

"Miss, he got agitated," Allison said in a calm and authoritative voice, "It happens often. I can handle him. Best thing is, I take him away."

"Are you sure? The doctor's gone, so I can't ask her."

"I've already called a car. He doesn't need a taxi."

"You're talking about an adult man," Rob said. "I'm not going anywhere, except where I want to."

He wiped his forehead with the bed sheet in a clumsy manner, grabbing the menu as part of the action, and pushed his blanket off while stuffing the menu into his underpants. "Get this woman out of my room, so I can talk to you alone. She's dangerous."

"You're the one who threw the basin," Allison said. She turned to the aide. "You see what he's done already. You don't want to be alone with him if he's in a temper, Miss."

Rob heard gruff words coming from the hallway. He recognized the voice. His muscles sent their strength to his brain. He could see the thick black eyebrows before they appeared. The right one had a bald patch in the middle. Check. The muscle man's long arm had a serpent tattoo. Check.

Rob pointed to the muscled man. "He's got my phone."

He must have trouble finding shoes big enough.

Allison arose. "Here's my helper. Popa and I'll take the boy off your hands."

Cindy's not gonna be pleased if I don't show.

Rob's hand went to his underpants.

Later, the triage nurse tidied her desk. When she picked up a crumpled menu, she deciphered:

Rob W k'napd. PH cops

She acted.

~

Cindy, behind the window pane, had the sensitive pale skin associated with Scottish ancestry, or generations of winter in Nova Scotia. She soothed her bleached hair with rinses, pampered her skin with creams, and painted her face to emphasize her fine jaw. The chemical mix sent her grandmother into fits of sneezing whenever they met indoors.

She didn't need or want another spy in her life, but this silly twit of a student might be amusing. They'd have dinner, unpack a few boxes of kitchen stuff, and then she'd whack her forehead with her hand, remember her previous commitment, and wish the sharp-boned, frizzy haired spy-child goodbye.

I can't invite her to the Iceboat Race with my operatives.

She put a bulb of garlic and two quiches to bake in the oven. One quiche was flax, lentils and spinach. The other was the same, with bacon. Cindy never skipped meat on her vegan-lapse day.

While she waited for Natasha's return, she reshaped her iceboat, which had been re-solidifying in the freezer. It was a mess.

Not enough papier mâché? Too long out of the freezer?

What if my fingers get—what do they call it? Chilblains, or frostbite? Can't happen with the air twenty degrees Celsius.

Her fingers burned from the cold, but when she dipped them into her soy-yogourt container of papier mâché, its room temperature soothed them. She coated her boat with a layer of the pulped paper.

"In the name of Michelangelo, I christen you *HakaHaka*. May you sail far and long."

She returned her reinforced boat to the fridge's freezer, alongside her insulated lunch box.

Remember, gir-r-rl. It's for the Cause.

She checked the Iceboat Insiders' Poster for errors, again—*Per-*

fect.

ICEBOAT RACE MEєT-UP

5th September 2020

6 PM Atlantic

Gaspereau River Tubing push-off Site

All Regional Operatives invited

Bring your boat, mask

&

Playful Plaudits & Plaints

Post Race, Action Plan Agreement

Five o'clock, Natasha was still not back.

She's more of a twit than I thought.

Cindy bit into a slice of bacon quiche. Saliva flooded her mouth. *I'm glad I switched to the vegan-lapse option. I'm gonna tell Rob we should sell 'Lapse Certificates' for the Cause. When you crave meat, buy a 'Lapse Certificate', and you may indulge in one meat-loaded meal. We alleviate your guilt, and you finance our cause.*

Perfect. Like my poster.

She picked up her lunchbox, with *HakaHaka* inside, and then locked her apartment. She put the key under her mat, and a note on the door: "Natasha, help yourself to dinner. I had to go out. Key is under the mat. ♥Cindy."

Rob has a cell. I know he's gonna be at the race, unless he calls. We're running this cause right.

~

Cindy, now at the push-off site, checked the time on her phone. Six-thirty.

No Rob. No anybody. The old guy down west is sick, but the operatives in Middleton never miss a meet-up.

A child's black t-shirt lay at the water's edge. No kids were around. No laughter to lighten the moment.

"What the hell."

She placed *HakaHaka* on Gaspereau River's edge. Her warship braved the current until it ran into a fallen branch and melted into the river. The twenty-two centimetre ice warship had floated a grand total of four metres. A few bits of shredded paper clung to the branch or continued their travel on the dark water's surface.

"Five hours to shape. Five minutes to float. Better than most of my creations," she said in a flat voice, to an audience of zero.

She trudged back to her white car, Fitzi.

Wasn't the best colour choice for life in the land of red mud, was it? Maybe I should have asked for the Chinese assignment. I thought it'd be easier here, where I know the culture and can speak the languages.

She tuned Fitzi's radio to the government update. 'Don't touch your mask' and 'Keep within the Atlantic Bubble'.

She switched stations, looking for something lighter, and caught a local news report.

"—this afternoon, a one-car accident in Middleton. Police suspect reckless driving. The alleged driver's injuries are life-threatening. Positive identification of this person is impossible. There may have been a second person in the car. If you have information about a Natasha, or Tasha, in the area, contact the police or our Anonymous Tip Line."

Cindy could not imagine what had happened.

~

The windscreen glass had shattered into crumbly pieces. Natasha had floated straight ahead in clear autumn air, until she skidded to a stop, face down, beside a disposable coffee cup on the concrete sidewalk.

Natalie saw herself from all angles at the same time. Scattered above, below, and around her were pottery shards. This was new. She liked to play being out of body, but never before had she achieved such a magnificent sensation or maintained it for so long.

People rushed to her from the nearby bistro. A young man phoned 911.

"I know first aid," an older woman said. "Don't move her."

She knelt beside Natalie. "We're with you. Help is coming."

The ambulance siren pierced the air, and its red lights flashed. It arrived in four minutes.

~

"In other news, a Caucasian man may have been kidnapped from the hospital in Middleton. If you know the whereabouts of Rob Williams, or his cell phone number, contact the police, or Citizens' Crime Preventers."

How can media people read tragedies with such glee?

Cindy drove her Fitzi east to the convenience store to park. Her eyes were red, her cheeks wet, her heart pounding, when she called the police. "I'm acquainted with a Natasha who intended to drive to Middleton this afternoon."

She headed, then, to Highway 101 and turned west toward Kentville, where she phoned the Citizens' Crime Preventers hot line. "Rob Williams said he would take part in the Iceboat Race Meet-up at Gaspereau River this afternoon. He didn't show, which is out of character."

Rob's a decent man. Why would anyone want to harm him?

Cindy drove toward her new apartment in Wolfville. She relaxed her shoulders and took a deep breath. It was easier on the eyes and safer driving at this time of day, with the sun coming from behind.

Six minutes before she arrived home, a man with a well-chiselled face had parked a black car across the street from her apartment. She didn't notice him sitting in the car, or the vehicle's sturdy antenna.

In front of the door to her apartment, she lifted the corner of her rug where she had placed her key. The key wasn't there. It was close to the other corner of the rug. This she did notice.

Once inside, she engaged the security bolt, the first time in her life she'd used one, and then tiptoed around the apartment, checking closets and under the bed for an intruder. There was no one.

She fastened the windows, then filled a tall glass with Cabral Port.

If they've taken something, they've taken it. Too tired. What else can happen?

~

"I'm glad to see you back in one piece," Cora said. "Did you see the accident? Was it as bad as the radio said?"

"Awful," Mona said.

The scraping sound from the metal on pavement and concrete. A thud when the body landed.

"By the time I realized what happened, the ambulance was blaring, so I stayed out of the way. I don't know why anyone would have a crash there."

"I'd give you another martini, but it wouldn't—"

"I'll take it."

"Okay, one."

Cora plunked a basket of tomatoes, zucchini, and kale on the deck table. "No rush for the basket. You might want an excuse to talk to another human."

An ambulance zoomed by, its siren blaring. "It's going toward our place. I hope Doug hasn't—"

Mona ran off, without her martini or veggies.

And there the ambulance was, dominating their driveway. Her kitchen seemed full of large bodies in uniforms, plus Doug.

"What did you do?" She stood inside their kitchen door and gasped between words.

"Your damn phone. Don't need an ambulance. Cancelled the call, 'cause I pulled myself up. Send them away. I don't want a damn ambulance."

"An ambulance was called in your name, sir. We should examine you. Make sure you're not at risk." The first responder spoke as if patients screaming at him happened every day.

"Gentlemen, I'm his wife, Mrs. Berenson. It looks like he had a problem while I was out. I'll sign for the ambulance charge. And watch that he's okay." Mona smiled and nodded like a bobblehead.

They watched the EMTs clump away to their ambulance. The junior guy was shaking his head.

"Where did you put my keys?" Doug said.

"I'll find them—after you tell me why you have a second mailbox key."

"If you have to put your nose in, I got a job. It's for buying presents."

"Now I know. Shall I pick up your secret mail?"

"Go ahead. I can't get it myself." When his next bout of coughing ended, he said, "I need to lie down. The air's too thick."

They plodded upstairs together, and she settled him before going out for the mail.

Both boxes were full. One letter in this mystery box was unsealed. Mona made little sense of its message about code names, forwarding procedures, and recompense by positional advancement. It contained an iceboat race poster. The letter was signed, *Cindy.*

Is Cindy a person, or a code name? I don't see honest money coming, whatever the game. It's difficult to know what's serious. And if it is, is it dangerous?

~

Cindy woke in darkness, at three in the morning. A half-full glass of port sat on her bedside table.

I was out of my mind to pour that much.

She switched the light on when she entered the kitchen for a glass of water. A metal disc the size of a loonie caught her eye. It was attached to the wall above the sink.

There are two of them. I don't remember seeing them before.

She went to the bathroom. Similar devices were there.

I'll check the bedroom and living room in the morning, when it's more natural to be in them. If this place is bugged, who's behind it? The Captain hasn't alerted me to such measures.

She composed a ditty on bugging, similar to schoolyard chants of the 1950s, which amused her until she slept again. But times have changed, and if asked, she would claim to have forgotten it.

She woke next to daylight, filtered by the towel she had stuck up with duct tape for lack of a curtain rail and curtain. It was seven o'clock. She made a mental groan. *I'm too awake to go back to sleep.*

She yanked her duvet smooth and laid out clothes for later—shorts, a t-shirt, undies, a bra. *Yes, a disk on each wall.* Her search for a book in the living room revealed the same result.

Keep cool gir-r-rl. What would I do, if I were dumb enough to not notice?

She made her latte, slathered her toast upside down with butter, flipped it and added an insane amount of strawberry jam. *Check.*

Next, she used the Cause's private watermarked paper to write four versions of a report to the Captain. She crumpled the ashes of the three that admitted complete failure.

Heavy metal music and a smokey smell that wasn't tobacco leaked through the wall she shared with the other upstairs apartment.

She re-read her report.

> Dear Uncle Captain,
>
> I ran the seasonal IBR yesterday, the fifth of September 2020. My HakaHaka won. She braved the waters for a total of four units of distance, and five units of time. I am proud to continue research which was encouraged by a great leader, during the Second World War.
>
> Conditions in Southwest prevented attendance by usual

race contenders, and therefore our expected plan for muihtil is on hold.

It is HOT here today.

Our mail is slow, because an essential worker is ill.

Are further IBR team safety measures required?

Seeking direction,

C

4: A bad day in Manhattan

Garry Leeson

Doug Berenson knew he should have been more careful with that key. He should have explained it yesterday; he had planned to, but that damned ambulance came rushing in with sirens blazing. He was so scared, shocked and dizzy that, even though he finally realized that he had accidentally dialed 911, he felt he might actually need their assistance.

But Mona, good old Mona, as usual, was there to rescue him and; but she had been giving him the silent treatment ever since. F*unny, she didn't even ask me why the shotgun was leaning against the wall at the foot of the stairs, just out of sight.*

Now he would have to come clean and tell her everything. But what did that matter now? If the doctors were on the money with their diagnosis, he wouldn't be around much longer: Stage 4 lung cancer, inoperable, terminal—a year to live and nine months already gone.

He sat on the side of his bed, rehearsing what he was going to say to Mona while he waited for her return.

He heard the back door open and close. Suppressing a violent coughing fit as best he could, he struggled to his feet and made his way cautiously down the stairs, holding onto the railing for support.

Mona was surprised to see him coming into the kitchen this early. It had been ages since he had been there for breakfast. "Sit down, you silly man. You shouldn't be up. It's too cold in here; you'll catch your death."

It was something that, later on, she wished she hadn't said.

Doug almost fell into his chair pointing to where she always sat opposite him.

"I'll sit, Doug, but first let me get you a cup of tea; you look awful!"

"No tea, thanks, Mona. Just sit and listen. This is important."

Mona reluctantly turned the burner off and moved over to settle in her chair.

Doug began speaking, pausing to take laboured breaths. "There's something that I have wanted to tell you ever since we first met, but couldn't."

"What, what now?"

"Just bear with me, this isn't going to be easy. I don't know if you used that other mailbox key, but if you did, please let me explain."

"Who is she?"

"Oh, that it would be that easy! Don't be ridiculous. There is no one else. Ever since I met you and your ready-made family, I've never even thought of anyone else. I love all your kids and their kids—I think they feel the same way about me. But I need to explain something about my life before we met. I couldn't before but it's imperative that you know about my other life."

"Your other life? What the hell are you talking about?"

"Please, Mona, just hear me out."

Then, in an effort to get her to understand the seriousness of what he was about to impart, he shouted, "My name is not Doug Berenson!"

"What...?"

"At least, it hasn't always been Doug Berenson. My given name was Henry Williams, and that was the name I used before I moved to Nova Scotia."

"But why did you change it?"

"I had to change my name. My life was in danger and, not only that, I need to tell you that I was married before and that our kids have a step-brother from my first marriage."

"What...? Did you get a divorce? God, I hope you got a divorce."

"Don't worry about that, the FBI made sure it happened."

"The FBI...?"

"Okay, this is going to be a long pull, so I think that you better go and make that tea for us, after all, and then sit down and let me start at the beginning so I can tell you the whole story."

Mona did as he asked, wondering what on earth was in store for her, almost hoping that his worsening condition had made him delusional. She looked quizzically at his face as she passed his cup over to him, sat down and took a careful sip of her own tea.

"Fasten your seat belt, Mona; this is going to be a long and dangerous ride."

"Stop; wait. Before you spin any more story, tell me about this son you say you have."

"He's real. His name is Rob. He's, what, twenty-two, twenty-three—"

"You don't even *know*?"

"I've been out of touch with him since he was a baby."

Mona looked around the kitchen. There was nothing that was going to wake her from this nightmare. She took a deep breath. "Okay, then. You have to tell me the rest."

Doug took a deep breath. "As I said, my name is, or was, Henry Williams, and I was not born in Toronto. I was born in New York City. I was married, but my wife—well, she died quite a while ago. I thought I'd struck gold when Maria agreed to marry me. I really loved her. She was a beautiful woman and part of a very wealthy Italian family.

"Her father took a shine to me and set me up in a well-paid position with one of his construction businesses. He gave us a house on Long Island and we settled into a happy, pretty-privileged lifestyle. Maybe I was naive, maybe I should have sensed that there might be more to her father's business than building hotels for local tycoons, but I didn't. Do you know what the Mafia is, Mona?"

"Everybody knows about the Mafia, but what's that got to do with you?"

"It has a lot to do with me and I wish it never had. I was busy working on one of those high-rise towers in Manhattan about a year after we were married. One night I got worried about a special job I was supervising and went on my own to make sure everything my father-in-law wanted was shipshape. He was a perfectionist. The neon lights were just coming on in Times Square. When I was up in the building I went over to the side of the unfinished penthouse to take in the view of the city. It felt like the top of the world.

"When I heard the sound of approaching voices my first instinct was to call out to whoever it was. It had to be somebody from our company; we were the only ones with access to the building. But something in the tone of their voices made me stay silent and hidden in the shadows.

"There were five men and one of them was not a willing participant. Two of them were big guys who were always around my father-in-law; just there, never saying anything. I won't go into the gory details of what I saw, other than to say that there was heated conversation. A redheaded man who developed hotels and golf courses was complaining that my father-in-law had overcharged him on one of his projects. He wanted recompense. My father-in-law pointed to a little man and asked if this was the fellow that had collected the money from him. The redhead nodded. My father-in-law motioned to the two heavies. They picked up the little man and threw him over the ledge. My father-in-law then turned to the developer, handed him a thick wad of bills and said he hoped this, and his accountant's unfortunate accident, had settled accounts. The developer just chuckled and they all headed down and out of the building.

"I went home to Maria that night a terrified, angry man. I couldn't say anything to her. She was due to have Rob any day and the doctor had said that she needed to stay calm and quiet or things might not go well for her.

"It was a year before a full investigation began into what the papers were calling a mob hit. All the senior managers at our firm were persons of interest, including me. At my first interview with the NYPD, I claimed to have no knowledge of the incident and that I certainly didn't know that the New York Mafia was the company's silent partner.

"Don't ask me why I had a change of heart, but I did. I cut ties with my wife, my son and her family, and agreed to testify about what I had seen up in the tower that night. Maybe it was because Maria had started to confide in me about some of the things her father had done before; I mean, she knew! I didn't want to be associated with any of her family and their businesses. It meant giving up Rob, but I just couldn't stay quiet, and I figured once he was older—oh, hell, I don't know!

"The FBI knew that my testimony, or even the threat of it, would amount to a death sentence for me, so they put me into a witness protection program. I gave evidence during that trial and again during the period of appeals. My father-in-law was found guilty and sentenced to thirty years, even if it was in one of those minimum security prisons for mob bosses, corrupt politicians and crooked business tycoons.

"The safe places that the FBI found for me in the States proved not to be safe at all, so they decided to send me up here. That's when I met you, and the rest is history—the best history!"

Mona sat silent for quite a while before she asked, "What about the letter box? Is that how you keep in touch with the FBI?"

"Good Lord, no. They wouldn't do that. It was something completely different. About a year ago I got a letter for Henry Williams but care of me, Doug Berenson, and I knew the jig was up. 'They' were onto me and it would be just a matter of time before an accident of some sort would find me. I've always tried to keep a low profile, but I guess I let my guard down when I let that magazine publish the story about our new business and they printed a couple of pictures of us. I thought it would be just local, not something somebody would post on Facebook.

"Anyway, whoever penned the letter seemed in no hurry. They seemed more interested in letting me know about Rob. They instructed me to get a post box so that they could keep me up to date on his whereabouts. I was curious, so I agreed."

"But why did you tell me the box was just a business account for presents? I guess I wasn't being ridiculous and jealous when I asked who 'she' was. Who is Cindy, anyway?"

"You read the letter?"

"Yes, of course I read the damned letter!"

"Can I see it?"

"It's your letter."

Mona went to where her purse was hanging on the kitchen door, took out the envelope and tossed it over to Doug. She was still in a bit of a huff.

Doug pulled the letter out, opened the folds and silently read for a minute or two. Then he turned to her.

"First off, I'm not sure what this Seasonal IBR, *HakaHaka* and Muihtil mumbo jumbo is all about. This is nothing like what I've been getting in the past. Maybe it's code—I have no idea. This looks like a photocopy of a letter for someone else that got passed on to me."

He had to pause for a bit to deal with a bout of coughing. Mona didn't shift in her seat.

When he had his breath back, he said, "What worries me is that it seems to have been sent by a 'Cindy', and I was informed by my FBI contact that somebody named Cindy was living with Rob."

"This is getting too crazy, Doug. I don't know what to believe. And why the hell was that shotgun loaded and sitting at the bottom of the stairs yesterday?"

"The ambulance had me scared."

"Why on earth would you be scared of the sound of an ambulance?"

Doug passed a hand over his face. "Back in the States, there were a couple of attempts to kill me before the trial. One attempt was two guys disguised as policemen who arrived at my safe house in a cop car. The other was with an ambulance and two goons disguised as paramedics. Back then the FBI was there to save my ass, but I'm on my own up here."

"You're on your own." Her voice was flat.

"You know what I mean. I guess I was having a flashback. Nobody was more relieved than me when I recognized the EMS guys. I phoned my contact at the FBI and told him what was happening, and he said he wasn't surprised. My father-in-law's lawyers have arranged for another appeal, here it is, twenty years later. Killing me off would be tantamount to the court finding him guilty again, so I didn't have too much to worry about. Their big worry was my going to New York to testify again—a sure way to keep my father-in-law in prison. I thought I was in the clear once and for all.

"That's when the FBI guy told me about Rob. My father-in-law had my silence all figured out. He had arranged for the 'Family' to pay for my son's postgraduate tuition at, get this, Acadia University, oh, so close to me. This is their key to my silence, I guess."

"He's at Acadia? How long have you known this?"

He hung his head. "For a while."

Mona was looking at him as if she had never seen him before. "You never said a word. And you never went to visit him? Even to *look* at him?"

He shook his head. "If I go to him, I could start all sorts of things rolling down on all of us."

"Wait, you've never even talked to him?"

"What would I say? How would I start?"

She opened her mouth a couple of times, then shook her head. "Why couldn't you just be having an affair?"

He laughed without mirth. "Now what am I supposed to do? I was never there to protect him for his whole life, Mona, but now I've been given a second chance. I have to do something. My agent told me that he had arranged for someone at the university to keep an eye on him. The last letter I found in the box had Rob's cellphone number and the address of an apartment he's been sharing with some girls."

Mona's eyebrows shot up. "*Some* girls? Like...six or something?"

Doug shrugged. "Who knows? College kids. We never did this stuff back in my day. But one of them is a girl named Cindy. It's got to be the Cindy who sent the letter, but how the hell would she have known where to send it unless she is involved?"

"Why do you think someone sent that letter to you?"

"Who knows? I'm having a tough time figuring it all out. I think maybe they wanted me to know they were telling me the truth, and really meant business or else: sort of like the proof of life conditions demanded in kidnappings."

"But why is it so complicated, why the subterfuge, why all the crazy code stuff, why don't they just come out and say what they want?"

"I have a feeling, Mona, that someone besides the Mafia has their oar in this."

"Ha, ha, nice Maritime reference, Doug, but what do you mean?"

"I haven't been back to New York in years, but I've kept up with what's going on down there, so, knowing what I know about the people involved, I can read between the lines.

"The Mafia is not like it was in the old days, when it pretty well controlled anything and everything it cared to. There are more players on the scene now and it's all about finance. Half of the elite properties, like those high-rise towers I used to work on, are now owned by Russian investors. They move their money around through international banks. My father-in-law was and probably still is heavily in debt to some Russian oligarch. Anything that happens to him affects their investment, and they are ruthless."

"What does that have to do with you and this Cindy?"

"Maybe the investors are involved in what's happening. It would be easy enough to slip someone into Acadia as a foreign exchange student, that's for sure. My contact said that he couldn't understand why everybody was so set on keeping me quiet. He had heard that my father-in-law was set for a presidential pardon anyway, so I don't see where I fit into all this."

Doug sat back in his chair, exhausted like he had just run a race. "So that's it, Mona. All I know. All I can say is that I'm so very, very sorry that I have made you part of this."

"But what about your son? What about Rob? What are you going to do?"

"Anything I have to."

5: A view with a room

Grace Keating

Rob looked out the window, trying to make sense of his exact location. He could almost spot the rail trail. Not that he could really see the pathway but he could make out a straight-line cut in the trees that stretched from his right to his left. His window faced north and his view was across the Annapolis Basin to the North Mountain. To his left, he could see Digby Gut and the lights from the ferry terminal. Assessing the landmarks, he figured the building he was in was on the highway side of the trail, not far from where he'd fallen when he'd been running.

He could also see there was no simple way out of his predicament. He had a cast on his right foot and couldn't put any weight on it for another week, at least. He had no means of communication and was, in essence, cut off from the rest of the world.

He'd had a visit from Popa early on.

"Don't try to leave. We're trying to help you, not hurt you." Popa had said.

“Who exactly is ‘we’?” Rob said.

"All in good time. There are things going on that we can't tell you about, just yet. Not sure why you lied about taking the bus here. That was just plain dumb. A bus? From Wolfville? We all know that would've taken hours you didn't have. Did you think we didn't know where you were coming from? Did you think we wouldn't find your car? You can maybe play us, but don't play us for stupid. Nice car, by the way. Alfa Romeo Giulietta Sprint. Granddad buy that for you?"

Popa unzipped Rob's backpack and continued talking as he pulled things out. "Hmm, computer science...that your area of interest? What's this, *Artificial Intelligence: Principles and Methodologies Involved in Artificial Intelligence*, nice light reading, then. I took the liberty of tossing your sandwich. It was a bit soggy. Lots of food here, you shouldn't have any problems making yourself some meals or pulling things from the freezer. Occasionally, I might bring you a dinner, in which case, I'll let you know early on in the day. Save you preparing a meal. And just for a bit of company, I might stay for dinner and bring someone along, so you're not too surprised."

Disturbingly, all this sounded to Rob like he'd be there for a while.

Popa reached in and pulled out a few more things: books, an Academic Calendar, some pens, notebooks, earbuds and chargers for his missing laptop and cellphone.

"Nice water bottle. A for Acadia. Did you have to pay for this, or is it bling? Don't answer. Honestly, I don't care.

"You're going to be here for a bit, so get used to it. We'll get that TV working for you tomorrow. What'd the doctor say? Keep your foot up. You'll find some pain-killers in the medicine cabinet. If you need anything, that's a direct line to the big house. Just call.

"Hmm, what's this?" he asked, as he pulled a piece of paper from the pack. 'Ice Boat Races'? Sounds like some student thing to me. Looks like you missed it, anyway."

He frowned at the page. "'All Regional Operatives invited'. Are you a regional operative, Rob? I don't suppose you'd tell me even if you were, and I don't suppose you'll tell me who this Cindy is. No?"

Rob had been well trained at keeping his mouth shut. Growing up in a mafia family had certain pluses, so it wasn't a problem to not give an answer, but he hadn't really fooled them about anything.

~

A light breeze made Natalie turn her head toward the water, a smell of, a sound of water. Children dressed in teal, every one of them, danced in a circle. Hands and giggles...the smallest child floating...sits in the tree, a solid limb of the old black walnut...what's she doing at the cottage with mom and dad...? Who's the slim woman, clutching her purse, sitting with them...? The child sings in an angel's voice...the willow bough bends over the bridge...doves fly above...

"Natasha, can you hear me?"

Yes, I can hear you. And my name is Natalie, not Natasha. No need to shout. What a thing to ask. Can you not hear me? Can you see me? We should go for a coffee. Why is everyone holding a balloon? Did you not see the lady in red go into the white house on the corner? Who's whispering?

Cindy was listening to the doctor. "We're not sure if she'll make it, but it helps that you're here. We'll keep her in a coma, at least until the swelling goes down and we can monitor her progress. I understand you're her next of kin, so I'll leave you with her for now. Talk to her, even sing to her as though she can understand. There's no guarantee, but there have been studies that indicate it may even help."

Cindy wasn't exactly sure why she'd driven to the Middleton hospital to see Natasha. There was something about the girl that Cindy was drawn to and it wasn't only that they found each other attractive. Finding out exactly who Natasha was and whether or not she was connected to the Cause would be especially difficult now, given her state. But she did have to try. Besides, she wanted to be there when, and if, she woke up.

It hadn't been difficult to get around security, since Cindy was the only person who showed up to see her. Natasha was allowed one regular visitor during the state of emergency, and it was easy enough to establish that that one should be Cindy.

"Natasha, I don't suppose you can hear me, but what sort of a spy are you?"

I CAN hear you, I can hear you. And it's Natalie. Who's Natasha?

"Listen, I'm really sorry I laughed so hard, I didn't mean to hurt your feelings or anything. It's just that you seem so unlikely to be a spy of any sort. I suppose I can tell you, 'cos it's obvious that you can't tell anyone else, but I'm actually a sort of spy myself. Spy, agent, operative, call it what you like. I could've gone on assignment to China, or the Philippines but I chose Nova Scotia 'cos my mother's family was from here. That's a few generations ago now though, and I haven't been to see any of them since I got here, even though we visited lots when I was a kid. All this COVID stuff makes visiting people so difficult. Probably good timing on everyone's part. I can't imagine what it'd be like to be in total isolation for two weeks."

Wow, Philippines...seahorses floating...bubbles of pearls...divers on the great wall of China...did you see where I put the money from my used books...bridge, over the bridge...is that where you come from? I'd like to go to China...nice lips...you have nice lips.

"Really, Natasha, I don't want to insult you or anything but...you being a spy, is this a carry-over from reading too many Nancy Drew novels, or *The Princess Spy*? I don't know why I'm drawn to you or what role you play in all of this but I need to know what you know. Are you some computer whiz-kid, or counter-intelligence? Are you with the special unit? You just seem so young to be with any assignment unit or the RCMP. But, then again, I've been out of touch with recruitments of late. Uncle Captain tells me you're in third year music at Acadia. I know you can't tell me anything."

~

On Monday, Cora sat with Mona in the afternoon sun overlooking her garden. "I know it's been such a difficult time for you Mona. First Doug not feeling well, then the mailbox, and now the accident with the girl. Do you know anything about her? A pity we can't just visit her in the hospital but you need a special permit or something. Or you need to be a relative. Have you heard anything?"

"No, nothing," Mona replied. "A student from Wolfville, that's all I know. It was such an odd place to have an accident, I don't remember there ever being an accident at that corner, right by the service station and across from the bistro. She was lucky there were people there, I didn't even have my cellphone with me. If it had been when everything was closed down, there might not have even been anyone about. The ambulance was there in less than five minutes, and they say it's because they got her to the hospital so quickly that there's even a chance she might make it."

She gave a little shrug. "I've been trying to convince Doug to go into Halifax to see Jimmy and Beth, and the grandkids. They always cheer him up and he seems so down right now. But he's not wanting to travel anywhere. Says there's things he needs to be at the house for."

"Mona, what did you find in the mailbox? You never did tell me. Or maybe you don't want to say anything. I certainly don't mean to pry. I'm just being curious, that's all. I should just go and mix up that martini we never seem to get to finish."

And with that, Cora was up and gone before Mona had to figure out a way to answer.

~

Wednesday, four days after Rob had fractured his ankle. Classes would be starting in less than two weeks, orientation was this week. He was lucky there, he'd already taken care of registering during the summer semester.

Of course, the flip side was, other than Cindy, Liz, and Shannon, his former and current roommates, he wouldn't be missed until he didn't show for classes. Two weeks.

Taking stock of his situation, Rob realized he wouldn't be able to drive for at least a week, that was if he could escape from his 'prison' and locate his car. He was being well looked after. They'd provided a wheelchair and everything was on the one floor, the TV had been set up, complete with a DVD player, and he'd found a closet full of hoarder's toilet paper, boxes of tiny bottles of hand sanitizer and a shelf full of paper towels. The fridge and freezer were well stocked and if he knew how to make bread, there were bags and bags of flour.

He had access to a large deck with too many steps to navigate, but that would change soon and he had to make sure he was able to act if the opportunity presented itself. The one good thing about his confinement, was the view.

In the four days he'd been observing things, he'd made note of several strange comings and goings.

First observation: Allison had been right, no one ran that section of the trail.

Second observation: off to the right, he could see the strange building he'd spotted when he'd fallen, its mystery now revealed. Twice a day, a small helicopter would exit the hangar, lift off and return, each time being wheeled back into the facade of the double garage. Each trip lasted exactly an hour and ten minutes. Clockwork.

His third observation: once, and only once, he'd spotted Allison with her arms around someone quite a bit larger. It was hard not to let his imagination take him away with what he saw. But, in reality, it was Allison with a man who could've been the pilot, or he could've been a passenger. The complete activities close to the hangar were out of view and Rob knew he was lucky to have been at that exact spot at the right time to see that much.

His fourth observation: the title of his textbook, *Artificial Intelligence: Principles and Methodologies Involved in Artificial Intelligence*, had saved him again. Popa hadn't even cracked the cover to see that the title had nothing to do with its contents.

~

Liz called up the stairwell in a loud voice, "Shannon, have you heard from Rob lately?"

"No. Why?"

"He hasn't been around for days, not since Cindy left. I know you and Cindy aren't talking, but I've called and texted both of them and left messages and I haven't heard anything back. Just wondering if either of them have been in touch with you?"

"Hang on, I'm coming down."

Shannon and Liz leaned against the counter in the kitchen and went over the timeline. Shannon had received a text on Saturday afternoon from Cindy and then nothing more.

Saturday 6:15 PM

have you seen Rob? he's not returning my calls

no havent seen him - sorry about everything - hope youre ok

I'm ok thanks - except I'm supposed to meet up with Rob

and can't find him LOL
k bye

Liz showed Shannon the last text exchange she'd had with Cindy.

Monday 2:47 PM

hey Cindy, have you seen Rob? haven't heard from him for a few days
no trying to get in touch with him too
where are you and how's the new apartment
it's great. BYe can't chat right now

"Should we report him missing?" Shannon asked.

"I don't know. Are both of them missing? Cindy and Rob, maybe they're together."

Shannon responded with a look somewhere between hurt and shock.

"Oh, sorry, I didn't mean it that way." Liz knew she'd touched a nerve. "No, they can't be together, Cindy was asking if we'd seen Rob, which was on the Monday and Rob's been missing since Saturday. Leave it with me, I'll get in touch with his faculty supervisor or someone and ask what we should do. I don't think we have to worry about Cindy for a few days, at least I hope we don't."

Liz made a phone call and arranged a meeting at the faculty rooms. Once at the building, she let herself in and waited for Gin Buttons.

"Rob's not come back from his run on Saturday and I don't know what to do," she blurted out the moment the professor appeared.

"When did you last see him, Liz?" He had a way of tilting his head to show he was 'actively listening'. Normally it irked her a little, but not today.

She recounted the timing of phone calls and text exchanges.

He nodded. "Check in with me tomorrow. I'll see what I can find out. Have you reported him missing with anyone else?"

"No. I thought it best to come to you first."

"Good, good." Gin sat back as if they had accomplished something. "That's the best route just now. I'll call you tomorrow, then, and we'll take it from there."

~

Rob was sitting on the deck, taking in the last of the day's heat and the fresh air. He stared out into the almost black night, drinking in the vastness of the sky, the soft sounds of far-off water lapping the shore. He welcomed the coolness of the night's soft breeze. It was close to 10 PM and virtually nothing could be seen.

Just off in the corner of hie eye, he noticed a bobbing light around the double garage. Not just one light, but by squinting and peering into the darkness, Rob counted three distinct lights. A slight whisper of a breeze rustled the leaves of the nearby trees, but other than that, the night was dark, quiet and motionless.

Following the movements of the flashlights, Rob imagined his rescue could easily be at hand. The flashlights could be Popa and Allison, but for Rob, for that night anyway, it meant he'd been loc-ated.

He spent the next half hour making sure all his possessions were stuffed in his pack and ready at a moment's notice for escape, his hospital crutches handy.

~

The lake water is always so warm in summer...dad is on the bridge with mom and someone else...is it the lady with the purse? or the lady from the white house...hammock stretched across the posts of the porch...it's such a drifting feeling...swinging in light breezes. Where's he gone, mom? Where's he gone...? My father suddenly dis-appeared, you know. I say suddenly as though it could be anything other than that, but, I don't imagine anyone ever disappears slowly. Intelligence work for the RCMP...his whole working life, you know...I could never hide anything on the computer...he was smart and he'd spot it...but I was just beginning to outwit him...three years ago when he...gone...my mother said he was having an affair, which I know wasn't the case, I know she was trying to comfort me...the children in teal are back...

"Natasha, do you know anything about someone named Rob Williams? Ring a bell? He's only in Nova Scotia because his father's in the witness protection program and—you can't ever mention you've heard this, but are you part of that whole thing? Or have you heard of muihtil? Do you work for the Cause? Someone has been observing me. That afternoon, the day we met, I came back to find someone had been in my apartment. And later on, there were all these cameras, well, I think they're cameras, on my walls. Somehow, I'm supposed to walk around and do things as if I don't know they're there. They're so obvious. Do they have anything to do with you, a Nancy Drew partner, maybe? Whoever's monitoring must be having a pretty boring time. I've hardly been there since then and I haven't said a single word."

...witness protection...protection...face mask...face masks in the courtroom...yes, protect dad in the courtroom...no...RCMP...he disappeared from...

Cindy left the hospital and checked in at the mailbox she shared with the other operatives before her return to Wolfville. She grabbed an envelope addressed to her and left one behind for Doug.

Sitting in her car, she carefully slit open the envelope, pulled out a small piece of paper and read:

> Agent C
> *Boat Race Numbers 4 and 5. Noted.*
> Uncle Captain

6: Quick as a summer storm

Angel Flanagan

Laurie got out of the shower and decided to make a pot of coffee. Coffee was what she always wanted, day or night. She stifled a huge yawn.

Black coffee in her mug, she opened her laptop and typed in Rob's cell number again. Bing! A little pin popped up on the map.

She took a slow sip and watched the pin blink. She zoomed in and saw it was blinking by the old rail bed people used for biking, hiking and walking. She shuddered, not her idea of fun, it was wood tick heaven out there.

Her skin crawled at the thought of the little hitchhikers waiting in the long grass. They didn't have ticks where she grew up and the little buggers really freaked her out. Maybe after she lived here for a while she wouldn't mind them as much, but she doubted it. How do you get used to living with those bacteria-carrying bastards?

Laurie knew Rob liked to run, it was pretty much all she knew about him. Why go so far? The trail was nice, but not that nice. Fewer people around, for sure, so easier to social distance. That was probably it. He wouldn't want to wear a mask while running.

She didn't mind wearing her mask. It kinda felt like a disguise and made her feel less anxious around people.

The little marker on the screen hadn't moved. Laurie was starting to worry. She better go look for him and make sure Rob was okay. She had been following him all week. He was pretty boring. Until he disappeared into thin air.

Laurie keyed his number into her phone app, started her car, and headed west. After far too much bland farmland, she reached and drove through Annapolis Royal, with one eye on her tracker.

Finally, she chose a spot to park along some dreary part of Route 1 where it looked like she could walk down to the rail trail. There was no sign of Rob, or anyone else for that matter. It was a grey, dreary day.

She sat in the car and smoked a joint watching for walkers and joggers. No one passed by at all.

Looked like the ticks would go hungry today. That at least made her smile.

It would have been much cozier at home with a blankie, a book and a joint. Instead she walked around and along the trail, and kept checking her phone. It was showing Rob was here somewhere. She scanned the sides of the trail and searched for any sign.

Then she saw it, a cell phone on the ground. She *was* in the right place. That was why it wasn't moving on the map, Rob must have lost it. She scooped up the phone and slipped it into the front pocket of her hoodie.

This was the first time Rob had let his phone out of his sight. Like most people these days, he always had it in his hand. It wasn't like him. Something was definitely wrong.

Her phone rang in her hand. She jumped, a little startled. The screen said it was an unknown number, except she knew exactly who it was.

Laurie took a deep breath, exhaled, slid the green button across the screen. She answered the phone with a curt, "Yeah?"

"Where is Rob? What have you found out?"

"I'm working on it."

"You better work harder."

"I'll call you as soon as I know anything."

The phone went dead. They had hung up on her. How rude.

Or the call had been dropped. Could have been either one, hard to tell with the crappy cell service around here. The phone bills kept getting higher and higher with the excuse of better coverage but the phones never worked any better. Rural life at its finest. Only the big city mattered to most companies and still, no service in some spots there too.

So, where was Rob? How was she supposed to know he was going to disappear into thin air? There had to be some clues on the shiny black Samsung rectangle.

Laurie was going back to the apartment to see if she could unlock it and find out all his little secrets.

Once home, she did a quick strip and search for wood ticks and took her second shower of the day. She had to be sure she wasn't being bitten by one of the tiny bloodsuckers.

That done, Laurie rolled a joint, lit it, and tried to figure out Rob's phone.

Didn't take her long, it was a much easier puzzle than she had expected. The password was the last four digits of his mom's phone number. He might as well have made it 1111. Rob was such a Mama's boy.

She had unlocked it with her first guess. Luck was on her side, at least for now.

Laurie scrolled through the camera roll. There wasn't much to see. It proved what she had been discovering over the last couple of weeks, that Rob was a quiet, boring guy. No pictures of girlfriends, parties or pets. Just a couple of screenshots of his fall schedule at Acadia. She had expected a lot more fun in a university town.

She was tired of sitting around, they weren't paying her enough for this, but she didn't really have a choice but to chill here and wait for Rob to return. They just wanted her to watch him. It was supposed to be easy.

She shut off Rob's phone and pulled the sim card out. Laurie had to do what she was told, she had to find out what Rob was hiding and be done with this place and these people.

~

Doug and Mona had opened their own small business. It was really a micro business, but people loved to promote local. To their surprise they got a lot of attention for their little self-serve roadside stand.

Doug loved to garden and grow food. His tomatoes were so big and sweet you only needed one slice to cover the whole sandwich. Mona loved to cook.

Word of mouth spread fast and people were hungry for good news, and organic foods. They sold out nearly every day. People couldn't get enough of Doug's organic veggies and Mona's homemade jams, jellies and sweets. The colourful green, blue and pink free-range eggs were the biggest seller. Her favourite part of the whole thing, was her chickens. Doug knew she loved hatching time the best because she spent lots of time watching the incubator waiting for the babies.

It was fun controlling everything until it was time to meet the new chicks. It was always so amazing when the shell started to crack and the little peeping noise began.

Doug was a good carpenter and had built the little stand and chicken coop to match. It was a hit with Mona and the community. They ended up in the local paper and were local celebrities for a little while. The fame lasted long enough for the mafia to find him again. Now he was sick and he couldn't wait any longer to tell Mona.

He dialed Rob's cell number again while he waited for Mona to come home. He didn't even have to look at the paper anymore, he had it memorized. He didn't know what he was going to say to Rob if he got an answer, but he kept calling the number over and over anyway. What was it they said about doing the same thing over and over and expecting a different result?

~

Mona rushed into the bedroom, quick as a summer storm. "Well, captain, I'm glad to see you up and dressed. You must be feeling a little better. Have you been listening to the radio?"

"No, I just got up," Doug answered with a yawn.

"I think your son is missing."

"What, since when?" Doug was wide awake now.

"I don't know, I just caught the end of the news when I pulled in the driveway. Maybe you should call the police?"

"And tell them what? My secret Mafia son I have not seen in 20 years might be missing? They will think I'm a nutcase or on drugs and lock me up."

"Well, you have to do something, don't you?"

"I'll try to contact the FBI and see if they know anything."

"Go ahead, then. How do you do it?"

Doug smiled a sad smile at her. "Sit down, Mona, I have something important to tell you. Sit down."

"Something important? More important than you having a son and lying to me every day for 20 years?"

"Yes. I'm sorry I couldn't tell you it all at once. It was just too much, for you and me."

He started coughing and held up his hand for her to wait. Mona grabbed some Kleenex and handed it to him.

Doug's voice was ragged and quiet. He decided not to beat around the bush any longer. He had to get it over with. She couldn't get any madder or more disappointed in him. "I have cancer."

"What...? No, don't be so foolish, it's just a cold, maybe even COVID..." her voice broke and trailed off.

"No, dear." He took her smaller hand in his two big ones. "I was sick long before this cold or virus or whatever I have that's wearing me down. I wanted to tell you sooner, but I didn't want you to worry."

"How far has it progressed? Can chemotherapy or radiation help?"

He shook his head. "I'm sorry, dear, it's stage 4. There is no point in treatment. It's too far gone."

"How long do we have?" Tears were running down her face.

"Not very long."

"I wish you would have told me sooner."

"Telling you sooner wouldn't have changed anything, except made you worry about it sooner. I just wanted to spend our little bit of time as happy as we could."

He hugged her tight. "I love you, Mona," it was muffled because he had his face buried in her hair. But he was sure she heard him, even though she was crying, too, 'cause she hugged him tighter.

~

Mona went out to feed the chickens. She needed a distraction from everything going on. Doug was going to do his mysterious FBI thing and find out what, if anything, was going on with Rob.

And the accident was really bothering her, she couldn't get it out of her mind. She knew it wasn't her fault, but she still heard the terrible sounds every time she closed her eyes.

It was just too much. She thought she just might lose her mind, maybe she already had and this was all a dream. Wishful thinking on her part. Mona needed time alone to think.

Her favourite member of her little flock was the big Brahma rooster, Chip. He was a gentle giant and would eat right out of her hand. Mona had him for many years and he had sired many of her chicks. She didn't name the hens, just called them random names like henny or girly.

Soon as they heard her open the gate they came running as fast as they could. They knew she was the food bringer. Their favourite people food was watermelon. They went crazy for that juicy red treat. It made her happy that they were glad to see her, even if it was only because she brought them treats. Their happy coos and clucks always brightened her mood.

Today, even the happy hens couldn't make her smile.

~

John watched Cindy enter her apartment, then drove away. He didn't have to stay; he could monitor her with ease from his hotel room. She looked harmless enough.

So far he hadn't heard anything out of the ordinary. Just lots of sobbing and crying. He guessed Cindy wasn't very happy with her recent move.

For a second he wondered why the boss was having him watch her. There must be more to her than he was seeing. Oh well, he didn't question the boss. No one ever did.

Rob's mom wanted John to take over the family business. The old man was locked up, and he was old and sick, but he still had lots of power. The old man had people watching Rob, the FBI probably had people watching Rob. Seems he was a very popular guy.

~

Allison just had one of those faces. Her hair was shorter now and blonde, instead of long and brown. She wore tinted contacts instead of glasses, but she still heard it often, like a bad pickup line: "Have we met before?"

At least she did before COVID. Now the only people she saw the whole faces of were Rob and Popa, and she didn't think Rob liked her very much. She didn't care if he liked her, but he had to help her.

Allison couldn't believe it when Rob fell right into her lap. She had come all the way here to find him and he found her, it had to be fate.

"Popa, what should we do? We need Rob on our side, but he doesn't seem very happy with me."

"He will listen or I will crush him."

"Crushing people is your answer to everything. This situation requires us to be more gentle."

"Rich boy isn't going to turn on his family. Just let me crush him."

"He might. Once I tell him how bad they are. That they are the ones responsible for what happened to my daughter. Amie was just a baby, she never hurt anyone." She broke down crying.

"I'm sorry, Allison."

Popa tried to hug her in a clumsy, muscle-bound, one-armed embrace.

Allison was having none of it. She straightened up and quickly wiped away her tears. "It wasn't your fault or mine, it was theirs. I want them to pay, every one of them. They can all rot in jail forever and I need Rob to help me put them there."

Allison sipped the sweet tea Popa had brought her. Her hand shook and she spilled a few drops.

"How are we going to get him on our side?"

"I'll just...talk to him. Explain my story. He has to see that they are evil and only out to help themselves, no matter who they hurt."

She paced back and forth. "I wish I had enough money to take care of this outside of the law."

"No, if you tried that, then you might be the one who ends up in jail."

"I wouldn't care. Nothing matters to me without my daughter."

Allison stared out the window without speaking. The leaves were blowing in the light breeze, it was mesmerizing watching the big maple tree branches wave and dance.

A hummingbird came to the feeder for a sip of sweet sugar water. Another green beauty darted in and they both zoomed away in a flash. Soon they would be gone for the season. She would miss their quick visits. A bright fleeting zap of colour, easy to miss if you weren't watching closely.

Popa closed the door quietly and left Allison to her thoughts of birds and babies.

~

Tony had left the black t-shirt by the river, just like he was supposed to. The man in the black car didn't say why he wanted that little job done, but it didn't matter to Tony, 10 bucks was 10 bucks, especially to a 12 year old with no job. Maybe it was a TikTok prank.

He didn't wait around to see what happened next. It looked like an old Frenchy's shirt no one wanted anyway.

Tony had been watching all week for the big car to come around again, hoping for another well-paying errand. His pockets were empty as usual. But so far, no luck.

~

Rob waited all night, but no flashlight-carrying cavalry appeared to whisk him away to safety. He awoke in the same place and there was still a cast on his foot.

He couldn't believe this was happening, what did they want from him? Why wouldn't they let him leave? He hadn't done anything but try to get some exercise, a little outdoor stress relief. *Boy, has that ever backfired*. He had to be dreaming.

Rob kept thinking he would wake up in the hospital. This had to be a fever dream, but so far he just kept waking up here.

Cindy would be looking for him, she would be pissed he missed the races. Seemed like lately he was always pissing people off without even trying.

7: We were just students

Carol Moreira

Doug struggled up from his favourite kitchen chair, an ancient rocker placed in the afternoon sun, and moved toward the stairs.

Better lie down.

It had been hard to believe in his cancer. The disease had almost felt like one more subterfuge he had created, but it was becoming real. The exhaustion that dragged his chest and limbs was transforming from fatigue to body-felling exhaustion.

Hurry, Doug told himself, his hand on the banister. And, for the first time, he felt fear shift in his gut.

It was a relief to arrive in the bedroom and see the large, comfy bed he shared with his wife. He smiled to see the headboard, remembering how Mona had insisted they buy it one sunny day in Mahone Bay where they'd driven for lunch while her folks took the kids.

Mona had pressed her nose to the handsome panel of red cedar and declared that she must have it, that she would sleep well every night if she breathed in sweet cedar whenever she closed her eyes.

And we have slept well here together, Doug thought as he dropped onto the quilt her grandmother embroidered with splashy purple lupines. *Mona shouldn't have slept in the spare room these past few weeks. I should have told her the truth—about the cancer, about my past.*

Hanging on to my secrets has only made us both lonely.

He closed his eyes, stretched out his limbs, and thought how he would not see the grandkids grow up. How many more Berenson

Bulletins of childish news and jokes would he receive from the Toronto clan? How many more times would he visit the family in Halifax?

Simple things...so achingly precious now he was losing them.

His mind turned to the missing piece—the New York son he'd never known well although he had met and chatted to Rob, thanks to Cindy. He'd been interested to see his boy was slight, like runners are—he got that from his mother. Rob also had a swift intelligence and an all-embracing grin. *Some good stuff he got from me.*

If only I'd been able to reach him, have a proper conversation, apologize, explain who I was, how it was.

But, on the whole, it's been a good life. How glorious it had felt to watch Mona's family grow up on the water. Sailing and canoeing. Sunfish and minke whales.

He smiled as he felt again the warmth of those days, the heat of the love he'd felt for his wife's children. *Who'd have thought I, Henry Williams, a career-obsessed guy from New York City, could wind up happy in rural Nova Scotia?*

Where is Mona?

Was she dousing her anger in martinis with that buddy of hers, Cora? His wife must resent his behaviour. She maybe feels that subterfuge has underlain their marriage like mould under carpet.

And poor Mona's been feeling down since the accident that put that girl in a coma. It's been a lot to handle. Mona's a good woman, but no saint.

A saintly wife would have been dull.

"Doug?" He heard a voice, and knew it was his wife, seemingly summoned by his thoughts.

Mona is calling me.

He tried to open his eyes, to say, "Hello, my love. I'm so glad you're back." But his eyes were cancer-weighted, and he managed just a glance before his lids dropped.

In that brief moment, he saw his wife, standing in the doorway, looking slight and panicked beside Cora's generous bulk. Mona's face and tone told him he must look bad, and he wondered how he did look. He was not dead yet, but maybe his face has already folded into emptiness like Mona's dad's did.

"Doug, oh, Doug."

Footsteps moved toward him. Martini-scented breath filled his face as he relaxed into the touch of kind hands.

~

"I'm not even sure I want to commercialize it," Cindy said. "I mean, we all talk about sustainable development, respecting resources, but how often does it really work out that way?"

"Cindy," Shannon said, and she fixed her former lover with her green eyes, then paused for emphasis: "It's us. Of course, we'll do it right."

"And there's all the fossils," Cindy said, unconvinced, and not wanting to gaze into Shannon's eyes—the attraction still stung; an ember not a flame. But it was good to have her here. Cindy was glad the COVID rules were being loosened.

She looked away from Shannon, and instead of seeing the white hospital walls, she recalled a long-ago trip to Joggins Fossil Cliffs with her uncle and cousins, and the beautiful, fossilized prehistoric fern they'd dislodged from russet rock.

"The Fundy cliffs are still full of fossils and treasures just waiting to be revealed. I don't see how we'll protect them if we mine the rock," she said. "And of course, there's other people—thieves who will steal our idea and run with it without any concern for the environment."

Shannon said nothing, just glanced down at the tiled floor. They both knew word had already got out that they were working on producing a replacement for lithium, the fine white metal so essential in the batteries of electric vehicles.

It was exciting to be a small part of such thrilling science, but Cindy wished the science could be undone. She longed to lock the secret away like fossils were locked in Fundy's ancient rock seams. She rarely even said the names of the three essential components of their replacement product aloud, even to other members of the team, but her mind always filled with images of the sandy silt that lined Bay coves, and the dense red dulse gathered from Bay waters.

They were all being surveilled. There had even been a break-in at the university. None of them knew who they could trust.

We'll screw up the environment. We may not mean to, but we will. And if we don't, someone else will.

"Even this girl here, Natalie, could be a spy for all I know," Cindy said, gesturing to the sheet-draped form in the bed. "She seems goofy, like she's pretending to be a spy to lessen the boredom of lockdown, but...she could be the real thing."

They gazed at Natalie's face above the hospital gown; calm in the repose of continuing coma. Natalie's fine features were beginning to emerge from the bloody swelling and disfigurement caused by her accident, but the trauma to her brain was not resolving as quickly. Cindy stared at the white bandage around Natalie's head and felt grief and sadness rise in her eyes.

Please get better.

"How do you know her?" Shannon asked. Her eyes searched Cindy's, and for a moment, Cindy's heart lurched with the thought that Shannon might be jealous.

Don't be silly, she told herself. *It's over.* And she realized she was beginning to be at peace with that fact.

"She bought some plates from me," Cindy said. "Those ones with the willow pattern. She was very sweet—*is* very sweet."

"I've been worried about you," Shannon said, "You know...worried as a friend. You're here all the time. You look...distressed."

"I'm okay," Cindy said, touched. "I'm just concerned about Natalie."

She felt a moment's shame about her own deceit. Here she was, sharing her fear of spies, her fear of the potential damage to the environment, and she was a spy herself.

She had only gone to Acadia University to infiltrate the team around Shannon and Rob. The news that students were creating a potential replacement for lithium had been of great interest to the American government—as it was to any government that heard of it. Few countries in the world had big reserves of lithium. A new, man-made source would be literally golden.

Cindy had assuaged her guilt about spying on Canadians—after all, her mom's family were Canadian, so she was spying on kin—by telling herself that at least she was acting for a friendly government, not some hostile, authoritarian state.

"You do understand that we must go ahead with commercial production?" Shannon said. "Not only for ourselves...It would be so great to have the money to pursue scientific projects without applying for grants. And there's the planet. Our method will be better —cleaner."

Cindy nodded. "I know."

She trusted Shannon and Rob. *They are good people, powered by intellectual curiosity and the desire for human progress*. It had been a joy to act as their lab assistant. She had fallen for their quick minds and warm personalities. They had even given her shares in the new company.

Their generosity had made her own subterfuge harder to bear, though somehow she had borne it.

"Where is Rob?" she asked. "Did he turn up?"

She shuddered as she recalled hearing the news of "a Caucasian man's kidnapping" on the radio. That had to be Rob, didn't it? Should she discuss it with Shannon? Could one of the government spies have kidnapped Rob to make him reveal the lithium formula?

Shannon shook her head. "No idea where Rob is, and I need him. We're on the verge of applying for a patent." She frowned. "It's not like him. Did you notice anyone new in his life? Hear him mention anyone?"

"No." Cindy shook her head, but her heart lurched. *I shouldn't have interfered*, she thought, *shouldn't have introduced him to his dad*. Maybe the Mafia have got him. Maybe Doug isn't the good guy he appeared.

Doug had certainly seemed like a good guy. He was a convert to the cause of veganism, having grown attached to the chickens he reared. Cindy's Ice Boat races were a cover for the vegans' meeting.

Sailing their ice boats across the water, they planned the group's activities in the open air, free of prying ears and eyes. Some of the group favoured extreme action such as releasing farm animals; action Cindy supported but feared might draw unwelcome attention. Still, the movement was growing. Cindy hoped it was the start of real change, that soon the only meat people consumed would be grown in a lab.

Doug was also into electric vehicles. He was the one who'd first approached her and offered to keep his eyes and ears open for strangers asking questions about research work at the university. That's when Cindy realized Doug was not the man he appeared. When her operatives told her of Doug's background, and of his connection with Rob, she was intrigued and began to notice familial resemblances between these two men she was becoming fond of.

And now...where is Rob?

The door opened and she jumped, her mind rushing ahead on the hope it might be Rob turned up safe and well. But it wasn't Rob. It was Professor Gin Buttons. He must have snuck into the hospital. Each patient was allowed only two visitors so he must have been stealthy.

"Hello Professor," Cindy nodded politely although she'd never liked the academic who oversaw the lithium-replacement project. He was seemingly a good man, intellectually supportive and encouraging. His only fault seemed to be his over-fondness for Wolfville's many bars and pubs.

The subtle scent of gin entered the room with him now. Cindy didn't judge. She liked a drink herself, and her fondness had grown during the pandemic. She'd had the prof's background checked; he'd come up clean.

"Hello," Shannon said, turning to the academic, seemingly without Cindy's undercurrent of dislike. She glanced at the young woman in the bed. "Do you know Natalie?"

"I do," the prof said, as he moved into the room. "She is also a student of mine."

He looked at the patient, and his eyes saddened. "Natalie is a brilliant young woman, brilliant." He shook his head. "It is terrible to see her like this."

"I should go." Cindy got to her feet, keen to get away from the professor she just couldn't warm to.

~

Rob, on the deck, thought about the woman he'd seen waving at him from the trail.

She couldn't have been waving at me. How would she know who I was?

But it had certainly looked as if the woman—youngish with dark hair and standing on the stretch of trail where he'd fallen—had been trying to attract his attention. She had swung her arms about then made motioning gestures toward her own chest.

I can't just walk out of here, lady.

He had been about to gesture back when he'd heard Muscles coming up behind him, and he'd swivelled his gaze from the trees and back to the path.

"Hello," he said, and from the edge of his eye he saw the woman dart into the trees. Muscles' gaze also turned in her direction.

He saw her.

Whoever she was, Rob had no way of knowing, and he put her from his mind as he sat on the deck in the late afternoon sun. He was growing accustomed to lazing on the deck, listening to the sounds of the ocean rinsing the shore. Fall felt glorious in Nova

Scotia—the way summer dropped into restful days enlivened by the first scarlets of the season. Each morning came cool, with mist on the water, then the mist dispersed as the sun warmed water and land.

You're not on vacation, he reminded himself as he watched the heat shimmer on the waves and treed shoreline. But he did feel calmed, even though he was a prisoner, even though Muscles hovered in the shadows, a gun slung over his one good shoulder.

Allison, he hadn't seen for several days. He assumed she would turn up and act either strangely hostile or oddly friendly.

He hoped she would finally explain what was going on. In the meantime, Muscles brought him food—they clearly intended to keep him alive—so he was aiming to enjoy the peace and not panic.

Life had been so hectic. Who'd have thought their lithium project would progress so fast? Who'd have thought they would establish their very own startup to commercialize the technology?

We were just students, Rob thought, *just testing out an idea*.

But when the idea showed promise, they'd moved fast to incorporate their company. There had been paperwork—lots of it, though Shannon as CEO was responsible for applying for patents and other authorizations.

Chief Technology Officer. Rob muttered the words to himself. *I am CTO of Tidal Bay Solutions.*

"What did you say?" Muscles and his gun shifted out of the shadows.

Rob's pulse jumped—he had almost forgotten Muscles' presence. The sense of menace, of imprisonment returned, and Rob thought of the lights he saw bobbing around the double garage after dark.

What are they up to? Is it about the lithium? Have they been spying on us?

"Nothing," Rob said. "Just thinking aloud." He instinctively flexed his injured ankle. It was healing, and his bag was by the bedroom door ready to be grabbed should Muscles show a moment's inattention.

I must get back. Shannon will be furious with me.

Alerted by the sound of footsteps, he turned to see Allison striding across the deck toward him. Once more, she reminded him of an actor; maybe it was her fine blonde hair, the white pantsuit.

"I need you to help me," she said as she approached, speaking with an openness that Rob had not heard before and which made him wary. If she needed help, why hadn't she just said so? He was a good guy, got a kick out of helping people, actually.

"What do you want me to do?"

"It's your biological father," Allison said. She sat down on the wooden decking opposite him, crossed her legs and leaned over them, gazing at him with wide eyes that neither threatened, beguiled nor shifted. "We—I—need you to enlist your biological father to...somehow get close to your adoptive father. *We* need to get close to your adoptive father."

She glanced up at Muscles, who had moved to stand beside her, and who was now gazing down at Rob, gun poised. "Yeah, we are going to hurt him," Muscles said in a gruff tone that almost made the threat sound amusing.

"I have a tragedy to avenge," Allison said. "Don't pretend you don't know what your family are, Rob." Her eyes darkened, and she glanced away for a moment, toward the peaceful water, then returned her gaze to Rob, breathed deep.

"A few years ago, your father's men were chasing me. I was doing some work for them. Yes, I admit it...And something went wrong—through no fault of mine. But they blamed me, as I'd known they would. And, when I was fleeing, your father's thugs pursued me, rammed my car...killing my daughter, Amie."

"Oh, my god."

Her eyes filled. "I haven't been able to get near them." She glanced up at Muscles, and Rob wondered about his relationship to the tragedy.

Her gaze brightened. "But *you* can get close, Rob. And your biological father can. The Mafia have found Doug, you know. He won't escape them, but if he's clever he can take them down with him."

She paused. Rob didn't know whether she expected him to express opposition or a willingness to turn on his own kin. What would happen if he refused? *So, it's not about the lithium..*

Not knowing what to say, he said nothing. Her face hardened as she waited for his response.

But Rob actually had no words. It was hard to believe, but his life had just gotten even stranger.

8: He could feel the water rising

Carol Ann Cole

Robecca wondered if anyone had figured out that the boy she gave birth to, while she was Maria and married to the guy now called Doug, had his name tied to hers. Probably not. The family had suddenly changed her name without consulting her, just days after Doug left. That's when they took her into 'the big tent', to be trained by The Boss himself.

Some time ago she had decided to talk this out with The Boss if she ever had the chance. Just one more thing that reflected the long arm of this branch of the Mafia. If they don't like your given name, they change it.

On occasion Robecca got to speak with him, more than likely when he wanted to give her a change of assignment or get an update on her current project. It was never personal.

The Mafia owns me, she thought. *Doug was the smart one. He got away from the Mafia...and us.*

As she drove toward the medium-security penitentiary in the village of Dorchester, New Brunswick, Robecca wondered when it had been downgraded from a maximum-security prison. Until recently, her father was in a federal penitentiary in Ontario. Millhaven was a maximum-security lock-up and for many years Robecca had believed her father would live the rest of his life there. The Boss was no longer in a federal penitentiary and she was happy to hear that.

While others called him 'The Boss', Robecca called him 'father'. But only on those rare occasions when they were alone. He seemed to like it.

~

During their courtship and the early days of their marriage, Robecca and Henry, now Doug, knew very little about the Mafia. Robecca couldn't help knowing a bit more, but she avoided talking about it.

But once he started to learn their connection to 'the family'. Henry simply couldn't leave it alone. He had an obsession with all things Mafia.

And then the murder happened. He could never un-see that.

From the day Henry had hidden behind a pillar to watch a man fall from the top floor of a building, he had been consumed with guilt and with fear. Might this be his fate?

Once Henry had accepted the great job offered to him over their first Sunday dinner with the in-laws, they owned his ass. He had been slow to realize this, but Maria had known and was happy to let him fall into the trap. He was convinced of it. His own father-in-law had had the sorry sod thrown off a ledge.

Henry had rushed home to share details of the terrible things he had witnessed. He was in shock.

He was further shocked when Robecca said, "Did you really not understand who these people, *my* people, are? Are you really so blind?"

"It...I guess it never occurred to me," Henry said. "They seemed so, well, ordinary."

Robecca laughed. "Yeah, they eat with silverware and tan by the pool. But they are not ordinary."

"But what do we do?"

"About what?"

Henry wiped a hand across his face. "They kill people. They do, uh, crime things."

Robecca fixed him with a look he had never seen before. "You can't change a glacier or a star in the sky. They just *are*. My family, and what they do, just *is*. They are the reality, not whatever you were thinking."

"And you're happy with that?"

"Happy doesn't come into it. I will always stand behind my father."

Henry made a helpless gesture. "We might have talked about this before our marriage, don't you think?"

Robecca had gotten up to leave the room. "I thought I was marrying a grown-up who knew how the world runs. Was I wrong?"

But Henry could not remain quiet. He went to the police.

The death of Brian Zinck was still under active investigation and Henry's testimony was music to the ears of the detectives working the case. When he had done all the police asked, the next stop had been the witness protection program. Henry became Doug, for better or worse.

For some time he had questioned his decision to leave every*thing* he loved and every*one* he loved behind, basically to save his own ass. The witness protection program had saved him, so far, but at a heavy price.

~

Robecca had moved home with her parents. Her baby, Rob, was safe there, insulated away, until he became an adult. She knew the family would call on him then.

She had thought she had a plan to save her son from the Mafia. As it turned out, this was nothing more than a dream. She had turned out to be no wiser about the world than Henry.

But that was then. She was much more in the picture now.

She wasn't sure exactly when she had changed her mind about who should be next to become The Boss when her dad reached his best-before date. She made a show of supporting John, but that was it: a show. *Fooled John, at least.* But that was just a way to buy time while she monitored Rob, her clueless son, for a few more years.

When clarity came, Robecca had smiled, thinking back to when she and Henry had brought the tiny baby home from the hospital. But that was another time, another world.

Now she had the map program pointing to the weedy little village of Salisbury, west of Moncton, where the helicopter would land. It never seemed to get closer as she drove and drove. But that's where part one of today's plan would happen, and from there they would drive the hour to the barbed wire at Dorchester.

Robecca flexed her hands and tightened her grip on the steering wheel. *Okay, Daddy. Let the games begin.*

~

Mona lost it when Doug began his morning with, "Thanks for breakfast in bed yet again, dear, but...ah, we need to talk."

She felt a fist grip her stomach. "More revelations?"

"I have to tell you something that I'm ashamed to say involves righting a wrong. I kept it from you to protect you, Mona, and I hope you will see it that way."

Mona was fuming. "I can't imagine what else you have lied to me about. I'm already feeling our entire life has been a lie. I think I need to get out of here and away from *you.* And *that's* no lie!"

With that she was out of the room and turning to go down the stairs when she heard Doug shout, "Mona, Rob's mother is not dead. She's been in touch."

She was back into the bedroom like a shot. "How many times have I asked you if she was dead? *How many times?* I don't know if I should believe another word that comes out of your mouth."

Mona felt her whole world begin to crumble, not for the first time.

She shoved Doug's yesterday clothes off a chair. She needed to sit down. She leaned forward, put her elbows on her knees, and chin in hands, and took a couple of deep but shaky breaths.

Then she looked up at him. "Talk to me. Don't make this a long story, I couldn't stand another one from you. Doug, I can hardly look at you so *give it your best shot.*"

With that Mona focused on the photo of the two of them, taken during happier times, sitting in its silver frame on their dresser just by Doug's right shoulder.

"Mona, my first wife is called Robecca now, for some reason. We have had absolutely no contact. But she called me the other day to say she was going to visit her father in prison."

"Why is that any business of yours, Doug?"

"Something is going to happen when her father dies. Something involving Rob. My Rob."

Doug looked at his wife. "Say something, please."

So many questions. Too many.

"Doug, I really do need to get away from you. This is too much. Too much."

~

Rob had started questioning everyone and everything. *Paranoia looks good on no one,* he continued to remind himself. But he couldn't help it. He was certain no one was his friend and everyone knew something about him.

He could hardly stand to be around himself...he needed a plan. Rob felt like he was drowning.

His healing ankle was able to withstand some weight bearing... maybe enough to test his leg and determine how much energy he could muster to get himself out of wherever in hell he was.

He could feel the water rising. He knew he was in danger.

He was in the dining area. Popa was tidying things. He picked up Rob's empty glass and waggled it in the air.

"Good to see."

"What's good to see?"

"That it's empty. You drunk it all up."

Rob began to feel uneasy. "It was water."

Popa added dishes to his tray. "Mostly water, yes. I have to run a little errand and you're going to be alone for a bit."

"Okay." Rob tried to keep the suspicion out of his voice.

"I didn't want being alone to go to your head. So I added a little sleeping aid to your water."

"What the hell?"

"You'll be fine. I just don't have to worry what you're up to while I'm out."

~

Popa returned, errand complete, to find Rob flat out on the floor.

Impressive, he thought. *He should not have had the energy to even keep his head up. Here he is dressed and ready to make a run for it.*

With a shrug, Popa prepared for the next little task. Probably for the best Rob would sleep through it.

~

A voice was saying, "Wake up! Rob, wake up."

Rob assumed it was either a dream or a nightmare. He had been having lots of those.

Now someone was slapping his face. The room was spinning and seemingly going up and down, up and down.

He felt somewhat ill but smelled strong coffee very near to his face, and just like that his senses aligned with his need to wake up.

Sheer panic enveloped Rob as he opened his eyes. He was in a vibrating metal something, surrounded by a deep rumble like the sound of a waterfall. He tried to touch his ears, and found that big somethings were covering them. And there was a cup of coffee waving in front of his face.

He focused past the cup and saw Popa. He had a headset on, covering his own ears. Beyond him were the walls of...what?

He shakily took the coffee. "Where am I?" His voice sounded far away.

Popa spoke in a kindly tone, one that Rob had not heard from him before. "You're in our chopper, heading for New Brunswick. You're going to meet with your 'family' at the Dorchester prison."

"My mother is in jail? They arrested, charged, convicted and shipped her off of to prison while you kept me in la la land with your drugs? How long have I been out of it?"

"Not at all, Rob. All is well with your mother."

"Then why—?"

"Your mother is visiting your grandfather, and they want you there. He's the one in prison, remember?"

The flight bounced around and seemed to be headed in every direction. "Is there a chance we won't make it to this meeting alive? Who is flying this thing and why is it so noisy? Gotta be a very old chopper, no?"

Popa indicated past Rob.

He turned and met the pilot's glance. "Allison? Is that really you?"

She raised her eyebrows, conveying, *What did you expect?* then turned back to her task.

Lowering his voice, Rob turned to Popa. "Our transportation is in the hands of the woman who wants to kill The Boss because she believes the Mafia killed her little girl? We sure are living on the edge."

"I can hear you," Allison said calmly through the headset.

"Don't you worry about a thing," Popa said. "We have a contract to deliver you alive. That is exactly what I intend to do. Today Allison is our pilot...nothing more."

~

Project MUIHTIL seemed to have a lot of students...too many students for Cindy's liking. There were six around the table, in this too-small room at the Legion they sometimes used for meetings, plus Professor Buttons and two gray-haired guys she had not figured out yet. And they were all talking at the same time. Shannon kept trying to catch her eye; Cindy did not feel like playing that game with her any more. She turned and looked at Laurie, who, curiously, would not meet Cindy's eye. There was more going on here than she understood.

Cindy had joined the project, and even room-mated with Laurie, Shannon, and Rob, to gain the inside story. *If an inside story even existed.* She was working for the American government. Her goal was to steal the project's body of work, if there was any worth to it.

She had quickly learned, though, that there were a number of spies who might have the same goal. There was a guy with a fancy car who was sometimes outside her apartment building. Who was he working for? There were the listening devices...where did they lead? She smiled inwardly, remembering that Natasha was another spy, one she didn't mind at all.

Cindy had one soft spot that Shannon had trampled all over, and that now was all wrapped up in her attraction to Natalie/Natasha.

Knowing Natalie had family living along the rural shore near Port Maitland, she was eager to get a day or two off to check it out. She hoped the following weekend to make the trip to Clare, on the Acadian Shore. More to learn, perhaps, down that way. She was close.

A problem was that Rob was missing. Cindy was less than happy to see their little group suspended because everyone was on the 'We have to find Rob' train.

"He can't be the only techno-nerd on our team," she said above the chatter. "I realize he's the CTO, but finding a replacement for lithium falls to every one of us on this team. Should we not put our heads down and work on our project?"

Some people nodded. Some had 'Not me!' written on their foreheads. Gin Buttons was gazing off into space.

Then Laurie said, not looking up, "We have to find Rob first. He knows where everything is."

Shannon stood up. "No point sitting here with a certain person accusing us of not working. I have better things to do." She started for the door.

"Wait..." Cindy said. But the tide was on its ebb. Soon the only other person still at the table was Professor Buttons. "This is crazy," she said.

The professor brought his gaze back into the room. "Not untypical, though," he said. "And sometimes doing crazy takes you to interesting places." He eased himself to his feet and left at a sedate, almost cautious, pace.

Cindy scooped her papers together and turned to leave. She crashed into a beautiful man who was filling the doorway as if to block her exit. Six foot five inches, give or take, shaggy blond hair, glasses with light blue frames to match his light blue eyes.

Cindy's mind registered all of this. Somehow she knew those

eyes. "Sir, if I was straight, I would take you home!"

The giant was having none of it. "I'm looking for Natalie. Natalie Mayne. I understood she would normally be with a group meeting here, and yet you seem to be alone. Fill in the blanks for me, please. I have travelled some distance. You will direct me to Natalie's location. Now, please."

"You're talking like a freaking robot. Who are you and why are you looking for Natalie? And why such a clipped tone? Does that work for you when you meet strange women? Let me guess, in case the little woman is frightened by the big bad wolf—"

"You're wasting time, young lady. My name is Darcy Mayne and I am here to see my daughter."

"Oh. *Oh*. Follow me, Mr. Mayne."

Cindy tried to stay two steps ahead of Darcy so she could think. She didn't even know if Natalie would want to see her father. Natalie had not mentioned him. Not once.

However, the hospital was not that long a drive away and she was certain she was doing the right thing to take him to his daughter. Plus, it would give her an excuse to compare Natalie's face with her dad's.

"Mr. Mayne, are you aware that your daughter was in a terrible car accident? She was behind the wheel. No other car involved."

"Just take me to her, please. I am aware that my girl is in a coma and might not live."

Cindy couldn't help herself. "Don't you dare say that. Natalie will recover. *She has to.*"

~

The old man was stooped and his skin had a transparent greyness that spoke of illness. His mind, though, was as sharp as ever.

"They took their time getting here."

"They're here now," his permanent guard said patiently. "The family-visit room is ready for you."

The old man gave himself a tiny shake, as if adjusting stiff armour. "Family visit. Happy family." He started toward the door of his cell. "My strong daughter and the grandson I hardly know. My heir-apparent."

9: Revelations

MJ Foulks

Rob watched as his mother waved to him from her car, just before driving off. The second the car was out of sight, the roaring of the helicopter starting up left his ears ringing. Popa carefully helped Rob into the helicopter, jumped in himself, and pulled the door hard behind him. Rob grabbed his headset and jammed it on to deaden the noise.

"Well?" Allison said in his ear as she took the metal pod into the sky.

"Well what?"

"Did you do it? Did you tell him you would take over for him like we told you to?"

Rob said nothing, but gazed at the cast on his foot. It was hard for him to believe that, in this moment, getting kidnapped was the least of his concerns.

"He did," Popa answered for him.

"...Good. Did he buy it? Or are you *actually* going to take over for the Mafia, Rob? Don't think it hasn't crossed my mind."

I've about had it with her raging bipolar disorder, Rob thought. Popa had been coming around to him. Or, at the very least, he didn't suffer from Bitchy Bouts Syndrome.

"Mancini was pleased," Popa said simply. "Rob did well."

It had been a rather surreal experience. After Rob hugged his mother tight, she and Popa had exchanged what Rob could only describe as a knowing nod.

Once they were in the family room, his grandfather, looking pale and sallow, had shifted himself through the doorway and sat at the table, waiting to be shackled to it.

His voice was hoarse. "Dominic, you have brought me my beautiful daughter and grandson. For this, you will be rewarded handsomely."

Popa, or apparently 'Dominic', bowed in thanks.

"You will stay and enjoy some time with the family." It wasn't a request.

"I'm honoured, Mr. Mancini." Popa had bowed again and took the seat next to Robecca.

"Hey!" Allison shouted through the head set, pulling Rob out of his recollections. "Don't doze off back there! I need to know what happened."

"Then get it from Dominic over here," he spat, jerking his head in the direction of Popa even though Allison couldn't see him.

"In time, Allison," Popa said soothingly, "it was an intense visit...for all of us."

Allison was silent. Rob watched as Popa lifted the seat next to him and pulled a large, black cloth out from its storage.

"Just for the ride back. I'm sure you understand."

Rob gave a sarcastic grin, and Popa gently blindfolded him. *Good job of it, too.* He couldn't see a thing.

"How is Robecca?" Allison asked, and Rob felt a sharp sting go down his spine.

"She's well. For now, at least." Popa answered.

~

The Muihtil team were ready to resort to drastic action. If they didn't get their CTO back, no other member of the team could do what Rob did. Cindy was trying hard not to find this admirable. She was supposed to be spying on them after all.

Their only lead was Laurie's, who had reported where she had found Rob's phone.

Cindy opted to go with Laurie and Shannon, further down the trail Rob must have been running that day. She was willing to put up with the presence of Shannon to keep an eye on Laurie. Something about Laurie made Cindy...uneasy.

Other members of the group decided to go back to Acadia and do some canvassing. Professor Gin Buttons decided to stay at Middleton Hospital, not giving a reason other than 'Someone should be here in case he comes back.'

The trio waited for the cover of nightfall, then took out their flashlights and headed down the empty trail. Cindy had put on Natalie's black beret that had just been sitting unworn in her hospital room. *Keep her close.*

"We should split up," Shannon whispered. "Cover more ground."

"Like hell," Cindy hissed. "Rob disappeared here and you want to split up?"

Cindy didn't have to see Shannon's face to know it was beet red, complete with furrowed brows and a withering expression.

They came to a part of the trail with residential backyards to their left, and fancy, waterfront houses to their right.

Cindy's phone vibrated in her pocket, making them all jump. She pulled it out and looked at the caller ID.

Mate

"Excuse me for a second," she said. She stepped a few feet back as she answered the call.

"No, go ahead," Shannon muttered. "It's not like we're on a harrowing rescue mission or anything."

Laurie snickered.

A dog appeared from nowhere. He came up behind Shannon and startled her. He was friendly, wagging his tail as she smiled and petted the top of his head. Laurie took a second to pet the sweet little guy herself.

"Sorry," Cindy said, shoving her phone back into her pocket.

The sweet dog went from Jekyll to Hyde, his hackles raised and his bark ferocious. Lights began to filter through windows one by one...he was waking the residents.

"Tippy? Tippy!!" They could hear a woman shouting.

"Hide!"

They darted for the nearest patch of trees and and climbed as swiftly and silently as they could.

Cindy watched a pretty blonde woman come out to greet the dog. She looked around briefly, then headed out of sight, with 'Tippy' following behind.

Cautiously, the girls climbed back down to the ground and resumed their search, trying with difficulty to put Tippy, and his many teeth, out of their minds.

Laurie stared into the darkness into which the woman and her dog had disappeared. “I have a hunch,” she whispered, motioning for them to follow her.

To Cindy’s great surprise, Laurie’s hunch was right. There, sitting calmly on someone's back deck, was Rob.

“Quick, turn off your flashlights!” Laurie commanded.

“Why?” Cindy asked, but the why became clear right away. A man who was nothing but muscle had just appeared on the back porch, carrying a tray with a plate of food and a glass of water. He set them down on the table and went back inside. Without a single sip, Rob dumped the water out onto the deck.

The girls acted.

“Rob!” Shannon whisper-shouted once she was close to the deck.

Rob turned his head, and his mouth fell open. He looked around for a second, as if checking for his captors, then hobbled to the banister just above them. *A cast,* Cindy thought. *Great.*

“How did you find me?” he muttered with his back to them.

“Never mind that. Let’s get you out of here,” Laurie whispered urgently. “Just throw yourself over the edge. I’ll catch you.”

“Are you insane? My ankle—“

Do you want to stay here?” Cindy snapped.

Rob looked to the back door. Then he rose and clumsily threw himself off the deck. In an amazing show of strength, Laurie successfully caught him. Then Cindy, not to be one-upped, carried him on her back all the way back to their car.

“You guys are—”

“You’re welcome,” Shannon smiled from the front passenger seat.

"I'll be so happy to be back home," Rob breathed as he closed his eyes and let his head fall back onto the headrest.

"You're not going home. Not yet," Cindy said.

"...where am I going?"

"To Middleton Hospital," she replied gravely. "There's someone there you need to see."

~

Rob found the room he was looking for down an eerily empty hallway. After taking a deep breath and adjusting his mask, he entered. The room was shrouded in darkness, save the glow of monitors and blinking lights. No one was there except the patient, his biological father.

Rob let the door close behind him with a little click. Doug's eyes opened just the smallest bit.

"Rob?" he croaked, trying to lift his head.

Rob rushed to his side. "Don't overdo it."

Doug gave a weak laugh, one that sounded like a death rattle.

Rob hooked his finger into the loop of his mask and removed it. He knew the risk, but was willing to take it.

"There's... so much... I need to—"

"No, you don't," Rob breathed. He could feel himself shaking as he heard the heart monitor start beeping faster, and saw Doug's eyes well up with tears.

"You know," Doug managed to say.

"I know."

"I'd give anything...for more time...with you..."

"It's okay...*Dad*," he whispered soothingly, grabbing his father's IV-less hand.

A nasty coughing fit made Rob jump a bit. He'd never heard anyone cough so hard. Cindy had said he had cancer, and likely wasn't going to make it out of the hospital this time.

"Listen, I don't have...much time. Please...grab my phone. I need you to do me...one little favour..."

"Anything."

Rob fumbled around, looking for a phone. When he had it, Doug gave him the code and he unlocked it. The screen immediately went to his most recent calls....most of them to Rob's lost cell phone.

"Video...record a video."

Rob turned on the room's lights for a better image and hit *record*.

"My name is Doug Berenson, formerly Henry Williams...I am giving my testimony against my former father-in-law, Mr. Roberto Mancini."

He took a few deep breaths to ready himself once again. Rob was careful to remain behind the camera and silent.

"Mr. Mancini is the current head of a powerful Mafia family. He has committed atrocious crimes...including the killing of an...innocent woman's young child. I personally witnessed him murder Brian Zinck...but there's more...so...much...more..."

Desperate coughing. Hacking. He was growing more pale by the minute.

Doug's testimony went on for twenty painful minutes as he detailed his experience with the family, and with Rob's mother and grandfather. The sick feeling in Rob's stomach, the one that started with his mother's confession and grew when he learned of what happened to Allison's baby, had returned with fury.

Finally, Doug made the 'cut' motion with his hand, and Rob stopped the video.

Doug suddenly began to weep, silently but openly. Rob grabbed his hand once again, feeling tears run down his own cheeks.

"My wife....my dear Mona...please tell her..."

"I will, Dad," Rob managed to choke out. "I will."

"I'm...so sorry...my son..."

Doug's voice trailed off and his eyes closed. He subsided into a deep sleep.

Rob took his phone and pocketed it.

As he hobbled out of the room, a thin, older woman rose from her chair. Her red-rimmed eyes contrasted sharply with her blue paper mask.

"Are you Rob?" she asked.

He nodded.

"Thank goodness you're okay," she breathed in relief. "I'm Mona, Doug's wife. I guess that kind of makes me like a step-mother to you in some weird way? I'm sorry, I'm rambling, but this whole hidden wife, hidden son, hidden…connections. It's really getting to me. But I'm so happy you made it out okay. We've been so worried since we heard about your kidnapping. What happened to your foot?"

She looked from right to left before leaning in to whisper, "Did the Mafia hurt you?"

Rob couldn't help but chuckle. Obviously Doug had told her a thing or two. *Did the Mafia hurt me? More than you could possibly know.*

"It's just a minor strain," he said. *How sweet of her to worry.* "How are you holding up?"

"You know how it is," she said with a fake smile visible in her eyes. "Girl meets boy, boy and girl get married, boy hides former family and cancer diagnosis from girl until it's..."

The rest of her words seemed to have retreated back into her throat.

"You should go see him."

She nodded and went into Doug's room, leaving Rob alone with his thoughts. He sat in what had been her chair.

"CODE BLUE," the PA system shouted after just a few moments. "CODE BLUE. ROOM 108."

The doctors and nurses were rushing by so fast they didn't even notice Rob was there. His heart pounded.

Mona was pushed out of the room. Rob stood as she turned to him and their eyes met. She rushed into his arms and sobbed.

"He's gone, Rob. Oh my God… he's gone! He's gone...he's gone…"

She kept repeating it over and over again, sobbing into Rob's chest, mourning a man she had thought she knew, the father Rob would now never get the chance to know.

"I yelled at him, Rob!" she cried, forcefully pushing each word out of her body. "I left him alone...it was all so much...*and now I'll never see him again....*"

Rob stayed with her...for a minute or an hour, he hardly knew. It was the least he could do for his new sort-of stepmother, to hold her until she needed it no longer.

Then, with no thought to his injured ankle, Rob escorted her to the parking lot. Mona kept her hand clutched to his forearm. Outside were Cindy and a sturdy older woman with a kind face and no mask in the outdoor air.

"Rob?" the maskless woman asked, and he nodded. *Everyone seems to know who I am these days.*

"Cora," she offered in return. "Are you ready to go home, Mona?"

Her eyes glazed over in shock, Mona managed a slight nod. As she let go of Rob's arm, she turned to look at him and removed her sodden mask. *Not like it was doing her any good anymore.*

She reached into her purse for a pen, and quickly scrawled her number onto the back of an old receipt.

"Keep in touch, son," she said in a near-vacant tone. "Text me and let me know you're okay."

Deeply touched, Rob lowered his own soaked mask. "I will. I promise."

Then Mona was gone and Cindy was beside him with a hand on his shoulder. "I'm so sorry, Rob."

"Just...take me home. Please."

But Cindy seemed hesitant.

"Come on, don't mess with me. I've been injured, kidnapped, sedated, my biological father...I just want—"

"I need you to visit one more room. It won't take long."

Out of her bag she produced a fresh paper mask and handed it to Rob, but he just looked at her like she had completely lost her mind.

"Please...it's important. To me, at least."

Rob let out a sigh. "I suppose you did just rescue me."

Cindy hugged him.

~

Allison was in bed, but far from asleep. Her thoughts drifted from the visit to the prison, to Rob's reluctant cooperation, to Popa's unwavering loyalty...to Amie...Mr. Mancini strung up by his neck...

A loud knock pounded on her bedroom door. In the dark, she fumbled for her robe and slipped it on before opening the door just a crack.

Light from the hallway streamed in, but she still saw Popa through squinted eyes.

"Rob is gone," he declared. "They came and took him."

Allison's mouth curled into a smile. "Perfect."

~

Cindy's heart leapt when Rob agreed to go with her. She hadn't been to see Natalie since the day her father had popped up out of nowhere. For some reason, his presence had begun to make Cindy worry more. Something about him just didn't sit well with her, though she couldn't quite put her finger on it. He had seemed cold in the presence of his gravely-injured daughter, as if he couldn't be bothered to care whether she lived or died. *So why on earth was he there?*

Darcy Mayne...even the name sounded made up. Clearly a false name. Perhaps Natalie actually was a spy, not just some silly little girl with cabin fever from COVID isolation. And if that were the case, who was this 'Darcy', really? She wouldn't be surprised if they were both spies. *The Muihtil team is crawling with them, for crying out loud.*

Their progress toward Natalie's room was maddeningly slow, given the pace at which Rob was limping. She wanted to scream at him to move faster, her insides squirming as they inched their way toward her lovely little mystery.

Cindy adjusted the black beret atop her head.

Just after they had left the elevator and turned down the hallway, Professor Gin Buttons had appeared, coming toward them.

"Professor! We—"

"Found Rob? Yes, I can see that. Good. Very good."

And with a nod and a wave, he was gone into an elevator. Rob and Cindy exchanged befuddled looks.

"Come on." She pushed him impatiently, not wanting anything else to distract her from seeing Nat.

Once they finally reached the room, a jolt went through Cindy at the sight of the closed door. Hanging from the knob was a black T-shirt...the same kind of shirt she had seen on the riverbank at the failed Ice Boats Race. Cindy wasn't sure what it meant, but something deep in her gut told her it wasn't good.

Cautiously, she opened the door. 'Darcy Dark One' was nowhere to be found. She gazed at the beautiful face of her beloved.

Natalie's head rolled from side to side, and Cindy let out an audible gasp. She took her hand, and Nat slowly began to open her eyes, but her eyelids seemed heavily weighed down.

"Cindy..."

She had never loved the sound of her own name more. Without letting go of Nat's hand, she reached over the bed rail and pressed the call button.

"I'm here, Nat," she cooed.

"Brother....brother...John...need John...want Momma..."

A nurse knocked twice, then entered the room.

"She's awake!" Cindy exulted. "She said my name and rolled her head, and she mentioned a brother."

The nurse went to Natalie's bedside and called for another nurse to come in. Cindy stepped back to let her do her job and stood beside Rob, beaming.

"Sorry to drag you here," she offered, though she didn't mean it. "This is—"

"Natasha," Rob said in a hollow voice. "Natasha Mayne."

10: Ratsberry pie

Rhoda C. Hill

Liz winced as the hand sanitizer made contact with the thin cracks on her knuckles. She'd been wearing moisturizing gloves to bed for a little more than a week now, but, so far, it wasn't helping. She'd washed her hands more times over the past few months than she had in all of her previous twenty-three years combined. Her fingers felt flayed.

She could be the poster child for COVID-19 global. She followed everything by the book and then some: stayed in when she'd rather go out, wore her N95 mask like a religion, and changed it out more often than she needed to. It smelled like the Lysol factory had exploded in the centre of their apartment, and she'd sung the 20 second chorus to Dolly Parton's 'Jolene' so often while scrubbing her hands that the song was like a jumbled tape worm in her head now.

Although at the moment they were only allowed to stay within their Atlantic bubble, Liz had taken it upon herself to narrow her bubble drastically. Aside from class, she rarely socialized with anyone other than Cindy, Shannon, and Rob; and now that Cindy had moved out, her bubble would become even smaller.

So why the hell did she feel like shit?

She stood over the bathroom sink, her fingers gripping the sides of the vanity, as she tried to suppress the wave of nausea threatening to propel a cocktail of vitamin supplements from her stomach. *Fuck COVID-19.*

Any bouts of sickness from here on would automatically send her mind down the COVID trail. A trail that was fast becoming a full-fledged highway.

She started to rattle off the symptoms in her head.

> Fatigue?
> *Check.*
> Nausea?
> *Check*
> Chills?

She covered her gaping mouth, and pulled on the ties of her cardigan. *Oh God, I'm going to be sick. No, scratch that—I* am *sick.*

"Stop it." She pointed a finger at the mirror. "You're dizzy because you drank a whole bottle of cheap-ass wine last night. All. By. Yourself."

She activated the screen of her phone. Still no message from Rob. *Where the hell was the S.O.B.?*

She'd tried to be coy, tried not to bombard him with messages, but now, with him missing, she was sending him text after text at fifteen-minute intervals.

When he did eventually look at his phone he'd deem her psychotic, and promptly find a new place to stay. Maybe he'd move in with Cindy. At least there was no chance of Cindy seducing him.

Liz hadn't seduced Rob, though, no matter how he twisted the story. *He* had kissed her first. The only reason they'd ended up in her bed was for convenience. Her bedroom was downstairs, so it had just made more sense to slip in there rather than do the whole romantic-comedy thing, slobbering over each other and stumbling upstairs, shredding their clothes as they went.

In the morning he'd disappeared. No 'it was nice, but' note. No 'let's forget this ever happened' text. Not even a nudge awake to tell her he'd picked up her clothes before Cindy and Shannon discovered them strewn along the hallway in a path to her door. Not even a simple dismissive peck on the cheek.

She knew it was a one-time deal. He didn't have to tell her that. Maybe his silence was just that—a P.F.O. of epic proportions. A bit dramatic, but what else could she expect? A beautiful rich boy with a trust fund, a souped up Giulietta Sprint he called Baby, a weekly allowance from home, and a free ride to university, versus a poor, plain Mi'kmaw girl with a student loan, a size seven mode of transportation she called feet, and no real place to call home. She was so out of his league she may as well be on another planet.

She wavered as the room spun for a second around her, and right when things started to settle back into place the doorbell rang. She jumped, sending the room in a tilt-a-whirl all over again. Her image blurred in the mirror before her, and she fell forward, her cheek pressed into the glass.

"I'm coming." Her call-out was so feeble she doubted anyone in the next room would hear it, let along out on the deck.

The bell sounded again, and then a click, a thud, and another click, and she knew something had dropped between the two doors.

She groaned. It was probably another parcel for Cindy. She better get her mail redirected to her new address soon. Every other day a new parcel arrived.

Liz scoffed. Rich people and their forever trail of never-ending money. How many handbags, pairs of shoes, and pallets of Estēe Lauder make-up did one girl really need?

She held on to the furniture as she made her way to the front door, pulled it open and picked up the parcel. Mounds of packaging tape cinched the plastic wrapping around whatever was inside. She turned it in her hand, seeking out a name.

Denali Sylliboy

What in the actual hell?

It wasn't her birthday and, even if it was, this didn't feel like the scarf her mother typically sent her, and it was far too big to be a cheap birthday card with a $20 bill inside from her father. No one knew Denali Sylliboy, aside from her parents and a few close relatives who didn't really give her the time of day. No one here in this world of pretend knew who she used to be.

In this world she was quiet, perfect Liz, the girl with all her ducks in a row, with her whole life planned out, and everything falling perfectly into place. Denali would be so out of her element here. The person she used to be was locked away, being fed a slow poison so that one day she would not exist at all. That was the plan, anyway.

Tucking the parcel in the crook of her arm, she pulled open the outside door and looked up and down the walkway for any signs of the courier. He was long gone; Speedy Gonzales.

She closed the door and, for reasons she couldn't quite put her finger on, slipped the deadbolt into place.

The X-Acto knife ripped a perfectly frayed X across her given name, and she tugged on the paper, tearing Denali Sylliboy to shreds.

She couldn't deny the thrill of excitement as she cut away the layers of tape. She'd never received anything in her life without a reason. This might be the first *just because* gift she'd ever received.

Another first for Liz. Good things happened to her now that she'd slipped out from under the shadow of Denali.

A book.

The green, white, and black technical grid, stretching across the back cover in an abstract wave, made her eyes cross. She closed them and shook her head, trying to stave off the threat of dizziness.

Flipping the thick book over, she read the title: *Artificial Intelligence: Principles and Methodologies involved in Artificial Intelligence.* That was a mouthful. Whoever approved that title must have been getting paid by the letter.

Now the question was who had sent it, and why. She did have a small interest in A.I., but she couldn't remember ever saying that out loud to anyone, not even to Fancy and Booker, and she generally told them everything.

She took the book and the crumpled packaging into her bedroom, and sat cross-legged on the bed. The book balanced on her knee as she activated her phone again. Nothing. This silence was getting old, quick. He better be dead, or at the very least fingerless.

She leaned over and popped open the door of the rat cage. Booker, a light brown rex rat, quickly stepped into her hand and started a mad scamper up her arm to her neck, tugging gently at the elastic at the end of the braid hidden beneath the folds of her thick dark hair.

Fancy, a blue fancy rat, was too cool for that. She waited for Liz to suspend the customized bridge from the door of the cage to the footboard of the bed, and only then did she scurry out, down the bridge, and under the pillow, searching for any Cheerios Liz may have hidden. She hadn't hidden any, but she'd eaten puffed chips in the bed earlier, so she knew Fancy's search would not be fruitless.

With the gentle sound of Booker bruxing in her ear, she opened the book, hoping for an inscription, and maybe a clue as to why someone had given it to her in the first place.

There was no inscription. She turned it on its spine in order to riffle through the pages with her thumbs. Halfway through, she stopped. There was an anomaly.

An Altoids can nestled deep in a neat cavity in the centre of the pages, and a momentary switch and a power supply were etched snugly into the four-inch border around the can. Liz had seen stuff like this in spy movies; never in life.

She used the attached finger bracket, typically used on a cellphone, to pull the can from the pages of the book, and popped it open. A small computer component nestled in the can. There was a note scrawled in red marker on the underside of the lid:

Raspberry pie @ six? Write!

What the hell?

Booker moved to her shoulder. She instinctively held her arm out, and he climbed down to the bed to be with Fancy.

"What do you think?" she asked and held the computer component out for Booker to sniff. Fancy sidled over, her twitching nose studying every inch of the can in Liz's hand.

"Hold on," she said, and flipped the computer part out onto the palm of her hand. "Check," she commanded. The rats nudged the can a bit more before turning to the computer component.

Sensing no trouble, they turned away and disappeared beneath the folds of the blanket again.

Feeling more confident now, Liz turned the part over in her hand and studied it. There were ports on the side, but she certainly didn't feel comfortable attaching it to her computer. She needed her computer, and she didn't have readily-available money to purchase a new one or have it serviced should she mess anything up or, worse, fry it.

But why would someone send this to her if she was not supposed to explore it? It just didn't look like anything she'd ever seen before. It was small like computer memory, but computer memory didn't have ports.

She held it closer. She could see a processor, and Ethernet chip, a 40 pin header, and a reset board, but black marker covered any markings that might give her any more clues.

She reached into the drawer in her night stand and removed some rubbing alcohol and a Q-Tip. Within seconds of rubbing at part of the black marking, she could make out the symbol of a white raspberry.

A simple internet search told her all she needed to know. In her palm she held a Raspberry Pi, a complete operating system. She need only connect it to a monitor and turn it on with the momentary switch provided.

Using the end of a pen, she pried the switch from its bed in the book's pages and connected it to pins five and six on the little device. Then she hauled an unused computer monitor from beneath her desk, plugged it into the wall, and inserted an HDMI plug to both the monitor and the Raspberry Pi in her hand. Balancing the tiny computer on her knee, she activated the switch and watched as the monitor sprung to life.

As the system powered up, Liz watched as Fancy and Booker flitted in and out of the folds of her quilt. She pulled a mouse from her desk drawer and plugged it into the Raspberry Pi. Amazing what the little thing could handle.

The machine ran on the Linux operating system, of course, and the only program she could see installed was called Write!

She searched for files and found a small collection of photos, but there was nothing to view them with. Easy-peasy: off to the internet to find, download, and install a photo viewer.

Flipping the Altoids tin, she reread the message inside.

Raspberry pie @ six? Write!

She could cancel out *'raspberry pie'*, and *'write!';* those she understood. All that left unfigured was *'@ six'*.

She lay back on the bed, Booker and Fancy moving up and down the length of her body, and ran scenarios through her head.

Someone had gone to great pains to deliver this book to her, although it was not the book itself that they wanted her to have, but rather the contents hidden inside. There was definitely something special about this device, so important that they'd felt compelled to use a coded message to convey it to her.

Liz sat up, and the whole room started to spin again. *Shit.* She'd thought it had passed.

She held her head as she multi-tasked, trying to slow her dizziness while she twisted the coded message in her head.

Activating the screen again with a nudge of the mouse, she returned to the pictures. They had numbers. Number 6 was a placemat-quality picture of Cape Blomidon on a touristy afternoon. Nothing special there.

She closed the image viewer and looked thoughtfully at the Altoids box lid. On a whim, she right-clicked picture number six, and moved to *'open with'*. She chose *Write! f*rom the short list of options.

The program was slow to open, and when it finally did a whole series of symbols flowed down the page: the code that told the image viewer what to display. She scanned it slowly, looking for anything that stood out.

And there it was: an equation.

This was not her area of expertise, but Liz knew an equation when she saw one. She couldn't make heads or tails out of it, but she could see it involved manganese and scallop bivalve shells. Mixed in the jargon were the words 'used for temporal change' and 'phytoplankton sedimentation'.

Another knock sounded on the door, and her heart flew to her throat. In a mad rush she dismantled the Raspberry Pi and put everything neatly back inside the book.

The knocking was growing louder. She paused, her breath hitched.

She would need to be extra careful. The book, the contents, the code, the whoever at the door: Liz had a sinking feeling that it was part of a bigger puzzle. She could very well be in danger now, and so she would need to be on her guard even more than she usually was.

Lifting Booker and Fancy into her hands she brought them up close to her face. "Hold on," she said to direct their attention. When she was certain they were good and on guard she commanded, "Check!"

Then she slipped them into the pockets of her cardigan and went out to answer the door.

11: A ten-jellybean problem

Kate Tompkins

Liz pulled the door open slowly, peering out the crack to see who was on her doorstep.

"Oh, it's you." Some tension melted out of her body, skipping out along the wave of dizziness that flowed across her, leaving her trembling.

The large man with the scarred eyebrow pushed the door all the way open and stepped inside. "Hi, Sis." He hugged her with his one good arm.

"What are you doing here?" Liz hissed. "What if someone sees you?"

"So what if they do? I'm getting tired of all this play-acting. Like I'm supposed to be this big tough guy all the time. So bloody loyal to that big arse in the prison and the evil blonde bitch. God I'm sick of talking about crushing people all the time. 'Dominic, teach this guy. Dominic, break that guy.' It hurts my head. Got a beer?"

They moved to the kitchen, where Liz handed Popa a Keith's. He sat on her kitchen island stool, thoughtfully sipping on his brew. Close up, anyone could see the resemblance between them. She waited while he composed his thoughts.

"It worked, though, Denali. She bought it. Rob's rescue and all of it. Allison thinks she has all of us dancing to her tune, like she's the one who is in control, like she is the one who is poised to take over 'the business'. Bloody bleached blonde. She thinks she can play us all."

"Take it easy. Just a little while longer. Then we can duck out and leave them all squirming."

Liz tucked into a plate of bannock she had whisked onto the

counter in front of her brother. After a moment her brother took a hunk of the fried bread and disappeared it into his mouth.

"Do you know about this?" Liz plucked the miniature computer out of her apron pocket and carefully pushed it towards him. She showed him the formula she had discovered a few minutes earlier. "I can't figure out who sent it."

Popa picked up the gizmo and tucked it away in his jacket pocket. "I'll deal with this, little sis."

He tweaked her affectionately under the chin and left, still chewing.

As soon as the door closed behind him, Liz covered her mouth with her hand and raced towards the toilet. After a few moments of heaving her breakfast out, she sat back on her heels, exhausted. "Crap." She breathed through her mouth. "This was *not* supposed to happen."

~

Cora rocked silently on her porch, nursing an iced tea. She had insisted that Mona stay with her for a while. Mona was in la la land now, heavily sedated by the hospital doctor after Doug's death. Snoring softly upstairs, Mona was deep into a restorative nap while the mysteries of sleep's healing powers knitted her into something perhaps she could at least recognize and live with.

Poor lass, Cora thought. *Her whole world is in pieces.*

Cora shifted her substantial bulk into a more comfortable shape in her less than comfortable white wicker chair. Her face showed everything she thought, or so her son always said. At that moment, a watcher could have seen a veritable movie of emotions ripple over her face as she thought about her oldest friend, upstairs.

Mona was one of those friends who, even if you never saw each other for five years, it didn't matter, you could pick up the conversation right where you left it as if no time had passed at all. The kind of friendship that was more like being an old married couple. You know each so well you can predict what she will say and do next. You might get exasperated with each other sometimes, but so what? *Who will be there for me when I'm old and decrepit? Mona will, that's who.*

There was something niggling at the back of Cora's mind, though. Mona was hiding something from her, the witch.

She took another sip of iced tea. *It's got to do with that gal who did the face plant on the pavement in front of her smashed car. Why did Mona even think about that accident? Who was that frizzy haired girl, and what did she have to do with Mona?*

This is a ten-jellybean problem, Cora reflected. Jellybeans were how she calculated the importance and impact of any issue she had to mull over. You have your three-jelly bean problem, which you could dismiss with a nod. Your five-jellybean problem required a few moments of thought before it took you wildly blowing off on some possibly random adventure. But your ten-jellybean problem, now that is one that needs some pondering. One that needs not only a handful of colourful candy, but also at least a mint julep, if not a high-test martini to help sort out what the heck is going on.

She downed the iced tea in a gulp and headed for the kitchen to mix up a delectable, thought-pondering drink.

Over the clinking of ice cubes, Cora heard Mona mumbling upstairs. She smiled. At least she could look out for her friend now, even if she had no magic wand to fix all her woes and pains.

Now, back to that ten-jellybean problem. She settled herself again in her wicker chair to contemplate the world, feet up and a puzzled look on her warm, round face.

~

Professor Gin Buttons crumpled up the formal-looking letter with the university logo at the top. He fired it toward the waste basket in his home office with more force than was strictly necessary for it to hit its mark.

He had known for weeks that he was walking a dangerous tightrope. *How did they find out?* An uncharacteristic wave of panic spread up from his belly and ended in a grimace that twisted his normally-placid face.

In the way that arrogant types in lofty social positions often do, he had blithely assumed he was above such petty considerations as accountability and formal recriminations. But in the past few weeks, he had had to take steps that were more risky than his usual *modus operandi.*

So that Big Ugly Cheese in his walnut-panelled office wants to see me? I don't think so.

"Stanley, where did you put my umbrella?" His wife's breathy, high-pitched voice wafted in from the hallway.

He ignored her, a worried calculating expression on his face.

"Never mind, found it." His wife was out the polished oak door on her way to some dreary faculty wives' function.

Gin sat down heavily in his tall, black-leather swivel chair. He steepled his hands by his chin for a total of two minutes and a few seconds, contemplating his options. Then he leaped up and emptied his top desk drawer on the floor.

On his knees, he sifted through the contents on his carpet, plucked a single ledger sheet torn from a record book, and glanced at it briefly. Nodding approval, he opened his office's French doors that led onto the backyard patio.

The barbecue screeched a little as he lifted the lid. He lit the burner and watched while the blue flame devoured the records. The page browned, curled up on the edges as the incriminating figures disappeared into ashes. He pursed his thin lips and blew on the last wisps to help the wind carry them away into his wife's rose garden.

Wiping his hands on his pants, Gin returned to the house. He took the stairs two at a time and hurried into his bedroom. He grabbed a Gucci bag and stuffed it with shirts, a pair of pants, a razor and toothbrush, then a pair of clean socks for good measure.

He lifted the fake Renoir off the wall, exposing the home safe even his wife did not know about. After a few quick turns of the combination lock, he lifted a stack of bills from the safe's dark recesses and stuffed them into his bag.

On second thought, he picked up the bills and crammed them into one of his clean argyle socks. *Not that that will help!* he thought wretchedly.

Three more minutes and he was backing his Bentley down the driveway to the road. *I'll bet she doesn't even notice I'm gone until tomorrow.*

~

Allison stretched out her dramatically long legs and sipped at a glass of Beaujolais. A gentle breeze, just enough to catch a few attractively wispy blond locks, had her reaching for a sweater. Tippy, her blindly faithful hound, plopped down beside her chair and ever so gently inserted her damp nose under Allison's hand, pretending not to be demanding pats. Tippy dissolved in doggy ecstasy as, absently, Allison stroked her companion's head.

"Well, we're on our way, pooch." Tippy nuzzled her hand again to remind her human of her petting duties.

Allison gazed up at the incredibly blue sky, lightly studded with mashed-potato clouds. "Amie, I swear to you, my child: they will suffer."

The mission to scout out the prison had been successful. She was glad that somebody had rescued Rob from this very porch once she no longer needed him. He had been just a way to get close to his grandfather, who was always The Man wherever he went, even behind bars. *Gullible young pup. Manipulating him was not even a challenge. The same with that moron, Popa*.

Now her plans were crystallizing. It had taken her a few years of research, spying and lying, but she had eventually gotten to the bottom of her daughter's death.

Yes, it had been Rob's stepfather driving the car that killed her innocent girl. But the question had been—Why? There had been no connection between that criminal locked up in the prison and her family. Why would the old man order a hit on a small child?

It was only luck that gave her the answer. She had stumbled upon a witness: a cook's apprentice who worked for the Mafia family, when she was buying groceries for her well-heeled employers. Being invisible, the apprentice had eavesdropped on the powerful family, as any good servant should do.

Allison heard her talking a bit too freely to the grocery clerk one day, then followed her. Cornering the apprentice, Allison threatened all sorts of dire consequences if the girl did not feed her information once a week.

Gradually, the pieces of the story had emerged. Robecca, who used to be Maria, had brought her new husband into the family fold. But being married to the daughter of The Man was not enough. He needed to perform well in a test of his loyalties. Robecca's father had assigned a gruesome task to the fledgling mobster: kill a young child, no matter whose child, to prove he had the cojones to be part of the family.

Allison knew that she must find a way to kill the old man, prison bars notwithstanding. Then, maybe, she could find a way to take over the family. Failing that, she would destroy the organization. *I will make them all wish they had never existed.*

Her heart had ripped apart when Amie had died. Her grief had twisted her soul out of recognition. She knew her need for revenge was warping her mind.

She didn't care anymore.

~

Cindy sat, not quite reading, by Nat's bed. The nurse had been in to check on Nat's IV lines, plump the pillow and offer Cindy a bottle of water. Now, lost in thought, Cindy let her book subside on her lap.

What am I doing here? Anyone would think I actually love her. Do I? I barely know the woman. Why do I call her my beloved? Am I really that messed up? Lonely, for sure, but…maybe I'm more lost without Shannon than I thought. No, get a grip, girl. Close off that wandering mind. That's what operatives are supposed to do.

She tossed her book aside and headed toward the door. A glance told her that Nat was out cold, her chest rising and falling rhythmically.

A minor part of her brain asked, *What is that black thing doing on the door handle?*

The hall was more or less empty, a doctor scurrying the other way, an aide with a tray in hand, a dude in green scrubs with his head in a patient's chart at the nursing station.

Cindy turned left and headed outside. It was a cool day with a spineless sun, but that barely registered. What caught her attention was a black SUV poised on the edge of the parking lot. She was sure she had seen that vehicle before, but where?

She pulled out a flattened, sad-looking joint, then sighed and stuffed it back into her pocket. *Later*. Instead she lit up a cancer stick and breathed in two long, searing puffs. Then she stubbed it out, shoved it in with the well-travelled joint, and searched her pockets until she found a hard peppermint candy she had picked up somewhere. She had had it so long that the clear wrapper had stuck to the candy and put up quite a fight.

The sweet juice flooded her mouth. She closed her eyes and let the lazy sun warm their lids. She could hear a soft buzzing as bees gathered what might be their last pollen for the season from the weed-ridden sad excuse for a garden beside the path. *Does anybody actually look after this little collection of non-flowers*?

With a sigh, she turned back to the hospital doors, navigated the oh-so-earnest COVID checkers near the entrance, and glided back towards Natalie's room.

The hall was empty. No sign of life about. Cindy yawned as the heavy door to Nat's room swung slowly on its old hinges.

Two steps onto the ugly 70s-vintage lino flooring, Cindy gasped. She felt rooted in her tracks. She tried to call out, but no sound came. She tried to move towards the bed, but her feet felt nailed to the floor.

In fact, her shoes felt weird. Liquid was oozing into her socks around the cracked soles of her shoes. *Blood*. There was a pool of dark blood on the floor.

In that freeze-frame way the brain protects us from seeing what we cannot process, she stared at a small flower in the lino pattern, watching it succumb to the spreading pool of red that slowly obliterated it.

Cindy forced herself to look up to the bed where Nat lay. The top half of the bed was soggy with blood, dripping relentlessly onto the floor in little spats and plops. She could not make sense of what her eyes were seeing. Her ears were ringing so loud her thoughts were drowned out.

Nat's hospital gown was sopping with blood where she lay on the soaked sheet. It made no sense. Cindy simply could not comprehend the enormity her eyes presented to her. Across Nat's pale neck skin, a slash gaped, an obscene second mouth where none should be. Her throat had been cut.

Cindy could tell she was sinking, like she was watching from somewhere above and in front of her actual body, as it slid boneless to the floor. In spite of the shock filling her brain, one coherent thought poked in from someplace. *This was a hit.*

Then all hell broke loose. People jammed the room, someone lifted her not very gently to her feet and started firing questions at her. Beeps and buzzing filled the air. Someone was screaming. Just before she slipped into oblivion, Cindy noticed a black shirt on the end of Nat's bed. *What the…?*

With relief, she passed out.

12: Invisible Man

Andrew Wetmore

Cindy came awake slowly. She was lying on her back, under florescent lights that made her closed eyelids glow. People were doing things nearby, but she did not really want to move her head to see what they were up to.

Slowly it came to her that she was lying on a gurney, which meant hospital. Which meant maybe what she was remembering was not from a dream.

Then she realized that she could not raise her left hand. There was a zip tie fixing her arm to the rail on that side of the gurney.

Her eyes popped open. She tried to sit up, despite a wave of dizziness.

A hand pressed her shoulder back down on the gurney. It was a woman with a stethoscope around her neck. "Shh," she said. "You have had a shock and a bump."

"But what—?"

The doctor's voice was soft, but her eyes were hard. "You must be quiet for the moment. I will explain all, but not now."

"Why am I tied up?"

"All part of the explanation."

Cindy felt a mosquito bite on her arm.

"That will help you find some rest," the doctor said as she withdrew the needle, "and to maintain quiet. Soon all will become clear."

Cindy had eleven things to ask, to complain about, to object to. But before she could get them organized into a compelling order in her head, she found her eyes were closing and the sound of hectic activity seemed to be growing more and more distant.

The next time she found herself awake, she was still attached to the gurney, but the gurney was in a darkened room. She was chilly and needed to pee, and her head ached. All of her ached, in fact, from lying still on her back for so long.

"Hello?" she said through her dry lips.

After a time a door opened, flooding the little room with hallway light long enough for Cindy to see racks of towels and supplies, and closed again. Someone drew near her and she tensed.

It was that doctor; she could tell by the shape of her shoulders and her hair, even though a mask covered most of her face. "Hello, again," the doctor said. She picked up some little device and turned it off. "Baby monitor."

"What are you doing to me?"

"I am doing things *for* you. To keep you safe."

"From what?"

"The first policeman on the scene thought you might be a person of interest. You were unconscious, so of course he could not ask you. So he made sure you could not leave."

On the scene...Images flared up in Cindy's mind of the blood, the blood, Natalie's pale face.

"Things got quite hectic and confused, as you can imagine," the doctor said. "They are familiar with death here, but not so much with murder. In the confusion, and when the first policeman was elsewhere, I was able to roll you away. And here we are."

"My friend is dead."

"But you are not. And nobody is going to hold you as a murder suspect."

"Me?"

"You may have been the last person to see her alive. Or the second-to-last."

"I'm going to be sick."

"We don't have time for that. Drink this."

Cindy hesitated, but it was just water. She managed to angle her head so she could drink it and revive her mouth without pouring it all down her neck.

When she was done, the doctor said, "You need to get away from here. It's late on Monday and the authorities are finally getting their act together. Go home, eat something, then sit and grieve. Only tell your friends that you just heard the news. They do not need to know you were here."

She clipped the zip tie to free Cindy's arm, and another Cindy had not noticed that was securing one of her ankles. Cindy slowly sat up and the room did not spin too badly.

"Now pull those clothes off."

"Do what?"

The doctor dropped a set of scrubs on the gurney beside her. "You need to be invisible as you leave, so put these on. We'll put your clothes in a black bag."

Cindy started to pull her top off, then paused. "My shoes are bloody."

"That would be bad for someone to see. Put them in the bag and wash them when you get home." The doctor indicated a pair of flip-flops. "Those should fit you."

"You're not a real doctor, are you?"

She could tell the woman was smiling. "Only when I need to be. Now let's go."

~

Later Monday evening, a chance comment at a gas station in Middleton alerted Gin Buttons to a possible flaw in his clever plan.

"Nice wheels," the kid at the next pump said.

Gin glanced dubiously at the Bentley's white sidewalls.

"Can't be too many of them around."

"Well, if you appreciate high quality in a car—"

"You a doctor?" the kid said, replacing his gas cap.

"A doctor?"

"Only I saw a car just like this over at the hospital. 'That's a doctor's car,' I said to myself. 'But why isn't it in the doctors' parking lot?'"

"That must have been a different car," Gin said. He added, lamely, "I am in perfect health."

The kid shrugged. "Can't be too many of them around."

Gin drove away thinking furiously. *This will not do at all.*

He pulled into a motel that had parking out of sight from the street, got into his room as calmly and casually as his thumping heart would permit, and closed the drapes hard against the pretty sunset sky.

Timing, timing, timing.

He needed to say things to Popa that one should not say over a telephone. He needed to catch the first Digby ferry crossing he could manage. And now he needed to unload a car.

His brain ran furious passes through a maze of plans as the sun set and the room darkened. Gin thought how restorative a cocktail or two would be at this point, but decided not to go out and court further sightings. He nibbled on one of the energy bars he had stowed in his luggage.

After a time, with a revised plan in mind, he took two of those lovely little pills that knit up the ravelled sleeve of care, washed them down with stale water from the tap, removed his outer clothing, and lay down on the bed. At the last moment he remembered to set an alarm for the pre-dawn hours. *No more Bentley sightings if I can help it!*

Awake if not especially rested, Gin tooled the car through the sleeping Valley early the next morning, staying just about on the speed limit on the nearly-empty 101 highway. He took a risk with a stop for coffee and grub at a gas station in Bridgetown, then took to the less-travelled 201 through such metropoli as Centrelea and Round Hill. He felt like the Invisible Man.

~

"Huh. That's Gin Buttons," Shannon said.

"Where?" Laurie said.

"That car on the exit ramp. I'd know it anywhere. There can't be two of them in the whole Valley."

Laurie yawned. "What's he up to at this hour? Should we follow him?"

"Too late now. By the time we got back to the exit and off, where would he be? Anyhow, we have to get to Clare."

Cindy had brought Rob back from the hospital on Sunday in something like a state of shock. Well, that was natural after he had watched his father's last moments.

But Cindy had not stayed around to take care of him. "I have to go back to the hospital."

"Why?" Shannon had said. "Are you sick?"

"No. But there's a, a friend of mine there."

"A friend." Shannon felt her face grow tight. "So soon?"

"She was hit by a car, okay? I want to go sit with her." And Cindy was gone, looking something between noble and frantic.

So that had left it to Shannon, Laurie, and Liz to sit with Rob in his sorrow. And very soon it was just Shannon and Laurie, as Liz claimed she was not feeling well and disappeared into her room.

"Stay if you can," Shannon said to Laurie. "We'll tempt him with pizza."

Rob was barely temptable. He ate a bite or two, no more, and kept passing his hand over his face.

"What are you seeing?" Laurie said.

After a minute, Rob said, "The end of things."

"Your dad..."

"Not just him."

Laurie put a hand on his. After a moment he drew his hand away.

Shannon felt a prickle of irk. "You didn't really know your father, did you? It would be worse if you had known him."

"Worse than this?"

Laurie felt she should say something to that, but what? She hadn't even lost a hamster so far, much less a parent.

"I'm sorry," Rob finally said. "I think I need a shower and some sleep. Then I can make better sense out of this."

He stood up, took a step forgetting about the air cast on his ankle, and crashed face-first to the floor.

The mood went from gloom to something more silly as Laurie and Shannon got Rob back upright and then helped him clump up the stairs to where his bedroom and the bathroom with the shower were.

When they had made it to the second floor, Liz came up from her room. "Is he okay?"

"No worse than he was," Shannon said. "He wants a shower."

"He needs one," Laurie said from somewhere under Rob's right arm.

"I've been a captive, okay?"

They hopped him awkwardly into his room and he sat on the bed with his injured leg straight out, looking like a broken Ken doll.

"Can we help you with the cast?" Shannon said.

"Or your, um, pants?" Laurie said, bright pink.

Liz threw her a look.

"I'll be okay, I think."

The girls all went downstairs. Liz retreated to her room and Shannon and Laurie consoled themselves with pizza. After a while they heard the shower running; a while later, it stopped.

"This would be the moment to give him a hand," Shannon said.

"I'll wait to see if he falls over again."

But two minutes later she came out of the kitchen to find Liz halfway up the stairs, moving like a cat burglar.

"Knock first," Laurie said, and Liz jumped.

"I just thought..."

"Me, too," Laurie said. "But he's probably not in the mood."

They chaperoned each other upstairs to check, and he wasn't. Wasn't even gracious about it. So they had left him to his own devices for the night.

When Laurie and Liz were back in the kitchen, Shannon said, "I know what might help. Let's do that run down to Clare that Cindy was supposed to do."

"What's in Clare?" Laurie asked.

"Another ingredient for our project, maybe," Shannon said. "The last one. I think I know where it's supposed to be, and who to ask about it."

"Count me out," Liz said. "I don't feel like travelling."

They all had Monday classes, but by the time the pizza was truly done, Shannon and Laurie had worked out their plan. They would start mega-early on Tuesday, do the Clare thing, and be back Tuesday evening bearing gifts to cheer Rob up.

After their close encounter with Gin Buttons at Bridgetown, they went on through the Tuesday pre-dawn, Shannon driving and Laurie running the radio. They took no notice of the car, headlights off, that had stayed well back behind them from when they had set out from Wolfville.

~

Once Gin had snuck past Annapolis Royal, the back-roading got a bit more complex. In the pre-dawn light it was hard to see and avoid the potholes and absolute ravines that laced the Fraser Road, and the Bentley bucked like a mechanical bull. It was a desperate relief to finally roll up to the garage that had never heard about "location, location, location", that did not even have a signboard, and to see lights on in the house and the shadow of the garage man moving about in his kitchen.

Gin switched off the car, got out, and leaned against the hood. He fumbled in his pocket for his mask, but did not put it on yet. He didn't mind if this fellow saw his face.

The garage man finally emerged, hair uncombed, overalls all any whichway, scuffing in heelless slippers. "Not seen you in a while."

Gin made a dismissive gesture. "What is time? But I am here now."

"I can't work on that thing today. I've got a car up on the rack and another one waiting."

"I am happy for you that business is good."

"I can't never get caught up," the man said. "Nobody's cars runs as good as that thing there of yours."

Gin nodded. "Yet I am here to make a trade."

The garage man stared at him, then made a show of looking around his yard, where a collection of complete and partial Subarus sat in palliative care. "I don't have anything in that class."

"I know. What have you got that just runs?"

~

The next stretch of road was a bit better, and Gin was dropping down the long hill into Bear River before he had gotten very comfortable with his new ride, a station wagon the colour of sun bleach, with a faint aroma of disappointment. He remembered to make the turn that let him avoid the downtown, where, even at this hour, one or two regulars would be available to see and remember strange cars.

He tooled through lanes of dozing houses, crossed the tiny bridge at the head of the tide, and turned left. Soon after he was on First Nations land.

Gin encouraged the car uphill past the health centre, past the band office, past the place for outdoors events, and pulled in at the convenience store by the ball field. The car gave a sigh of relief as he turned it off.

In the store, a skinny-faced girl at the counter smiled a welcome and then slipped a mask on. Gin made sure his own mask was deployed.

"Help you?"

"I'm looking for Popa."

The girl looked blank. "Is that something you bake with?"

"He's from here. You must know him."

She shook her head.

"Quite large. He has a scar across one eyebrow—"

Her eyes lit up. "Oh: *Popa*!"

How can she make those two syllables sound so very different from what I just said? "Where would I find him?"

"He's off away working somewhere. Did you try to phone him?"

"If he appears, tell him..." He stopped just in time. *There is no good way to leave this message.*

A small frown had developed on the girl's face.

"No matter," Gin said. "I will phone him later."

He turned and grabbed a package of ginger snaps off a shelf. "How much for these?"

~

Tuesday morning, Cora came by with fresh-baked rolls, butter and jam. Mona, back in her own house, was awake, dressed, downstairs; but not herself. *Of course not,* Cora thought. *A death in the family is a train wreck.*

She went to where her friend was sitting, in a chair placed for a good view of the yard, if she cared to look. "Can I get you anything?"

"...I'm fine."

"Do we need to do anything? You know, about the funeral, um, the service..."

Mona gave a little flip of her hand. "Cremation. They will tell me when it's done. I don't want to go see it."

Cora moved to where Mona could not avoid looking at her. "What about the life insurance? And his bank account. You have to call."

"I will. Not today."

"I could call for you."

Mona shook her head and went back to not looking out at the garden.

While the coffee machine did its thing, Cora reduced the stack of dishes in the sink. She tidied up as best as she could in a kitchen not her own (*Why does she keep this here, rather than over there where it belongs?*), then found some sheets of paper and a pen and came to sit near where Mona was. She noticed that one of the rolls was gone, so that was something.

"I tell you what: you'll need an obituary for the paper. That's always a hard thing to write. So if you just tell me things as you think of them, I'll take notes and then we can knock it into shape."

Mona made a sound somewhere between a cough and a laugh. "I don't think this town is ready for his obituary."

"But people will be looking for one. It doesn't have to be long. Just something for all the folks around here who knew him."

Mona turned to look at Cora with a strange expression. "All the people around here didn't know him at all."

Cora set the pen down with a louder *clack* then she had intended. "Later on, then."

"Much later."

"Well," Cora said, "doing the dishes isn't enough for me. Oh, I know. I'll go check your mailbox. Never know what you might find there."

Mona was staring out the window again, but she smiled faintly. "You never know, indeed."

By the time Cora had marched back to her house to collect her car (never know, there might be packages for Mona), she had worked through some of her annoyance at her friend. *If you can't be pissy and remote while grieving, when can you?*

She had her own ring of keys in one pocket and Mona's in the other. With two mailbox keys. Good thing they each had a little label, or Cora would have had to spend the morning trying box after box. And the post office people probably frowned on that sort of behaviour.

She found Hollywood-movie parking—the space closest to where she needed to go—and took that as a good omen. *The next odd thing I see will be significant, I bet!*

Well, there was nothing out of the ordinary in her own mailbox; just junk to lug home and throw out.

Mona's first mailbox was stuffed: bills and advertising and a heartfelt message from their Member of Parliament about staying resolute during the health crisis. But there were also half a dozen small, squarish envelopes. *Condolence notes, no doubt. News travels fast.*

Cora thought she might have some suitable note cards somewhere at home. She would pick them up and try to get Mona started on the small, but essential, task of writing thank-yous. *Doing any small thing will help her find the strength to do the bigger things.*

The other box was a puzzler. It had envelopes with no stamps, a tiny package, even loose pages, folded once, with all sorts of people's names written on them, names Cora had not run into before. She paused for a while, pondering, then plucked out only the stuff marked for Doug or for 'Captain'. *Mona used to call him that.*

She stepped away from the box to where she could concentrate on fitting everything sensibly into her shopping bag without blocking other people's access to their boxes. She wondered whether she should read those loose pages, or maybe just look over Mona's shoulder while she read them. *My curiosity is itching. Maybe 'the next odd thing' is somewhere here.*

Then she glanced up, and saw a man approach the bank of mail boxes, studying them as if he had not been there before. There was something about him. *He's trying to look more casual than he really is.* Cora kept her face aimed at the papers in her hands, and powered up her peripheral vision.

The man was really tall, with a shock of blond hair, but he looked more like an athlete than, say, a scarecrow. What he did *not* look like was a guy with a Middleton post office box.

Cora watched him narrow his scan to a section of boxes, and then to a single box...the box she had just visited. He glanced left and right, his eyes registering and dismissing dumpy old Cora, then fetched something that did not look like a key from his pocket and addressed the lock on the box.

Is this when I raise a fuss? Very un-Canadian, but so is whatever he's up to.

The lock yielded to persuasion and the man swung the mail box door open. He picked up the tiny package, stared at it a moment, then slipped it into a pocket. Then he emptied the rest of the box, slowly at first and then in one big grab.

So now he will find the stuff with his name on it, and put the rest back. If I could remember what all those dang names were, I could check when he's gone and figure out who he is.

But he didn't. He swung the mailbox door closed, not even locking it, turned and walked away with that same super-casual gait that stood out a mile in this small town, holding the mass of papers in a way that was supposed to be natural.

Here's the next odd thing, all right.

Cora got to her car before the man got to his, which was parked where it shouldn't be, further down the road. She started her engine, fastened her seat belt, and wished she had a ray gun to power up, just in case.

Then she swung out into an opening in the light traffic, about three cars behind the blond man, and followed him out of town in the direction of Kingston and Wolfville. Her better angel was howling about the danger, the foolishness, the risk, but she stifled it. *When life hands you mysteries, you become a detective.*

13: What would Miss Fisher do?

Kerri Leier

What am I doing? Cora questioned herself as she followed the car from what she felt was a safe distance. She had no formal training in espionage, so her knowledge of tailing was limited to spy films and cop shows—not a particularly inspiring genre for her.

Not to say that she didn't love a mystery. She wouldn't be pulling on all the loose threads if she didn't. However, she was more of a "Murder She Wrote" or "Miss Fisher's Murder Mystery" fan.

Actually, Cora thought, *"Murder She Wrote" never made so much sense to me before*. The way the tall, blond man had dismissed her without the slightest of thoughts showed how powerful a woman of a certain age could be. Thanks to society's views on aging, Cora could maneuver many places without the slightest glance. Often this was incredibly inconvenient, like when she was waiting to be served at a store or wanted to speak at a town meeting, but in her new role as Middleton's Jessica Fletcher, it was a valuable asset.

Unfortunately, her age and curiosity were where the similarities between her and Ms Fletcher ended. She didn't have any crime-solving experience so she could only use curiosity and common sense. Luckily for Cora, she had an abundance of both.

She knew confronting a man who had no issue stealing someone else's mail was liable to end up in a situation she was not prepared for, so common sense dictated she should follow him instead. However, Cora considered, following someone who recklessly defied the law and did so in such a casual manner, was probably also unwise given her lack of experience and interest in proper espionage procedure.

She thought about calling Mona. However, after everything she had been through, that was probably ill-advised. What had the box contained? What other secrets could Doug have been holding on to? What was he involved in that people were sending him unmarked letters and mysterious packages? Why was Cora so invested and where the heck was this man going, and did she have enough gas to get there? Not to mention, what was her plan for when they got there?

She reached into her handbag and pulled out a handful of jellybeans....some problems you had to set aside counting your jellybeans for.

The blond man's vehicle signalled Wolfville and she followed it down the exit ramp. Rob, Doug's mysterious son, was an Acadia student-wasn't he? Could this have to do with him? Cora tried to make sense of it all as she followed the car onto Ridge Road, and then into the lesser streets of Wolfville.

When the car signalled and turned into an unmarked, nearly invisible driveway Cora drove past. It would be stupid to follow him down the driveway in her car.

What would Jessica Fletcher do? Better yet, what would Miss Fisher do? Miss Fisher was ballsy and clever and would definitely park her car a good amount away and sneak down there on foot.

Good Golly Miss Molly, that's a plan! Cora rejoiced, with a shiver, pulling her car to the shoulder and preparing to follow the gentlemen into the deep, unsettlingly quiet night.

~

If Darcy had been on his A-game, he would have been more than aware of his not-so-subtle tail. However, Darcy was horrendously distraught. His contacts at the RCMP had passed along the news of his daughter, and he was wracked with guilt. Nat's untimely demise would have never occurred if it were not for him.

Darcy Mayne was an operative for the RCMP's organized crime division. Years ago he had worked deep undercover in hopes to bring down Mancini's operation. He had posed as a low level enforcer, and had started a relationship with Rosa, a cousin of Robecca's, to further sell his cover. When Henry Williams had needed to get out, it was Darcy who had arranged it.

When Darcy prepared to return to Canada, he left Rosa behind. However, he hadn't known at the time that Rosa was pregnant.

Dedicated to his job, he was an emotionally distant and demanding parent, which is why Natalie had worked so hard to make sure she made him proud. Unfortunately, Darcy hadn't noticed.

The more he remained oblivious to his youngest child's desperate desire for his approval, the more Natalie's Natasha identity solidified. Natalie might never be the child her father noticed, but Natasha could not be denied.

Darcy had thought it was innocent, but Natasha's expertise as a spy had led her to explore Darcy's case files, which is where she had happened across Cindy—and that fact had likely gotten her killed. Darcy was monitoring Cindy as part of counter intelligence, especially since she was directly connected to Rob—grandson of The Old Man. It was all a little too Greek for Darcy, too many connections and all too close. Especially once you added Popa's latest information to the pot.

Darcy sat in his car, radio off, staring out at Blomidon as he contemplated all of this. Now his Natalie had been offed, and the hit had some all-too familiar signatures. Darcy's steely eyes narrowed as he reviewed the details: black tee-shirt at the river, black shirt on the door handle. A dramatic signature of one of Mancini's most notorious hitmen and a contender to take over the business for The Old Man: John Francesco Bernetti, Darcy's own son. It had to be.

For a split second, Darcy's stalwart composure slipped and he smacked his hand against the steering wheel in frustration and in pain. His daughter, brutally murdered, by his son?

It seemed inconceivable but, as this case slowly unravelled, the messy, seemingly unconnected pieces were all forming a terrifyingly tightly framed picture. A picture with Mancini's family business at its very core.

Darcy had thought his business there was long wrapped. Sure, he had kept touch with Henry over the years, carefully monitoring the cover they had constructed, but things had been almost tediously quiet. No quiet now.

Darcy shook himself, trying to recover his calm and tuck his emotions neatly back in their tightly locked boxes where he felt like they belonged. The knocking at his window scrapped that attempt like a car being crushed.

His head snapped up and he reached for his service pistol, hesitating when the round and open face of a burgeoning grandma type filled his driver side window.

"Excuse me, do you need help?" Cora inquired, embracing her very best Angela Lansbury.

~

Booker and Fancy moved in concentric circles around the white plastic test strip that was lying on the gray laminate counter in the bathroom. Liz, exhausted and annoyed about being so, sat on the floor as her friends guarded the process that might give her some answers.

Liz did not want to believe the test could be positive. She had, by anyone's estimation, gone above and beyond to prevent this particular outcome.

Her dark eyes travelled up to check in with her friends. Booker noticed and turned in a full circle. *No answer yet.*

Liz heaved a sigh and paused, freezing in motion for a moment, as the sigh seemed to stir more unsettled tummy rumblings. Then she relaxed back against the cabinets as the feeling passed. Her eyes travelled over the baseboards and she noticed the need to dust. Funny that she hadn't ever really thought about dusting them before. Wasn't that the way? You always noticed those annoying little chores when you were down on the floor feeling too sick to do them.

Fancy's squeak signalled that the wait for the result was over and she dismissed the dusty baseboards from her mind. Before she mustered the energy to check her fate, she tried to think back to when she noticed her symptoms. Was it after that night with Rob, or had it started before that? It was times like these when Liz wished she kept an accurate diary about more than just her experiments with training Booker and Fancy.

Fancy squeaked again, more insistently. Liz shot her a dirty look and slowly reached for the test.

"Okay, okay, enough. I know it's ready. I am allowed to take a dramatic pause, especially when I feel like crap. Give a girl a break."

Fancy seemed to give her an unimpressed look that said, "you're just procrastinating,", without so much as a squeal.

Liz rolled her eyes, then snagged the offensive piece of plastic off the counter, wistfully smiling as her rodent companions scampered down her arm to rest on each shoulder for the official viewing.

"Shit!"

She wasn't completely surprised at the two pink lines, but to say she was less than thrilled would be a gross under-exaggeration. Her mind immediately raced to everything that she would now need to do, and all of the things that wouldn't be possible because of those two vexing little lines. *Popa is not going to be happy. This is going to mess up everything!*

Liz heard the apartment door open and made out two muffled voices. Rob was home and, if she had to hazard a guess, Laurie was with him.

She took a breath and struggled to her feet, signalling Booker and Fancy to head back to her room. She checked the mirror: she had definitely looked better but the damage could have been worse. Still, for this conversation, she needed Laurie out of the picture and it was more likely to happen if Rob remembered that he was attracted to her...or had been at one point.

With a tiny bit of blush and swipe of mascara, she managed to make herself look like she hadn't spent the better part of the last two days woofing her cookies after every meal.

The knock at the door surprised her. It was not part of her plan. She froze, swiping the makeup off the counter like it were contraband and the test into her pocket. "Hey, just a minute!"

She checked her hair and bumped the drawer closed, wincing

that her voice had come out several notes higher than normal. She sounded ridiculous.

Pulling together her composure, she opened the door and stared into Laurie's face. Her agitation must have registered because Laurie looked apologetic.

"Hi, Liz. I'm so sorry and I know this is probably inappropriate but I didn't want to just step on your toes if your toes are indeed in the way and I just kept thinking about how awkward the other night was and then I was like, 'Laurie, this is silly. You are both grown women, just tell Liz how you feel and discuss it like adults.' So here I am," Laurie finished, still standing in the doorway.

Liz eased her way by her, nodding and trying to piece together the point Laurie was inarticulately trying to make. Then she smiled, Laurie had just handed over her own exit visa.

"I am so glad you brought it up, Laurie. My toes are definitely in the way, and I would so appreciate you stepping off of them." She smiled sweetly, and put an arm around Laurie, and propelled her to the door.

Laurie attempted to protest, trying to pull away from Liz's gentle but relentless guidance. "Thanks again for the chat and I am sure Rob and I will see you around." Liz batted her eyelashes with a smile she knew looked as fake as it felt and then bumped Laurie out the door, the way she had bumped closed her makeup drawer.

~

Rob returned from the kitchen with two glasses of Phonebox Red to meet a frowning Liz by herself at the front door. "Where did Laurie go?"

"She had something come up. How's your ankle? Hurting? Let's take these and sit down," Liz insisted, herding him into the living room with much determination. She propped his foot up on a pillow and ensuring he was properly situated with pillows behind his back.

Rob couldn't say he entirely minded being fussed over. She looked different, like girls did sometimes in photos with filters.

That wasn't to say that Liz was normally unattractive; just the opposite. Liz had the type of beauty that was ever-present, unstudied and uncomplicated. Which is what had led to them going from roommates to bedmates.

However, following that fateful night, which Rob had hoped would be the beginning of something-Liz had pulled back, claiming it to be too complicated. *Perhaps,* thought Rob, *Liz had a change of heart due to my accident and the sudden interest Laurie seemed to be taking in me.*

He could feel his chest puff up, with the sudden flush of cockiness in being the object of two women's desires. After the ordeal he had been through, and recovering with a good night sleep in his own bed, he was much more affable to their advances: it was a welcome distraction. He had almost allowed that feeling to spread to a slow, self satisfied grin on his face as they sat down on the couch.

However, it was immediately deflated as Liz placed the milky white plastic test carefully on the coffee table. Rob's brain immediately registered the pale pink lines and closed his eyes in resignation of the ramifications that such a small, innocuous piece of plastic could cause.

~

"So, we need to talk. And I need to be honest, it's a little more complicated than you think." Liz began, setting her untouched red on the table and turning to the man she now thought of as a friend, instead of a mark. She looked into his eyes, wondering how he would feel about what she knew she needed to reveal.

She was searching for a clue that he might know that everything, from their 'chance' meeting in freshman year, to becoming friends and roommates, everything except the night when Liz had allowed herself to go off script, had been orchestrated by someone else to keep him under their thumb. Everything except the test and the causes for it.

~

Allison rolled her shoulders and checked her go bag again for her supplies. She had absolutely everything in place. All the years of planning, all of the heartache she had endured, would soon be over. Popa had played his part well and Allison was grateful. He would be richly rewarded by being close to her right hand when she rose as head of the Mancini Crime Syndicate. She could almost taste it.

She strode to her mirror and expertly applied the subtle shade of murder red to her lips.

The plan was simple enough. Popa had arranged another meeting with The Old Man to discuss the details for Rob's ascension to the "head of the family". *As if that computer science nerd had any business running anything outside of a lab,* Allison thought bitterly, taming her freshly platinum locks into a sleek chignon.

She would be attending as Popa's assistant, hired to handle the paperwork and the legalize of the "business". It had been years since Mancini had laid eyes on her; he would never recognize her. When he had known her she had been a young actress, eager to make an impression, desperate to make her mark. She appreciated the opportunities that The Old Man had arranged for her, even if it meant acquiring some new skills.

Allison pulled the quiet gray nondescript suit out of the closet with an angry yank. *I got too good,* she thought, *and he couldn't let me go.*

She had been going to leave the business. Her acting was more than adequate and she had her beautiful daughter, she didn't need the danger and power of being the sharpest and most lethal torpedo in the game. So when the opportunity arose to keep her under his thumb, remind her who was in control, Mancini had done so in an insulting fashion—having a virtual nobody take the thing she loved the most.

Allison fumed, the edge of her sanity slipped as the memory of Amie's hit, and her subsequent banishment, flooded back with a vengeance. Sent to Nova Scotia under the watchful eye of Popa to "keep her out of trouble". As if anything as trivial as a handler could prevent her from exacting her revenge.

He had been a cool customer, Popa had, and it had taken a while. But Allison could be very persuasive and all he wanted was for his precious little sister to be out from under the influence of the mob.

Her cool elegant beauty twisted into a disturbed grimace, allowing the monster she had become to show itself unchecked for a moment. She shuddered, shifting it back into the shadows and replacing it with that veneer of classic perfection.

Allison rechecked her weapon, a needle which was concealed in a pen. All it would take was an accidental prick from a clumsy forgettable assistant and The Old Man would be taken care of. It would present like COVID, which was already a problem in the prisons, and then he would just never get well. Allison would have access to all the paperwork and simply transfer everything to herself.

She couldn't wait to return to the Mancini headquarters and rub her triumph into Robecca's stupidly smug face. And while she was doing that, Popa would be taking care of the little Rob problem in Wolfville, using COVID as a cover there too.

Allison sighed and shook her head in slight regret. She didn't really have anything personal against Rob. He had gotten her access to the prison plans and information that she desperately needed, but his death would be the ultimate twist of the knife for Robecca and her murderous second husband. *Everyone had a part to play,* Allison lectured herself, *no use getting sentimental at this stage in the game. Not when the poetic justice of the whole situation was so apparent and just too sweet.*

"An eye for an eye," Allison said with a cold grin, "A tooth for a tooth."

She slid on the oversized pair of glasses to complete her transformation into the mousy little assistant who would help usher in a new era of Mancini madness. Except this little mouse had claws and fangs and was going to bring down ruin upon the whole house.

14: The dome shatters

Gordon Wetmore

"Excuse me, do you need help?" the grey-haired woman shouted through the closed window.

Darcy took in her grandmotherly figure, the wispy curls framing the rounded face with the concerned expression, her wide eyes taking in his pain.

"I'd gotten on the wrong road," she said, "and was looking to turn around when I saw that you hadn't got out of your car and—"

Suddenly he broke down. Sobs wracked his body. He thumbed the down button for the driver's window and said, "I just learned that my daughter is dead. Killed. I..." and he could say no more.

"Oh, my dear!" the woman said. "Oh, how horrible! What—how can I…? Is there someone I can call for you? Any way I can help?"

Despite his breaths coming in gasps, unaware of the tears streaming down his face, he felt something like resolve return. "Thank you," he said, "but I have things I need to do. Responsibilities. And I can't look after anything from here. Do you know your way to where you want to go?"

"Yes. Are you sure?"

"Definitely. Thanks again, lady. You don't know how much you have actually helped me just now."

As she took one step back, he popped the car into reverse and bombed out onto the road, disappearing in the gloom back the way he had come. In his rear view mirror he saw the woman standing in the middle of the lonely road, shaking her head.

~

Liz and Rob talked long into the night. The prospect that they had created a new life rearranged the kaleidoscopic chaos that each had been living through. They discovered that, beyond the lust of that one coming together, they actually liked each other, somehow innately trusted each other. And both wanted to parent this tiny human, whose existence they had so casually created.

They both were aware of the possibly deadly consequences from any actions they might take. Rob was aghast to hear that Liz's big brother was Popa, his kidnapper, and that he was using Liz to gain control of Rob. Liz was terrified to learn that Rob had been anointed heir apparent to take over the Mancini family's "business."

"No way," Rob said. "They can't make me take that on."

Both were intelligent; they could see that being obedient to those who would control their futures would be as dangerous as rebelling. Worse, it would pit them against each other.

"We have to get out of this," Liz said.

"But how? We can't just say, 'I quit'."

They talked until both were numb with fatigue without finding even a glimmer of a plan.

Just before they parted to get a few hours of much needed sleep, Rob said," My head is too full. I can't process it all. The kidnapping, the rescue, which was way too easy, by the way, my real father died, everyone around me is acting, well, off—"

"I'm not," Liz said.

"No more than normal, no." He ducked her fake punch. "But Laurie's weird, Cindy's always been a bit of a flake, our 'academic advisor' is a boozing poser, your brother and Allison are probably still after me, this 'secret' project everybody knows about is stalled, my leg's a mess, the cops are going to want to talk to me, and... and...I need to get somewhere alone. To think uninterrupted, just for a few hours. I hope you can understand."

"Jesus! How come you aren't crazy? Where will you go?"

"Don't know. Somewhere off campus where people won't find me. But it's got to be within walking distance—okay, limping distance. My car's still in Deep Brook somewhere."

"As if driving around in an Alfa Romeo won't attract attention. Take mine. It's old, it's small, but it's filled with gas and it's an automatic, good for one-foot driving."

She handed him the keys, went up on her tiptoes to give him a goodnight peck, and went back to her room and her loyal rat guardians.

A wave of gratitude washed over Rob for this simple act of faith from someone who had every right to distrust and despise him. Then fatigue took over and he stumbled to his bed, vowing to hit the road early.

His worn-out body had other ideas, so it was 9:30 before Rob folded himself into Liz's cherry-red Toyota Yaris and motored off in bright morning sunshine and a crisp 15 degrees Celsius (which his American mind translated to 60 Fahrenheit), perfect for driving and thinking. He had a notebook—he always charted his thoughts before important decisions—two pens, a mechanical pencil with a fresh eraser, a bottle of water, two chocolate bars and an apple he had found in their shared fridge.

To avoid the increasingly congested areas toward Halifax, he pointed the car down the Annapolis Valley, rolling through hills, pastures and orchards and ever smaller towns. During the first part of the drive, he let thoughts and memories come and go as they pleased—emotional colouring was essential information.

His grandfather's naming him as next boss, with a capital "B", was a death sentence, for sure. The rest of the family would never accept it. Rob was too like his natural father, too much an outsider. Rob's big problem was his mother's obsession with his becoming the next Don Roberto to erase her shame of Doug's "traitorous" testimony against the Mancini family, and especially against her father.

Rob knew that the old man himself, once the undisputed lion who ruled the pride, had increasing dementia. The Roberto Mancini of his prime would never have been so careless as to be captured in Canada during a botched attempt to smuggle in a million dollars worth of cocaine by landing a float plane on a New Brunswick lake. Even before that, the old man had more and more depended on advice from Robecca over anything his saner advisers proposed. Rob had no doubt that within hours of the old don's death, the family would arrange Robecca's demise and his own. Maybe before. The kidnapping by Popa and Allison had to be part of that—unless they were exploiting the family's growing schisms for some reason all their own.

One person he hoped was not involved was Johnny B, his childhood nemesis. Johnny B was the child of Rosa, Robecca's first cousin, and some Canadian stud, rumoured to be a cop. Where Rob was quiet but high-achieving academically and athletically, Johnny B was a vociferous rebel, bully, gang leader. And merciless. Also very smart, determined to be the best of the worst. He spoke like he was brought up by the Soprano family and had "made his bones" before he was seventeen.

As they grew up, Rob was Johnny B's favourite target. Once, when Robecca sent her ten-year-old son to school wearing a tee-shirt with "Not Only Am I Perfect, I Am Also Italian" in big letters on it, Johnny B and his buddies beat Rob bloody and tore the shirt off him. They were suspended, but who cared? Message sent.

Rob never ran with a gang. He excelled at school and sports, and concentrated on his university studies until the family sent him north to take over the lithium replacement program and make sure its patent went to a family-controlled company. The potential for profit: huge. The danger to Rob if unsuccessful: extreme.

As he rolled through the peaceful countryside, these worries sliding through his mind, he failed to notice the car half a kilometre back keeping pace, neither gaining nor losing distance between it and Rob's little red carriage.

~

When Gin Buttons' car was finally cleared to board the *Fundy Rose*, he heaved a great sigh of relief. His was actually the last vehicle to enter, and he found himself parked on an up-sloping ramp almost nose to tailpipe with some bloated SUV. That was fine by him. The echoing boom of entry doors closing, roaring vibrations from the engines and ventilation system, bangings and rattlings of all fasteners to the shore releasing, all were soothing music to his ears. Safe at last!

Gin unfastened his seat belt, loosened his pants belt a notch, tilted his seat back to a comfortable angle, pulled a silver flask from his jacket pocket and took a sustaining swig of the liquid that earned him his nickname. He planned to stay in his car for the duration. A stop at a bank in Saint John, where he had a safety deposit box under a false name with a doctored passport and more funds to go with the $20,000 escape cash in his suitcase, and he'd have time to plot his next destination: somewhere where no one would ever find him.

He had just about dozed off when a loud rap on his window startled him awake. A burly man in a worker's coveralls shouted above the din, "Ventilation problem, sir! Everyone must go on deck."

"I'd rather stay here," he shouted back.

"Carbon monoxide, sir. You could die."

"Oh, all right," he grumbled, opened the door and squeezed outside.

"Follow me," the deckhand directed, and Gin did as he was told.

They climbed flights of stairs to a heavy door and stepped out onto an empty deck. The wind was biting cold. Gin could see Digby Gut receding in the distance.

"Where is everybody else?" Gin asked.

Without a word, the man grabbed Gin and lifted him almost effortlessly above the rail.

"Don't!" Gin screamed. "I have money! Lots of it! I'll pay you!"

The man stopped lifting with Gin's bum resting on the top rail. "Show me," he said.

"It's in the car!"

"Good to know," the man said, and toppled Gin to where no one would ever find him.

~

It took a hundred kilometres and much deliberate belly breathing before Rob's memories lost their power to freeze his thought processes. Finally he was able to review each scene as an observer.

He became aware of patterns, remembered conversations, some he was part of and some overheard, that contained snippets of valuable information. By the time he reached Annapolis Royal, he was ready to stop and find a spot to sit with his notebook and let his scientist's mind reconstruct the scenes, review each character's actions, words, body language, and find the hidden agendas of the different players.

He knew just the place: the "17 acres of paradise" called The Historic Gardens.

As a precaution, he parked the Toyota in the lot of the Queen Anne Inn, about a half block from the Gardens' entrance, hoping that his hunters, if any, would waste time looking for him there. Even with his walking cast and a book bag slung over his shoulder, he made the short hobble to the Gardens without too much trouble.

Oblivious to the gorgeous blooms, historically themed shrubs, ponds and trees, Rob headed to the southern edge of the grounds. He stopped where two paths converged and a bench sat in a small alcove of thick bushes. From there, he could see anyone approaching along the paths before they saw him..

Despite the beautiful weather, with the COVID-19 tourist restrictions and this being mid-week, there were very few people to worry about anyway. In fact, once past the entrance, he hadn't seen anyone.

Rob forgot that when he went into full analytical mode, he became virtually blind and deaf to the outside world. Thus, just as he was completing an analysis of the scene at Dorchester Prison, he was startled to hear someone say, "How's it goin', cousin?"

"John Francesco Bernetti," Rob said, his heart in his throat, "What hell are you doing here?"

"Aw, Rob," he pronounced it almost as Rob-uh, the Italian intonation deliberately exaggerated, Rob knew, "just saving the Mancini family from the total disaster of you being the new Boss. You're very careless, you know. I could have slit your throat before you even knew I was here. But, for old time's sake, I decided to give you a heads up before I took your head off."

"You mean you wanted to scare the shit out of me first. To gloat."

Rob got to his feet. He was taller than his lithe cousin and a few pounds heavier, but the deadly Johnny B was lean, very quick, and not encumbered by a cast on one leg.

"Totally. This is going to be a 'Family Special' kind of experience. I'm loving it."

Johnny B had been standing with his hands behind his back. Now he raised his right hand high and flicked open a gleaming switch blade. "Shall we dance?"

The two men circled each other warily, and then Johnny B feinted left and whipped right with a slash toward Rob's heart. Rob caught his wrist, pivoted on his walking cast's rubber foot, and threw a very startled Johnny B onto his back.

"Whoa, was that Aikido? Very cool," he said, bouncing to his feet. He folded the clasp knife and slipped it into his pocket. "Different strategy."

Johnny B moved in fast. Rob blocked a kick to the head, but he had no chance of stopping another to his right thigh. As his leg started to buckle, a roundhouse kick caught him in the kidneys, momentarily paralyzing him. Suddenly he was on the ground, helpless, with Johnny B standing over him. The switch blade was open again in his hand.

"Say goodbye, cuz," he said.

Then Rob heard a *phht!* sound and saw a pink spray shoot out of his cousin's left temple. Johnny B dropped as if all his bones had turned to jelly.

A tall, blond man with light-blue eyes that Rob knew from somewhere stepped out of the bushes and pointed a silenced pistol at him. He spoke with quiet intensity. "Is it true? Are you the new Don?"

"No!" Rob said, cringing away from the muzzle. "Never! It's a set up to get me killed so someone else can take over. I'm my father's son. I will never be their puppet again!"

The man pointed the pistol between Rob's desperate eyes. "Henry Williams was my friend and I don't believe a word you're saying."

"I have his deathbed deposition on my phone," Rob said. "It will bring the whole rotten bunch down."

"What?"

"I have it here. In my pocket."

"Get it out."

Rob scrambled onto the bench and pulled the phone from his pocket with shaking hands, praying that it hadn't been damaged in the fight. It hadn't. He found the saved file, pushed *play*, and the image of his father's face came on the screen.

> My real name is Henry Williams, but I am known here as Doug Berenson. I am dying, and so I am giving this deposition to my son Rob to be used at the retrial of Roberto Mancini, may he rot in prison and then in hell.

The blond man gestured and Rob stopped the playback. Then he exhaled audibly, stepped back and lowered the pistol to point at the ground. "You need to give that to Inspector Sean Nickerson, RCMP organized crime, Halifax, quick as you can. Repeat his name."

"What?"

"Repeat his name! You may be going into shock and I want you to be able to remember his name. Repeat it!"

"Sean. Sean Nickerson, RCMP, Halifax."

"Good."

"Who the hell is Sean Nickerson?"

"My boss." The man waved his hand at Johnny B's corpse. "But don't mention this. You were never here. Understand?"

Rob didn't but nodded yes. "Who are you?"

"That piece of garbage killed my daughter Natalie yesterday. Slit her throat."

"Nats! He killed Nats?"

"Of all you stupid kids, she was the only truly innocent one. Her Natasha the Spy thing? Just a delusion, poor crazy kid. But in poking around, she must've found out something that got her killed. The rest of you, you've all got your agendas. You're all less than innocent. Although he might have offed Natalie just to get at me."

"You? Why?"

"He was my son."

"What?"

"Shocker, eh? I was Henry's handler back in the New York days. Stuff happened. Get up," he ordered.

Rob stood on shaky legs. The man pointed with the gun to where a roof was visible above the trees.

"That barn. Head in that direction. There's a service gate that's not locked."

"And you?"

The man became very still. "'Life, like a dome of many coloured glass, stains the white radiance of eternity until death tramples it to fragments.'" He favoured Rob with a twisted smile. "Shelley. Surprising who reads poetry, eh? Well, here's hoping for something pure."

He put the muzzle of the silencer in his mouth.

Rob heard the *phht!* once more, saw another cloud of pink droplets hang in the air for a second and then rain down on the tumbled bodies of father and son.

Somehow Rob kept his thoughts together long enough to gather all his papers and stuff them in the shoulder bag, push through the bushes to a trail leading to the gate, limp down the driveway beside the tea house, get across the street and find the car where he'd left it. Somehow the cherry red of the Yaris did not seem so cheerful as before.

Despite his trembling hands and eyes blinking away tears, he pulled out onto the road without incident. Rob headed to Wolfville on old Highway 1, careful not to exceed any speed limits or draw any attention to himself at all.

15: Gin and vodka

Mark Shupe

The *No One* was not the sturdiest of fishing vessels, nor was it worth its captain's life. Yet the captain had died trying to protect it from the Russian mafia lieutenant who had commandeered it at gun point.

The lieutenant had no time for mercy. The operations in Atlantic Canada were going to hell in a hand basket, and unless he took direct action that basket would explode into a roaring blaze.

It was a sign of the inadequacy of their preparations for the Mancini transition that they didn't have more logistical assets at their ready. Their human asset based in Wolfville, despite his planning, had gone soft. If an assassin wasn't already after him, Moscow might give the order.

No matter. He had gotten the boat into the water in Saint John not long after the ferry had left the Digby terminal. He had hoped he could intercept and board the ferry in time to act before it was too late. Despite his illness and death, the captain in Middleton had left a network able to unearth and sell the most critical information.

The lieutenant had not been able to board the ferry in time, but one of his small crew had seen something bigger than a bread-basket splash into the wake of the ferry. If he had received the information about the assassin a minute later, he was sure he'd never have been in time to fish that fat ass out of the water.

~

Rob knew he shouldn't, but runners without running go mad. Nor can they think properly.

He'd stayed the night at the Old Orchard Inn, just minutes from the apartment he shared with Liz and Laurie, his COVID mask enough of a disguise, he hoped. His mind was throbbing with anxiety from all that was going on around him.

He had grown up in craziness, and somehow developed his easy-going personality to deal with it. He felt in his gut that this was the moment when he had better grow up. Nothing like losing your father, finding out you were going to be a father, and witnessing violent death to make you grow up fast.

Holy shi... He suddenly realized his child would be in line for the Mancini family leadership someday. It was one thing to be happy-go-lucky with your own self but quite another with another life at stake. He felt a bit like Shakespeare's youthful Henry the Fifth, taking life so casually until he got a good swift kick in the butt.

The analogy made him smile. If he was Henry the Fifth, he knew that his Falstaff was one Gin Bottoms, a hopeless braggart who had led him down some very self-indulgent paths.

The smile didn't last long. He couldn't get the image of death out of his head. Of course, it hadn't been the first he'd witnessed.

He pulled the cast off his leg and wrapped the tender joint with a bandage from Pharmasave. He had soaked the bandage with the illegal substance, CMSO, Cindy had got for him that killed pain unlike anything else he'd tried. He then set out on the mud of Evangeline beach to think.

It probably wasn't the best idea, but he had a seven-day rule. Seven days without a run and then he had to jog for thirty minutes, no matter the circumstances. He'd lost track, but he sure it was at least seven days since he'd run. He knew Liz would be pissed he was gone so long, but he needed the time.

It was nearing dusk, and there was no one on the beach. He'd parked in a hidden driveway nearby that was only visible if you were looking for it. No one had followed him this time.

Darcy's suicide had changed everything. He was the only one Rob knew he could trust not to be tainted. Darcy's command to contact Sean Nickerson was the exact opposite of comforting. His mother and Natalie had warned Rob about Nickerson. Obviously, father and daughter had not shared.

Rob was no longer sure his true father's testimony was the key to getting out of this mess. He had seen his family outwit the law too many times. There had to be another way.

The problem nagged under his skin as he ran gingerly across the beach, staying to the sturdier drier beach. A soft surface was not exactly the best for a weak ankle. He lost his train of thought as he tried to minimize his limp. After fifteen minutes of agony, he had to turn back, though no satisfactory course of action had come to mind.

Suddenly there was a gleam of light in his eye. His unconscious running mind had been working! There was only one solution. He had to influence who became the next head of the Mancini family, someone who could be acceptable to all sides, someone not him and not Allison.

He paused to look out at Blomidon. It would be nice just to stay here and work on the lithium project. Put away this family nonsense that had loomed like a shadow over him all these years.

But he had to get home and talk to Liz. He knew just who to nominate. The person wouldn't be pleased at first, but he knew it would work. Once she discovered her true paternity, and the power it would give her.

No one else he knew fought for so many causes. That would make the person a reasonable mafia don, right? Someone who didn't like animals getting hurt certainly wouldn't be too vicious, right? A couple watchings of Al Pacino's character arc in *The Godfather* trying to legitimize the family and she'd be ready for a new cause.

Rob was so excited he didn't even notice the blood oozing from his ankle wound.

After all, that CMSO was not only illegal.

It was also poisoned.

~

Nothing like telling your lover and father of your child he was the father, watch him take your car, and then not return to get your temperature up. Liz knew lots about chemicals and biology, drawing on her tribe's knowledge of plants to become a poison specialist for the mob. She had now turned that knowledge toward a degree in chemistry to find a way out of the mess her life had become. She was lucky her brother was there to help her. She was almost free, but things kept pulling her back.

Liz was a good seven years older than Rob, but she didn't think that mattered. In bed, she had been more than his match, and figured he would enjoy all she had to teach him. She'd be happy to be his lifelong instructor.

She wondered if Rob would be okay when she told him the Mi'qmaq name she had already picked out for their child. She was dedicated to raising her (she just knew it would be a girl) on the straight and narrow. No mob ties. Had to get that all settled.

Agitated waiting for Rob, she went back to the computer. She still hadn't cracked all the code, though she was making her way through what was clearly now a complicated organization chart. Not as good as Rob, maybe, but she was still a good hacker.

She had a sudden burst of inspiration as she noted one of the characters after encryption was an emoji that looked like a pink panther. The thing she most remembered about that old movie series was the music.

By Henry Mancini.

Her fingers flew over the keyboard. She called up an old music file, hit an icon on the screen that hadn't responded before, then played the theme from the pink panther. A new file opened with a much more extensive org chart.

Her mouth dropped open almost as much as when she'd seen the test result for her pregnancy as she realized what deep trouble she was in.

~

When Rob finally returned, he didn't see that Liz was too upset to be angry.

"Rob, we have to talk," she said as he gave her a gentle hug.

"Yes. But something more has happened." They sat on the sofa and Rob explained his idea and watched her reaction.

Her face was blank. Maybe she was just too scared.

"I have a way out of this," he said. "We have to nominate someone else to take over the family. Someone who can handle the danger."

"Laurie," Liz said rather hopefully.

Rob laughed. "Liz, my love, Laurie is the clumsiest spy of all. Clumsier than me, and I tripped into a ditch on my most important mission."

Maybe it was the adrenaline and excitement of the danger. Maybe it was the knowledge he was going to be a father despite all the threats of his life. He found himself exhilarated. He could do a lot worse than Liz- what he meant to think was, he was excited to share this danger with her. It had been horrific to see John killed, but it did take one more piece out of the equation. Allison was the true competition, and maybe one other.

He suspected the person he was about to suggest was the one person who could be ruthless enough to take Allison on. She may not look it, but that girl was tough.

~

Shannon sat alone in the research lab, staring into space. The trip to Clare had been more successful than she had anticipated. She knew now the lithium replacement would work.

But what had happened on the way back, at a gas station on the edge of Digby, bothered her. While Laurie was taking a pee break and Shannon was filling the tank, a man had brushed past her. She hadn't thought anything of it until later, when she found the envelope in her pocket.

Inside was a single sheet of paper. It simply read, "Keep your options open."

But it was signed with a picture of a red beetle. The symbol of the crime family she'd tried so hard to escape.

She destroyed the note without mentioning it to Laurie.

~

Liz looked at Rob anxiously. She had too many vulnerabilities. Should she interrupt him to tell him about the secret org chart she had unearthed? The one that had included his real father. Dated two weeks ago.

Henry Williams had not been inactive in witness protection.

She could see earnestness in Rob's face. Coming from the background he did, was he really this nice? This carefree? She thought so, but given her troubled life, it was not easy to trust. Her trust was what had ensnared both her and her brother. She was about to say something, but...

Booker suddenly appeared on Rob's shoulder. The rat didn't look happy, though Rob didn't seem to notice him. Booker looked her in the eye and thrust his nose skyward. She bit her tongue.

Rats don't give warnings lightly.

~

Gin stared at the vodka.

Until the vodka started staring back. And calling his name, his true name: Dimitri. He tried to hide the unconscious licking of his lips but gave up. His host knew he hated gin, drank it only to protect his cover.

It didn't matter now, did it? He was dead, drowned in the bay of Fundy. Some said the biggest tides in the world, but he'd say the smelliest.

"Am I dead?" he managed to sputter to his companion, or possible captor.

"Nyet," the blond man said. He had the worst dye job Gin had ever seen. It was worse than Gin's own.

"You may wish you were dead, though. Folks in Moscow are not happy."

Gin sighed. "That's a statement you could make 365 days a year."

The companion scowled. "You got fifteen minutes. Get yourself a drink and be ready. I got some tough questions."

The badly dyed man left the small room. It was then that Gin felt the swells. *On a boat.* And one not stable like a ferry, though the ferry hadn't done well for him. He'd almost have been better drowning.

He stood up. Barely. He reached for the vodka. The gin had helped cement his British cover identify so well, he was sure no one had suspected. Except someone had. *Did Popa leak that info?* Hard to believe. Popa had always been trustworthy.

His first sip was like a salve. It was true Russian vodka from the homeland. The next drink was a gulp, not a sip and Gin started to relax.

He was alive! Well, he'd been a star swimmer in his youth. Almost made the Olympic team for the motherland. He should be able to survive a few minutes in the Bay. He'd been lucky the oceans were warming; he may not have survived if this had happened when he'd first arrived in Nova Scotia. How'd he let himself go so badly since then?

All that training, third in his class, expecting to be a top agent. Then located to Nova Scotia. At first, he hadn't understood this cushy assignment, with so little Russian influence, but bit by bit it had built. Not enough to keep his full intellect engaged; he'd succeeded too well in accepting the good life in Nova Scotia, even began believing in Gin Bottoms.

Well, who wouldn't? Other than that bitch, Cindy.

Then suddenly, not one, but two major mission objectives appeared, one potentially lucrative, and one so complex, he could barely keep it straight. If he couldn't, he wasn't sure anyone could. He thought his complex plan could address the first task, but there were so many factors involved.

The vessel took a sudden lurch in a new swell and Gin wondered who was piloting the thing. He had to be careful. He wasn't out of hot water yet.

The dyed man returned, and sat down rigidly across from him.

"Good vodka," Gin said with a wan smile. Maybe he could seduce his captor, seek his protection. He laughed aloud. He was not the same man who'd slept his way to tenure.

"It's *great* vodka. Straight from the Oligarch's collection. It'd make a fitting final drink."

Gin got the threat. Moscow meant business.

"Tell me about lithium."

"Lithium is a rare substance used in—"

"Cut the crap, Dimitri. Leave your silly cover behind. This is serious."

"The replacement they are working on is feasible. I'm sure. These kids are brilliant."

"Our backers won't like this. Nor will the homeland. You know about the find?"

"In Zolesk. Perhaps the largest lithium deposit in the world, but not cheap to mine. This replacement would make it economically infeasible. And eventually destroy Russia's oil and gas sales."

Gin shrugged. *Things happen*.

"Then what good have you been?"

Gin felt the chill stare. He was in trouble. But as always, he had an answer. "I can stop them. I can stop the project. You just need to let me get back there."

It was dangerous. Maybe too dangerous. What choice did he have though? Better to live with danger than float out with the Fundy tide.

"Good. I'll send some muscle to help. Let me go arrange."

As the mafia lieutenant left the room, Gin breathed a sigh of life. Oh, yeah, he recognized him. The danger was very real.

Then he laughed. The lieutenant hadn't even asked him about the more complex initiative. Gin suspected he didn't know. Seven children of crime families, most who did not know their real identity. Bastards, stepchildren, forgotten kids, but all with ties to the most ruthless people in the world. All placed in Nova Scotia, in the genteel province, to test how ruthless they could learn to be, to see if they were worth recruiting into high-ranking mafia positions. Most became spies of one kind of another as their first great test.

With him nudging them along. *A friggin' Pygmalion of epic evil proportions.*

Not all were going to live up to their family legacies, but if he was a betting man, and he was, one or more were about to get very ruthless.

~

After a long silence, Liz asked, "Who? You've got me on pins and needles."

"I think you know. Who is the most committed to causes we know? Who is the smartest and has the fiercest temper?"

Rob looked at Liz expecting her to know, but if she did, she didn't let on.

Liz shook her head,

"Cindy."

"Cindy? Why her?"

"She was born in New York, just like me. Her father was a half Russian, half Italian mobster. She's the only possible candidate who will please everyone."

Liz still looked dubious, so Rob turned up his final card. "She doesn't know it, but she's also my cousin."

~

If Alfredo, the Rat Killer had had any doubt, hearing Rob's declaration through his headset as he sat in the black BMW was enough to convince him. Rob, that pain-in-the ass stepson, may not intend to get in Alfredo's way of taking over the family, but this asinine plan had too much merit. Time to stop him.

Robecca would be pissed. But she didn't need to know Alfredo was involved. Fortunately, he didn't have to act himself. An assassin to replace John was already in town. A very discrete assassin who'd already made a kill.

Robecca should have let Alfredo go to the prison in Dorchester to see the old man. Her first allegiance should be to him, her husband, not this milksop son of hers.

She had expected first to turn Henry hard and ruthless, and then Rob? It was just not in the genes. Didn't she recognize that? If she had heard the conversation, he just had... Oh, well.

The Rat Killer had never married Robecca for love, though she would surely help substantiate his position once Rob was gone.

He slid out of the car, and placed two black shirts by the back door of the apartment, then two more smaller, doll-sized, black shirts.

He had grown up in an unsanitary apartment in New York with a violent father and abusive mother. The Rat Killer never could stand rats.

16: Unexpected chemistry

Thibault Jacquot-Paratte

Cindy turned off the engine of her car, the rumble of which, once stilled, released her focus. She had, without knowing it, put all her anger, frustrations, and sorrow into the steering of her car on the long winding road to Scots Bay (where she had hoped the sea, the pretty or quaint houses, the forest enclosing the path to Cape Split, would wash away her sorrow; she had even considered trekking the trail to Cape Split in the dark, until she convinced herself she was being ridiculous).

She had concentrated so hard on her steering wheel that her grip around it had become so tight her joints ached now as she let go; her mind had been so set upon maintaining the right speed, and on the noise of her engine, that she now felt overwhelmed by the quiet tranquility of Wolfville's streets after dark.

Guilt overwhelmed her temporarily. *How much gas did I just burn? We're killing the planet, we're all going to die, and I just burned gas for no good reason. I advocate veganism so that individuals can lower their impact on the environment, and now I burn fuel for no good reason...*

She grieved for Natalie anew. *It wasn't useless, it was therapy. Maybe I need therapy. It's ridiculous that I cared so much about her...Maybe I saw her from afar once or twice at the university, but I'm not even sure, maybe I'm just making it up because I'd like to believe I did...I can't explain love at first sight any other way...What else would have made me so...at ease around a strange girl who broke into my freaken apartment!? Why is it that I loved her?*

Cindy reflected upon the gash in her heart, and in this reflection, she realized that, instinctively, she hadn't pulled up at her new apartment, but at her old pad—the house she had shared with Rob, Laurie, Liz...

She knew it couldn't be a mere accident. She knocked on the door. Shortly after, Liz opened it.

"I know I can be a pain in the ass, but I really need company," she blurted out.

"Oh no! Don't be sad!" Liz replied. "This is a happy day, and we were looking for you! Shannon just came back from Elliot Hall—the lithium replacement works!"

~

"What?" Gin Buttons repeated.

"*Ne ponimaiet,*" a short man with a Chechen accent snorted. He leaned against a wall in the blank room.

"*Blet suka*, you even forgot how to speak Russian? How did we communicate with you, Dimitri?" the tall, slender, black haired woman who had just walked into the room hissing orders, or questions, or both reproached Gin.

"Wha...what, well, it would have blown my cover! Gin is from Ontario, why would he have known our language? And Acadia is bad with languages—"

"Acadia is bad at everything. A second-rate university like every North American university. That is also why it was the perfect place for you, you scum."

"We, well, I... I meant it only has a small foreign languages dep....Department. Really it's not that bad..."

Gin shuddered, shaking the uneven legs of the chair he was tied to, making slight rattling noises on the worn wooden floor.

"Not so bad that we luckily anticipated your failure...though of course we would have rather not let it come to that," the woman roared in the slight accent she had, despite her best efforts.

"What do you mean?"

"That is none of your concern now, Dimitry. The question is now, how to make you take the fall for everything that's going to happen... not that it will matter anyway. Be happy; life in a Canadian jail is much nicer than what we would do to you otherwise. Until we figure out how we will make you take the blame and manipulate the government into covering up unsolved questions, you will stay right here with Zaurbek and his people."

~

Popa was sitting in the second-floor room he rented right across the street from the house in which his sister lived. They had been involved in shifty business their whole lives through, and he couldn't believe she wasn't more careful. Or didn't inquire into more questions for that matter.

He looked at the Raspberry Pi she had given him that day he had dropped in unannounced. She hadn't asked why he was in town, or why his visit was so brief, even though she knew he lived and worked on the other side of the valley. She knew that in this business, you didn't ask questions if you truly could not trust the other person (Granted, that meant most people). But couldn't she trust him, her own brother?

Of course, Liz, as she insisted on calling herself, wasn't the nosy type—not a good type to be—and she was polite enough not to pry...Nonetheless, he was afraid she simply didn't know enough about everything she got involved with.

He only wished he could come and keep an eye on her from this room more often. And not only because it was one of the only places where he could remain alone after work, without having to take on some persona or another—some metaphorical mask, on top of the actual COVID mask he needed in public.

He turned the dial on his radio to listen in on what the microphones he had planted recorded. He took a sip of mineral water to wash away the bitter taste he still had in his mouth from when he learned, through these microphones, that his sister was pregnant, and she hadn't even called to tell him yet. Didn't she think he'd make a great uncle? He couldn't wait...And yet, he wouldn't even had known if it hadn't been for his eavesdropping.

"I've been testing it all day," Shannon's voice stated. "I left the first one I made in the lab. This one I made just afterwards. They both work the same...Look at it! This is *neolithium*! This is the breakthrough we wanted! Cheap, efficient...and it was so easy, I mean...I almost can't believe no one ever stumbled upon it before us."

Rob's voice: "And what was it that you added?"

Popa had trouble not laughing as a loud fart noise filled his radio. He knew a couch was a bad place to put a microphone, acoustics-wise, but it was also a place where no one looked (he had found about $45 and a brassiere under the couch cushions while placing the microphone when Liz first moved in).

He wished the individual could have broken wind a few seconds later, as he was curious to know what the mystery element was.

The radio crackled through a delayed silence. "Who told you to add that?" Liz demanded.

"We were with Laurie, and Cindy. I told you, didn't I?"

Another loud—and long—flatulence interrupted the radio signal. Popa knew he shouldn't have been laughing, but he couldn't help himself. It was even funny wondering if the flatulent individual thought no one heard them, whilst everyone heard them, or if said farts were *silent-but-deadly*s that only resounded at the perfect pitch for the microphone.

He heard Shannon's voice: "—only at Clarence's in Saulnierville, for some reason."

Rob stopped her. "That can't be right... The charge, along with the iodine present—"

~

The Rat Killer had snuck in through the back door. Not too much sneaking was actually involved, as the door had been unlocked (the neighbourhood was calm except for a house down the road where a party must have been going on).

The floor didn't squeak, the door hinges didn't creak, and since the only voices came from the living room he was at ease. He had his silenced Uzi in one hand, ready to eliminate the lot of them, and a knife in the other, in case he should meet an initial victim on his way to the group.

He came up the stairs that lead to the kitchen. *People are pigs,* he thought, seeing the unwashed dishes on the table and, near the sink, dark stains on the counters that shone pale otherwise in the streaks of half-blue light oozing in through the blinds. *And alcoholics,* he added, almost bumping into an empty two-four, three empty wine boxes on top, five empty wine bottles next to it. *People are disgusting. Good thing that these ones will soon be out of the picture.*

The Rat Killer rejoiced when he had a contract. Of course, he could have gone around killing people here and there, like your average North American serial killer, but he didn't want that. He believed himself above that. He could have been like those imbeciles who offed a few dozen people in a single go, but he didn't want to be associated with the white male shooter assholes.

There was no ethnic, religious, or political source to his dislike of people; he simply disliked people. Any people, all people. Lone wolf shooters were clowns with conspiracy-oriented white pride; what did he care about that? *Yeah, let the whites die out once and for all, and me with 'em.*

He paused and shook his head—he was getting in one of his frenzies again. He couldn't let that happen; he was on a hit. A hit had to be clean.

Last time he did a hit while losing his calm in a frenzy was in Houston, and he had killed six extra people and smeared the inside of a hotel room with gore. He had been happy about ridding the world of the extra six people, but his bosses weren't. 'You might think we should have a world-wide genocide, but that's not what this organization is about. So either you go do your thing, or you do what we tell you, kapish?'

And he wanted to stay with the organization—he worked well, and they gave him money for doing what he loved to do: killing. They gave him the means to kill more and, over time, he would be much more efficient than those serial murdering psychopaths, and those alt-right moron shooters with their short-run sprees...as much as he enjoyed the show they provided.

The Rat Killer smiled. He could see the yellow light from the living room illuminating a section of the hall in front of him.

He put away his Uzi. *No need for a confrontation.*

Instead, he took out the device. The authorities would mistake it for a used-up makeup compact, though in reality, when turned clockwise, it would he would activate the detonator of the tiny, powerful bomb. Less thrilling than shooting them full of holes... though he had to admit he didn't know if Wolfville was a place where five bodies riddled with lead might end up a cold-case. Five bodies found dead, from an explosion...they might just think it was another cult thing. Even the Rat Killer knew Nova Scotia had seen enough cults throughout the years for it to be plausible.

He crept in the hallway, slowly...and suddenly stopped. He blinked; he was sweating. *Is it a mirror?*

Someone was crouching in the dark hallway, opposite to him. The rat killer did not budge a muscle. He looked up and down. The person was dressed in black, had the same mask as he did. *It must be a large mirror...*

He could have sworn it hadn't been there a second ago, though...

~

"Please! Aren't you are least going to tell me where I am, or—?" Gin Buttons blurted out.

"You lucky to be alive!" the woman said. "*Eta, paloshim, prailzashlo pa evo nevinnosti.* You can't expect me...especially when you don't even remember..."

"Remember..." Gin racked his brain in an attempt to decipher what she could be hinting at. "You don't mean...my dear! To say we were lovers, and I forgot?"

"*Kak idiot*!" She yelped as Zaurbek burst into laughter. "I'm your sister-in-law, you ass! *Bozhe* you have become even more pompous than used to be. I'll tell your brother he owes me even more for save your skin...for now. I vill be back for rest of the interrogation."

Without hesitation, she pivoted on her heel and left the room, a departure soon accompanied by the opening and slamming of a heavy door.

Gin Buttons looked down at his bare feet. At least the rescuing mobsters had gotten him out of his clothes; this being said, they had left him in the nude. Even though his wet clothes would have been much colder, he was still chilled.

The sheer awkwardness of being tied nude to a chair in a room alone with an unknown member of the Russian mob (at this point, more his enemies than his friends), caused him to focus on his goosebumps, and feel colder still. "Couldn't I get a blanket, or a pair of pants, or...anything?" he pleaded.

"You shut up! I am watching videos on my phone."

"Come on! It can't be fun for you to see me naked like this!"

"I broked out of Polar Owl maximum corrective facility for life imprisonment. There is no way for your hairy scrotum to make me more intimidated than I then had." he summed up in broken English.

"You know, I could help you with your English if you want. It can't be easy for someone to live here without speaking well."

"You think I speak not well, you must with the locals to speak. You have not? With the peoples, they say funny things like *I have wrote*. When I hear that from local, I stress no more for me." He laughed shortly. "Maybe I speak not so well, but this is okay."

"Even so my good man..."

"I stab seven prisoners Polar Owl detention centre—I am not yours or anybody's man!" he yelled angrily.

Taken aback, Gin Buttons insisted "It was a figure of speech, I assure you. I meant that I can make it worth your while if you help me out!"

"Make it worth what? I live in this nice house, nice wood house on Fundy Bay, close to beach, beautiful sunsets, nature. I have four-by-four Dodge ram truck, I watch series on Samsung Galaxy high-definition screen smart phone. Reception not perfect, but better than Siberia. If I kill enemy we feed him to lobsters, is no problem. Then we eat lobsters. Ha! And all I have to do is drive boat, retrieve crates underwater, bring them up, and work with Canadian dealers to put cocaine and heroin on the market. It's dream life—*pizdietz na'hooi*, what could you offer me?"

~

When the Rat Killer moved forward for the second time, he remained uncertain whether or not it was simply his reflection moving, or if the mirror moved as well. It would have been a feat amazingly difficult to manage, yet not impossible, especially in this thick penumbra, also the cause for his lack of acuity.

Had he a choice, though? He would have to throw his compact gas bomb inside the room or the odourless gas would disperse too quickly to kill them—or to say, there would be a minor chance of some of them surviving, and he couldn't take such a chance. If he were to gun them, he still had to get to the room. In any case he would also check to see if they were really done in.

And how could there be a moving mirror in front of him? It must be his frenzy acting up. Sometimes he'd lose sight of distances, spaces, the world would become a violent blur; when he became berserk, he could swear walls moved around him.

He made up his mind—like ripping off a Band-Aid. Or, rather, like opening a bag of chips in a quiet place. Doing it slowly, trying to be quiet, you'd end up making more noise than if you did it in one shot, two seconds of noise rather than a minute of annoying, slow crackling that everyone would notice.

He rocked backwards to gain some momentum before ducking into a combat roll.

~

Popa felt a jolt of anxiety equal to that in the voices in his radio. "Then a release of hydrogen combined with the electric charge—" Liz blurted before a thunderous explosion resounded through the quiet town. Liz,

Rob, Cindy, Shannon, and Laurie did not need to be there to know that this detonation was the sound of their neolithium generating an explosion of multiple megajoules, disembowelling the ordinary-looking brick building known as Elliot Hall.

"And you made this just afterwards?" Rob yelled.

"Get it out!" Laurie screeched, rising up from the couch.

They heard a soft thump in the hallway. Shannon, who was facing the hall, saw a man dressed in black roll into sight. The thump was followed by a loud crash—Shannon saw a mirror fall on the man in black's head, and another individual dressed in a military uniform rushing out from where the mirror had fallen.

The man in uniform bolted past everyone, grabbed Cindy by the waist, hauled her over his shoulder as if she weighed nothing, and kicked the door out of the way.

Liz didn't need another sign; she was sorry for her rats, but the rest was *just stuff*. She started running towards the door.

Shannon grabbed the neolithium battery prototype off the coffee table. Liz and Cindy were at the front door. Shannon panicked, stood still, turned towards the hall. Who was that man in black, inert on the floor? And the shards of broken mirror, reflecting the nauseating yellow light of the living room ceiling lamp...

"Go!" bellowed Rob, who had been frozen until then.

Laurie tripped on the coffee table and fell to the floor. Rob bent to help her up, became dizzy from the pain in his leg.

Shannon ran for the hall.

~

Popa stood up from his chair, mouth paralyzed in a mute scream. He didn't understand what was going on, but he knew the sound of an explosion when he heard one – he had set off too many himself, usually for sabotage more than for anything else.

His sister! His family!

From his window he saw the man in uniform rush off carrying Cindy, then he saw Liz in the doorway and then...a violent flash of light.

The blast, and an aggressive rush of air, lifted Popa off the floor. The window in front of him shattered from the impacting burst. Glass flew all over him, shards lodging themselves in the bulging bicep Popa had flung across his face.

He regained consciousness a second later; his head ached more than it ever had, he was wet. He lad trouble lifting his arms, but he could see he was bleeding abundantly. He touched his face; his nose was broken, and he was bleeding from there too.

Painfully, slowly, he stood. When he turned around, he almost collapsed. He saw the hole where his head must have broken the drywall.

Fucking hell, Dominic, you're stronger than this. "Liz! God dammit, Denali!"

Popa grabbed the hockey stick he had had behind the door to use as a cane. When he stepped out of his room, he saw the girl who lived in the room across the floor from his with a puzzled expression on her face; her expression turned to shock with one glance at him. "You're bleeding," she said. "You're bleeding!"

Popa could not care less if he lived or died – he had never cared about himself per se. Hockey stick in one hand, banister in the other, he hurried limping down the stairs, his vision a blur.

The front door had been blown open. A downstairs tenant stood next to it, afraid to approach. Popa almost fell down the few steps outside.

He crossed the street, and let himself fall onto his already aching knees next to Liz's body, which had landed on its back on the sidewalk.

Popa gently took his sister's head—her eyes wide open, blood at the corner of her mouth. *She's still breathing, is she? Is she still breathing?*

He lowered his head close to hers, opened her mouth, attempted mouth-to-mouth, cried. Sirens wailed in the distance.

He attempted CPR, his vision cloudy. "Liz!" Growing, burning, raging, agony spread though his arms, his ribs, his stomach.

A burst of flames came from the house as the living room window shattered. Intolerable heat radiated from the blaze.

Popa couldn't breathe. He tried to pull shards off glass out of himself, but they were too slippery with warm blood; he couldn't get a grip on them.

He lowered his head towards Liz's. "Breathe, Liz!" Tears were flooding his eyes.

~

Cindy started screaming only a minute after her abduction and the explosion—it had all happened so fast...*what had happened so fast?*

As soon as she started screaming, the man in uniform put her on her feet and held her by the shoulders. "Are you okay?" he asked calmly, though slightly out-of-breath.

At once she recognized him. "Ljubomir! I thought...in Bogota... But...and the others?" she mumbled

"No sentimentality, Cindy, you're a spy!"

"So are you!" she accused him.

He raised one hand, pointed an index finger under her nose. "No, I am an intelligence officer for the International Non-Aligned Commission of Vojvodina. That is not the same thing. A spy is dishonest."

"Oh, shove it! You take information that isn't yours, and you probably murder on occasion."

"Not this again, Cindy! I did just save your life!"

"What are you doing here, why are you wearing a RCAF major's uniform, and how do you and your government know what I'm doing?"

"It's a long story...!" He fumbled for words. "We've known everything since 1956—"

"Screw you! No you don't! You don't know anything! And my friends?! My friends are dead? Are they all dead?"

He gave her shoulders a gentle shake. "Shh...Cindy...Yes, very probably they are. And very probably they aren't your friends. You know how it is; sooner or later someone will stab everyone in the back. That's how it is in the east and the west. Agents from the USA, your own country, gave money to Acadia to run your program, hoping the technology would go to their partners, the multinationals; Rob from a mafia family—the mafia giving money to

Acadia hoping they would get the technology through one of their legal companies; Shannon selling information to the Russian Mafia to avoid student debts, with a job contract in one of their *legal* companies at the end of her studies, and the Russians putting pressure on Acadia to close the program; and that's not to mention the Japanese and Chinese students, that one English student, and the German teaching affiliate who casually stopped by because they liked science... It was all going to crash down sooner or later."

"You did this!" She raised one hand to slap him. Ljubomir caught her wrist and held her back.

"I will let you slap me when I deserve it. I did not cause the explosions. The Russians did. They fed Shannon false information."

"The bastards..." Cindy wept. A sudden craving for one of her cigarettes assaulted her nerves, and she remembered the old joint that still lingered in her pocket.

"I know more than you know. I told you, we know everything. No one ever suspects us. Listen: you are Rob's cousin and—"

"What?" she interrupted. "Why did the CIA sent me to spy on him in that case?"

"I don't know, maybe it's because the Mafia owns the US government by exerting pressure on it through multinationals, private arbitration courts and 'free' trade agreements. Maybe their legal companies are the partners your government are interested in. But we can talk about it later. Listen before asking questions. The Mafia will come for you. I can help you out of all this, and help you gain asylum in Vojvodina if you collaborate with us."

He stopped and turned her to face him. "I have a jet pack on top of Crowell Tower that will get us out of Wolfville without anyone noticing."

17: Rats are survivors

Wayne Currie

The taste of blood and tears assaulted Popa as he pleaded, almost prayed, "Breathe Liz...for God's sake, breathe!"

And then his prayers were answered. Liz slowly opened her eyes.

At first she didn't know where she was, or even who she was. Her head was ringing and she could smell, almost taste, the smoke and ash surrounding her as she lay on the ground.

Then it came to her: moments ago she was running from the apartment with Rob, after a man in a military uniform had captured, kidnapped, dragged away Cindy.

She looked up at Popa. "What's going on?" It was more of a slurred murmur than an actual question. "What's going on?", she asked again, this time more clearly.

Popa looked down at her and was ecstatic that she was alive. He gently hugged her using mostly his good arm, being careful not to hold her tight, fearful that she had broken something or, worse, suffered horrible internal injuries.

"Liz, Liz...." He couldn't find the words to express his joy that his sister was alive.

He slowly and carefully relaxed his arms around her. Popa never considered himself a "touchy feely" kind of guy, and throughout his life, guarded his emotions from his friends and family. However, these past couple of weeks had been a roller coaster of feelings and his emotions now exploded as he sobbed, "I'm so happy you're alive. Are you okay? Is anything broken? Do you feel any pain? Can you walk?"

It took Liz a few moments to calculate what had happened and to figure out what Popa was asking her. She slowly took stock of her physical state, mentally going through a checklist of body parts and how they felt before finally answering. "Yes...I think I'm okay and it doesn't feel like anything is broken. I'm sore as hell all over, but I think I can move. As for walking, help me up, and let's see."

Liz wrapped an arm around Popa's shoulder and he put his arm behind her back and gingerly helped her to get up. Liz put weight on her feet, one at a time, and determined she could stand with no difficulty, and therefore could walk. She gently pushed Popa's arm away to ensure that she could do it on her own.

She looked at him and asked, "Where are the others? Where is Rob? Are they all right?" She wanted to know the answers, yet was afraid of what they might be.

"I honestly don't know, Liz. My only concern was you and I haven't even looked around to see where everyone else is."

They both looked back at the burning building as they listened to sirens, seemingly coming from all directions.

At that moment, they could see someone, something, emerging from the building. Whatever, or whoever, it, he or she, walked like a drunken sailor staggering home from a night on the town. But this wasn't a party night, and the figure wasn't a sailor.

As the person got nearer, it was obvious who it was.

"Rob!" Liz yelled, and with all the strength she could muster, ran into his black, ash-covered arms.

~

Jet pack! Jet pack! What is he talking about? Cindy thought. Her mind was a complete jumble of crazy information.

She tried to connect all the dots, but they simply floated in the freespace of her mind as she followed Ljubomir toward Crowell Tower. *New York Mafia. Russian Mafia. CIA. The US Government, the RCMP, Vojvodinan Agents, Lithium replacement formula, trained rats! What next? Talking elephants and dancing giraffes?*

She tried and tried but could not make sense of the whole thing. It was as if she was in the middle of a whirlpool and kept getting pulled into the small eddies of it, before being pushed back to the swirling middle.

Ljubomir had said, "You would have seen it if you were paying attention," but she had been paying attention, yet she couldn't see the entire picture. Perhaps she was too close to it all, perhaps she was just a small leaf spinning on top of the whirlpool and would never actually escape from it, destined to spin for the rest of her life.

These were not helpful thoughts and she needed to clear her mind and start sorting this out in some logical way. In the meantime, she realized that in a few minutes she would be tied to a jet pack and shooting skyward from the top of student residence at Acadia University. She now wished to God that she had never heard of lithium.

She decided at that moment, she was not going to rocket off with Ljubomir. She needed to stay in Nova Scotia, in Wolfville, and sort this out. She would look for an opportunity to flee from this Vojvodinan man and get back to her friends.

Or were they her friends? She needed to know that...and a lot more!

When they entered the residence, nobody took note of them as everyone was streaming out to see what all the excitement was. Ljubomir guided Cindy towards the elevator. They got in and he pushed the button for the top floor.

As the door was about to close, a student rushed in and pushed the button for three. She looked at the two of them, smiled and said hello. Cindy thought, *This is my chance. I'll have to be quick.*

The door slid closed and the elevator started to rise. No one said a word. It stopped on the third floor and the girl got off.

As the door was closing, Cindy rushed off and quickly looked for the sign indicating the stairs. By the time Ljubomir realized what had happened, he was not fast enough to stick his arm in the door to stop it closing.

"Shit, shit, shit!" He was pissed at himself for allowing Cindy to leave the elevator like that. He tried the open door button, but by that time the elevator was on its way to the top. He hit the *four* and *five* buttons hoping it would stop at four. It didn't! By the time the door opened on five he was livid.

Now what? he thought.

Cindy was running down the stairs as fast as possible, hoping she wouldn't trip and break a leg or something. On the ground floor she went out into the lobby and quickly ran outside. She had to find a place to hunker down so she could think this through.

What I really need is a simple life. I don't need a replacement lithium formula, spies and mafia people in my universe. One way or another, I'm going to make this happen.

She realized that there was one place where she would be safe for a while. She had heard that Gin Buttons had headed for New Brunswick, and she knew that he had a cottage on Sandy Bottom Lake, close to Annapolis Royal, that almost nobody knew about. He had told her about it in a weak moment, and even told her where the key was hidden: in a maple tree beside the house. He wasn't around now, so she could use it as a safe haven until she came up with a plan.

~

Gin Buttons took stock of his situation. He was tied nude to a chair, in a place he didn't know, with a slightly crazy man who was a trained killer. Oh well, he thought, it could be worse. *I could be dead!*

He mulled that over for a few moments and then re-evaluated his situation. *Maybe being dead could not be worse at this point.*

He had to do something, so he spoke to his guard. "You ask what I could possibly offer you and I can tell you. I can offer you a better life. You say you have a nice truck, you live in a beautiful little house on the Fundy shore and you watch whatever you want on your television. You simply need to 'eliminate' someone from time to time and your life will continue to go on as it is now."

"Yes, is simple life, and I like that," the guard said in his heavily accented English.

"Yes, it is simple; maybe too simple. You live alone and no one bothers you, yet we all need someone to share our life with, even if it's for a short time. You know, a little social life, maybe some friends to get together over a drink, some hot sex every now and then or perhaps even a longer relationship. I could make all of that happen. I could fix it so you would be able to live in complete freedom, with no fear of the Canadian legal system pursuing you and no fear that the Russians will find you. That's life, a good life, a better life and that's what I can offer you if you will help me. Your name is Zaurbek? Is that right?"

It was obvious the man was listening, even though he was pretending to concentrate on the game on his phone. He stopped playing the game and looked up. "Okay...sure...you not here much longer anyway," he said, with a little evil in his voice. "Yes, my name Zaurbek. I know your Russian name, but your English too good. I call you Gin. So Gin, how you do this to make my life better? Could be difficult while you naked tied to chair." He said this with a doubtful smirk on his face.

Gin could see that, even though the man did not quite trust him, he was interested in what he was saying. He had now established a bit of a trustful relationship, having Zaurbek admit his name.

"Okay, Zaurbek," he began, "here's how it works. I have powerful friends in the Canadian government and in the RCMP. With their help I can get you a new identity, Canadian citizenship and a lovely condo in a big city where you will simply disappear into the crowded urban environment. You will be able to move around freely, make friends and enjoy all the things that a big city can provide. You can travel, if you like, and visit all parts of Canada, one of the most beautiful countries in the world. You will have more than enough money and you will live out the rest of your life a free and happy man."

"But you are correct," Gin continued. "I certainly cannot do this while tied naked to a chair."

"Russia most beautiful country in world!" Zaurbek said, almost shouting.

"Yes, of course it is, I agree," Gin said, not wanting to lose him at this point. "But Canada is also a lovely country, and you know you can never go back to Russia. If I'm correct, the reason they sent you here is that the authorities over there will throw you in jail for the rest of your life if you return."

"*Da vy pravy*, you are right," he said, almost sadly. "So, what I do? How I help you?"

Gin knew he had him. "Here's what you do. First of all, I need some clothes. Then you need to untie me. I don't know where we are, but you need to get your Ram truck and then you and I will get the hell out of Dodge."

"Dodge?"

"It's just a saying. Don't worry about it. Look, I have a cottage on Sandy Bottom Lake, just outside of Annapolis Royal, a secret place. We'll head there and lie low for a couple of days. I'll then contact my government and RCMP friends and I'll have you on your way to a new life in no time."

Gin was on a roll now, but he needed to wrap this up fast. "Where is that woman? Is she still around? What about your friends here? Are they around?"

"No, she go into town and will be a few hours," Zaurbek said. "And others, they are not my friends, they are...colleagues. We work together but not friends. They in downstairs den, drinking beer and playing pool. You are in house in Parker Cove, so not far to go to Sandy Lake Bottom. What we do now?"

"Okay, great. Let's get started. This will be easy-peasy!"

Gin was ecstatic his plan to escape was going so well. He was meant to be a big part of this lithium thing, and he wasn't going to miss out. Nothing and no one was going to stop him. Not even this big dumb Russian!

Zaurbek also seemed excited now. "Alright, I get you clothes."

~

Shannon came to in the hall with her head exploding and her mind in a blur. Jesus, what was that? she thought.

She looked around and couldn't see much as she struggled to get up. She was sure that she was cut and bruised, but couldn't quite figure out was happening. The last thing she remembered was a man rolling around in their living room and some guy in a uniform dragging Cindy away. She was sure that Cindy had been screaming, so there was definitely a problem.

She picked herself up and tried to figure out which way was out. Through the fog of her mind she staggered towards the door and saw somebody else bouncing around, trying to get out.

God, it's Rob!

She followed his dark figure out and by the time she burst into open air, she could see him wrapped around someone, next to a man she didn't recognize. What the hell is going on? she thought.

As she approached Rob she saw that he was with Liz. Both Rob and Liz were dark with ash and singed clothing and she thought that she must look the same to them.

"Are you guys okay?" she asked as she came up to them. "What the hell happened in there? What happened to Cindy?"

Rob now recognized Shannon. "Yes we're both fine, considering. What about you, any injuries?"

Shannon finally really took stock of herself and realized that she was okay, with no broken bones or great pain. "Yeah, I'm doing alright, as you say, considering."

"Shannon," Liz said, "this is my brother, Popa. He, uh, happened to be across the street when all hell broke loose and he came over to help me. Oh, God, has anyone seen Laurie?"

They looked at each other and it was obvious they all thought the worst.

"Let's look around outside here," Rob said. "If she managed to get out, she won't be far."

They started looking around. Then Liz exclaimed, "Booker and Fancy! Oh, shit, they're probably still in there. We have to go save them."

She started to run towards the house but Rob grabbed her arm to stop her. "Liz, they're rats. Intelligent rats, but rats just the same. Rats are survivors and they've been on earth for longer than most species. If they could have gotten out, they would have."

Liz looks pleadingly at him. "I hope you're right. I have stronger feelings for them than I have for most humans."

"Don't worry, they'll be fine," he said with confidence. "Besides," he gently touched her stomach, "you now have a human on the way and you will have the strongest feelings ever for our baby."

Rob had his own overwhelming feeling at that point and it just jumped out: "I love you, Liz!"

~

Gin and Zaurbek managed to sneak out of the house without alerting the others, who were in the den shooting pool and, by now, a little drunk. They were in Zaurbek's truck heading down the coast road and now turning right on another road, which Gin noticed had a sign that said *Parker Mountain Road*.

As they came down the steep hill and into Granville Ferry, Gin said, "Okay, I know where I am now. We've got about a half an hour to my cottage and we'll be safe."

The ride went slowly as neither man spoke, except for Gin who gave directions. They stopped at Lequille Country Store for enough provisions for about a week, but other than that it was a quiet trip.

As they were pulling into the lane of the cottage, Gin said, "See the shed over there? Just pull in behind it and the truck won't be visible from the road and even from the water side you can't see it. Nobody knows we're here so it's the perfect place."

"Thanks," said Zaurbek as he parked the Ram. "I know this was the right thing to do. I trust you and I feel safe here."

Good luck, Gin thought. *I hope not to have you around for much longer!*

~

Liz was left speechless with Rob's admission of love, but they had to look around for Laurie. Also, there was that man in the house who was hit by the mirror. What had happened to both of them?

The first responders had started arriving about 15 minutes ago, and they were all over the building. The little fire that resulted from the blast was now out, and some of the firemen were in the house.

Just then she noticed some of them coming out, carrying something. She let out a small scream when she saw that it was two body bags.

Rob ran over and talked to one of the fireman and returned to let them know what was going on. Liz could almost see through his smudged face that he had gone pale.

"They are bodies of a man and a woman," he finally said in a murmured tone, "and they came from your apartment. One of them must be the man who was hit by the mirror."

"Yes," Liz said, now crying, "and the other must be Laurie."

18: And all went dark

P. E. R. Sprague

The lights were off in the Old Orchard Inn room and Rob sat on the miniature couch in the descending darkness as the sun neared the horizon. He was at a loss for words. Everything had literally come crashing down. No more apartment, so here he was in an inn with Liz.

What life am I to live? A failed experiment, a child on the way, mafia ties...how many people want me dead? This is not the life I want for my child.

He continued to rub his sore leg, which seemed to be throbbing all the more since he took that run.

"What do we do now?" Liz asked as she came out of the shower and turned up the lights. She sat gingerly on the edge of the bed, her hair wrapped up in a white towel.

"Nothing...well, I don't mean 'nothing.' I just mean, for tonight, let's just rest and not think about it. Our problems will still be around tomorrow and we can deal with them then."

"I can't stop thinking about it. How can I rest?"

"Well, I can't think about it."

"But Rob, you have to—"

"No, I literally can't think about it. My mind is numb and seems to have blocked the explosion from my mind. Plus my leg is killing me. I should never have gone for a run."

"A run? With your leg? Are you an idiot?"

"Thanks, that's helpful."

"I'm sorry. You're right."

"The pain seems to have spread further up my thigh." Rob winced, grabbed his leg, and tried to breathe but his lungs refused to let any air in. “What the hell did I do to my leg?” he said between gritted teeth.

“You aggravated it.”

“In my thigh? I broke my ankle.”

He readjusted his position, his leg now resting on the top of the small coffee table. “Why did that dog have to come out at me...and why did it have to be next to Allison’s? Funny how I could have avoided a lot of this if I had chosen somewhere else to run.”

“Speaking of Allison, how are you going to topple her plan to take over the family? I know you think Cindy to be the best choice, but shouldn’t she be a part of this conversation?”

“You’re right. We need to talk with her.”

“But why Cindy? She’s a bit...I don’t even know how to describe her.”

“There’s more to her than meets the eye. She is CIA.”

“What!? Bullshit!”

“It’s true. Hired to come here to infiltrate our project. Now, I just hope she isn’t one of the American government who the Mafia have bought off. But I think her pride is large enough for her to avoid our family suckering her.”

Rob sat in silence for a moment, suddenly remembering the explosion. “If she’s still alive. I mean, she wasn’t in one of the body bags. So, there’s a chance she got out.”

“Cindy was kidnapped by some guy in uniform.”

“Oh yes...that’s right.”

“You really can’t focus.”

“No...my mind is a blur.”

Rob reached to grab his cellphone, which was on the edge of the bed, but his mind thought it was closer than it really was and he swiped his arm through the air.

“Could you pass me my phone, please?”

Liz stood, picked up the cellphone, placed it in Rob’s hand, and sat down next to him. “Maybe we should take you to a doctor.”

“No. No doctors.”

Rob unlocked his phone and searched for Cindy’s number in his contacts. He swiped her name and her number dialed.

"Who are you calling?"

"Cindy," said Rob as he placed the phone to his ear.

"How fuzzy is your mind? I just told you that she was kidnapped!"

Liz stood and loomed over where Rob sat on the couch. Her eyes contorted in worry, or at least Rob hoped it was concern. "Rob, you're starting to scare me."

"I remember what you said, but I just—Cindy! Hi, you answered!"

"Hey Rob. I can't really talk right now."

Cindy's voice was muffled, almost as if she was speaking through an electric fan, and Rob could hear the roaring of a car engine in the background.

"I need to talk to you, and soon."

"I can't right now. I will have to call you back."

"Or we could get together later, speak in person."

"I'm not available later today."

"Cindy."

"Rob. I have to call you later, bye."

Rob heard the overbearing click of Cindy hanging up on him, leaving him in an awkward silence as he continued to hold the phone to his cheek.

Cindy was in a car, but where was she driving to? Wasn't she kidnapped?

Rob winced again as pain shot up his leg. He grabbed his thigh with both hands and tried to massage it.

"Let me see your leg, Rob," Liz said.

she helped him stand, unfastened his pants, and pulled them down. Then she gasped. The entire leg was red, and blue lines were spreading up towards his thigh.

"Oh my god, Rob! We need to take you to a hospital right now!"

Liz threw on a t-shirt and jogging pants, grabbed her keys, and helped get him down to the car as best she could.

~

Allison raced down the 101 from Wolfville, heart palpitating and her breath staggered. She got as far as the Greenwood exit and decided to get off the highway. *This should be far enough for now.*

She continued towards Kingston and stopped in the Tim Horton's parking lot to pull out her phone. Her nerves were so shot and she was so sweaty it took her three attempts to unlock her phone, but finally, *swipe swipe swipe*, the phone accepted the patter and she was in.

She found her contact, Katenka, made the call, and raised the phone to her ear. It went to voicemail right away, as it always did.

"I've done it. It's been sabotaged, there was an explosion and the apartment isn't even there anymore. The project is done, as you wished, and best of all—Rob is dead now, as well as a few others."

She hung up and stared ahead at the brick wall of Tim's. *Rob is gone, another person out of her way, the so-called heir.*

A man was sneaking into the apartment before the explosion, and she couldn't take her mind off of him for some reason. *Whoever he was, he's dead now, along with everyone else*.

Allison placed the car in gear again and backed out, this time deciding to take the more scenic route back down the valley.

~

It was late in the day and the sun was sinking below the trees surrounding Sandy Bottom Lake, casting an almost heavenly glow across the water. Gin Buttons couldn't believe Zaurbek had freed him and taken him here. *Could he be that gullible?*

Nevertheless, he was away from the Russian Mafia and was relatively safe. Now he just had to dispose of Zaurbek. But first, a gin.

Gin reached in the hollow of the maple tree out front and grabbed the spare key he hid there. Not long after he had scaled the four steps (which were in less than good shape, each board lifting from the stressed nails as he stepped on it) he was through the front door.

The living room, or salon, as his pretentious wife preferred to call it, held a stale and musty odour. He stood in the entryway and held the door open for Zaurbek and thought about leaving it open for a second to air the place out, but decided against it and locked it instead.

"Peaceful," Zaurbek said.

"Indeed it is." Gin made his way to the liquor cabinet, opposite the couch. He threw back one glass quickly, then refilled it.

"We come to cabin. You call powerful friends now."

"It's far too late in the day. I'll get on the phone first thing in the morning," Gin replied, desperately trying to buy time. This would at least give him the night to think things over and possibly come up with a plan to free himself of his captor.

"Alright. Then you sleep, I tie you up."

Zaurbek tossed zip ties onto the living room coffee table.

"That wasn't our deal!"

"Our deal was you make me better life. Our deal not yet happened. And I not trust you."

"Don't trust me? But I..." Gin stumbled over his words, trying to come up with something plausible that this dunce of a Russian would trust or believe. *Maybe a threat?* "I could have killed you! Yet here you are."

"How you kill me?" Zaurbek pulled his suit jacket back to reveal a Browning pistol seated snuggly in its holster. "I have gun, you have none."

"Damn it, Zaubek!"

"You think I take word of filthy spy? You sleep tied to bed or make phone call."

Zaurbek didn't even unholster his weapon. In fact, he replaced his jacket and concealed it again, knowing full well that the threat was enough.

Gin was backed into a corner. He, of course, had no intention of calling anyone. He only needed to get Zaurbek into the cabin, grab his pistol from the desk drawer in second bedroom, and leave Zaurbek's body at the bottom of the lake. Damn his reliance on booze! Why didn't he go straight for the desk instead of straight for the liquor cabinet? He certainly had no interest in passing the night tied to a bed.

As he stood numbly in the living room, gin glass half empty, a beam of light shone through the entry windows—headlights!

"You had us followed!?" Gin shouted.

"Absolutely not. You call police!"

"When did I have a chance to call the police? You haven't let me out of your sight! Not even when I took a piss at the gas station!"

"Sshh!" Zaurbek placed his finger to his lips. "Someone walking outside."

The two men stood with ears poised, straining to hear what was going on outside the cabin. But there was no need, whoever was outside made no effort to be silent. Gin could easily hear the crunching of leaves and snapping of twigs as the person walked. The deck boards squeaked again under the strain of a person's weight against the nails.

Gin's heart palpitated, and he could feel the gin making him flush. Zaurbek unholstered his pistol and held it tight between his hands, pointing it at the door.

Ding dong.

The doorbell rang. Yet neither man moved from his place.

Ding dong.

"Do we answer that?" Gin whispered.

Knock knock knock.

"Open up, Zaurbek!" It was a female voice with a slight Russian accent.

"Katenka?" Gin said to Zaurbek. "You had her follow us? You lying son of a bitch."

"I did nothing."

"Open the damn door, Zaurbek," Katenka said again.

The two men stood in silence, looking at each other and then the door, uncertain of what to do. Gin knew this would most likely be the end of his life. Katenka held a certain pride in herself and having her dumbass of a brother-in-law (her own dear words for him) try to outwit her and escape would have certainly offended her.

The last thing Gin was going to do was open the door to this madwoman. Evidently, Zaurbek felt the same way. He had also betrayed her, and he stood by the couch in stunned silence.

But soon enough the sound of gunfire broke the uncomfortable silence. The men dived for the floor.

There was a heavy thump and the door crashed open, revealing a huge man with a gun. Around him stepped a tiny woman.

"You try to betray me?" Katenka said.

Zaurbek scrabbled back further, even though his own pistol was raised and hers was not. Katenka had the ability to place the utmost fear in men.

"How did you find us?" Gin asked.

Katenka pulled out her phone and showed them the map on the screen. "The GPS tracker on Zaurbek's phone. I have trackers activated on everyone's phone, and this one can't put down the Candy Crush or whatever game he plays."

Gin turned to Zaurbek, "You didn't think to lose your phone? Even I wasn't dumb enough to bring my own phone."

"Enough. Men. Now sit down." Zaurbek and Gin obeyed with little hesitancy and sat themselves down on the couch. Zaurbek looked at his own outmatched gun and, as if embarrassed by it, put it on the coffee table

"I very much dislike traitors and cowards."

"I want—" Zaurbek started. Katenka's raised hand stopped him.

"I don't give a shit what you want! You have proven you can't be trusted." Katenka pulled out her phone again and made a call. "You can come in now."

They must have been poised outside the door, waiting for her command, Two more big men barged in. One was holding a bag and rope.

"We have something special for you, Zaurbek." She turned to the men. "Take him. You know what to do."

One of the men placed the bag over Zaurbek's head, muffling his screams, while the other tied his arms together.

Zaurbek fought, legs flailing and arms straining against the ropes. But ultimately, he was too weak and they carried him off into the descending darkness. Gin heard the trunk of a car slam shut.

Gin wanted to yell, he wanted to scream, to run, but his body was frozen. His body was a coward. "Are you going to kill him?"

"Now, Dmitri, don't concern yourself with him. He'll be fine; if he cooperates. Now for you."

"What about me? I have been following orders...well, except for this."

"We had specific plans for you, but things have recently changed. We were going to have you take the fall for the anti-lithium project —"

"I can still do that!"

"Please don't interrupt." Katenka stood over him, arms crossed like a teacher reprimanding a troubled child. "I received a call today. There was an explosion. Sabotage. So, no more need for you. And I especially can't trust you. Do you think you could be silent?"

"Absolutely! I won't tell a soul."

"You're right, you won't. Maybe if you hadn't run away we could have chatted. But you did."

Katenka raised the pistol, pulled the trigger, and shot a hole into Gin's forehead.

His body spasmed and immediately went still. His head rolled back and his blood, after a moment of stillness, flooded down his face and stained his brand-new couch.

~

The sun had descended well past the treeline as Cindy rounded the last bend and pulled into the driveway of Professor Button's cabin. A few days alone would certainly put her mind at ease, but also Buttons was hiding something. She never trusted him, and now something having to do with their project had exploded. She just knew Professor Buttons had something to do with the blast, and she was going to find out what it was.

But her expectations were quickly dashed as her headlights lighted up three vehicles and two giants of men standing by the front door of the cabin. They quickly pulled out pistols.

Cindy frantically searched for the gear shift and rammed her little car into reverse.

Hulk number one took aim and shot the two front tires, and the car stopped moving.

Before she could even scream. Someone wrenched her door open and a thick, rough hand covered her mouth. She tried to break free, but it was all futile. The man cut the seat belt and pulled her out of the car. His arms were like vice grips and Cindy could barely move a muscle. In fact, she was losing feeling in her left arm.

Her captor forced her toward the cabin; she could feel her feet making drag marks up the path.. The brute pulled her up the steps and hauled her indoors, where she found herself face to face with a middle-aged brunette.

Over the woman's shoulder, Cindy saw Professor Button's body. She tried to scream, but no sound came out.

"What we do with her?"

"What is your name?" Ketanka asked Cindy.

The man uncovered her mouth to let her speak, but Cindy refused to say a word.

"Very well. No witnesses."

"I didn't witness anything!" Cindy blurted out.

Katenka looked over her shoulder towards Gin and then back to Cindy. "This is witnessing something." To the man she said, "You know what to do."

The man cinched her tight again and dragged her to the door, but another man blocked their path

"I found this in her car," the man said. "Looks like she CIA."

Katenka held Cindy's badge and looked it over. "An American CIA agent in Nova Scotia...Interesting. I believe we have something else planned for you, then. Take her away."

They dragged Cindy out to the car that wasn't Professor Buttons' and tossed her in the backseat. A hand placed a soaked cloth over her nose and mouth.

She fought and struggled against it until she fell back into darkness.

19: Unless some other crazy happens

Carolyn Nicholson

Liz resisted going too much over the speed limit as Rob groaned in pain beside her in the passenger seat. She tried to will herself at the hospital getting Rob the help he needed. It was going to be dire; she knew that.

"Rob, I'm going as fast as I dare, but I want to avoid being pulled over by the cops for speeding. But we're almost there. Just hang on!"

His groaning had stopped, and Rob didn't reply, which only increased her anxiety to almost unbearable limits.

She turned into the emergency entrance to the hospital and pulled up to the sidewalk in front of the double sliding glass doors. Making sure the car was turned off, she ran into the reception area.

"My husband"—there was no sense trying to explain their relationship—"is in terrible condition. He may be, may be, may be... dead! Help! Please help!"

The attendants grabbed a gurney, followed her out to the car, then quickly loaded Rob onto the stretcher. Seeing Liz was not exaggerating his condition, they raced back to the emergency room, calling for a doctor. An admissions officer trotted along beside Liz, trying to get some vital information.

They wheeled Rob into a cubicle and closed the curtain, leaving Liz to find a seat in the corridor.

After an interminable length of time, the doctor pulled back the curtain and said to Liz, "Are you the next-of-kin?"

Am I? she thought. She ran through the options as quickly as she could. His biological father was dead, and his biological mother was a part of the Mafia, her whereabouts unknown. His stepfather was also Mafia, and his grandfather was in prison. As far as she knew, Rob had no siblings.

"Yes. I am pregnant with his child and am willing to act as next-of-kin."

The doctor sat on the chair beside her. "He is unconscious, and we need to amputate his leg to save his life. You will have to sign the authorization."

Liz heard a scream; somebody screaming, "No! No!" Then she realized it was her.

"We need you to be calm for his sake. Can we count on you?"

"Yes, yes."

She was crying softly now, rocking back and forth to try to calm herself and pay attention to what had to happen.

The doctor placed some papers before her and started to explain the need for emergency surgery.

"But he's a runner. He runs every day. I don't know if this is what he would want."

"He will never run again if we don't do this surgery." The doctor leaned in and waited until her eyes met his. "He has a flesh-eating disease which will be fatal without the surgery."

"But where did it come from?" she heard herself saying.

"That's a question for later. We must deal with it right now."

Liz signed the papers, her hand shaking so badly she hardly recognized her own signature.

~

Cora was sitting at the kitchen table across from Mona. Her friend was weeping quietly, speaking through her tears. "Sure, I was angry with him for keeping so many secrets for so many years, but I really loved him, Cora, and we had a wonderful life together. Now I can't see any future for myself. My kids are grown and gone, and I can't keep up the farm by myself. Whatever is going to become of me?"

Cora wished she had an answer to that question. She was glad when the phone rang, and she could break away from the intensity of the moment to answer it. *Maybe it might even be good news.* Cora was an optimist.

Mona looked up through her tears to see Cora's face blanch and her hand tremble slightly.

"We'll be right there. Just hold on, Liz."

Cora hung up and looked at Mona, her face now flushed and her voice a bit shaky. "Your husband's son, Rob, is in surgery having his leg amputated."

"What? But why?"

"That was his girlfriend, Liz. She tried to explain but I could not understand her. She could use some support. She's all alone. And on top of the surgery, she's pregnant!"

Mona looked stunned. "I don't even know anybody named Liz."

"Come on, Mona, we're going to the hospital!"

Cora expected resistance, more answerless questions; but to her surprise, Mona grabbed her purse and ran out the door towards the car.

There was a tussle over who would drive, which Cora won by virtue of being the first to sit in the driver's seat. Mona stomped around to the other side, got in, and they headed to Kentville and the main hospital for the Valley.

They found their way to the waiting room where Liz was pacing, her long, black hair dishevelled and her eyes red from crying.

The women took turns embracing her and then listening to the story of how Rob had broken his ankle and then taken a questionable drug to dull the pain so he could go running and now he had a flesh-eating disease. Liz left out all the information about spies and Mafia and neo-lithium and explosions, hoping it all was irrelevant to the present situation.

"And you're pregnant, Liz?" Mona asked.

"Yes, just a few weeks along, but the test was positive and I have morning sickness, so, I'm sure."

"Well, then," Mona said, "you're coming home with me while Rob is recovering and we'll visit him every day. I'm going to make sure you get the proper care. Then he can recuperate at my home."

Liz felt there was a small ray of hope for her and her baby. It would be what Rob would want for his child. *And Rob is going to make it; he has to make it; he just has to make it.*

Cora felt relieved for her friend. Perhaps she had a new purpose in life. But Cora had an inkling that there was more to Liz and Rob's situation than she was telling them.

And Cora was a curious person.

~

The blast had thrown Booker and Fancy into a corner. As Booker regained consciousness, he realized that Fancy was not moving. Distressed, he prodded her with his nose and squeaked his concern.

She didn't move. He looked around the blasted room: windows and doors blown out, curtains and blinds dangling at odd angles, furniture toppled over and—he stood up to try to get a better view—*was that a dead body?* It was dressed all in black and lying face down on the floor. He sniffed the air. *Yes, that was the smell of death.*

Determining that they were safe for the moment, he returned to Fancy and prodded some more, each time with more force, and louder squeaks.

Fancy slowly opened one eye, then the other, and looked at Booker, confused at first, and then the memory of the blast returned, and she shuddered. *Where was Liz? What had happened to all the people in the room?* And she could smell death.

Liz had trained them to search out small metal objects—why, they had no idea. You couldn't eat them, but they always got rewards for this behaviour, so they went along with it for the treats and to please her.

It was a mutual decision that they explore the dead body for metal objects. Perhaps Liz would be back soon, and they would have something to show for their time and earn a nice treat.

They began to explore what they now discovered was a man's black jacket soaked in blood, rather than a dead body. Just then Fancy squeaked, and he ran to see what she had found.

There were several small metal objects in a partly-open jacket pocket. Booker kept a lookout while Fancy hauled them out, one at a time. Then they both dragged them over to a corner behind an overturned living room chair. They hoped Liz would be pleased.

Now the more pressing need was to find some food. The food left out for the neighbour's dog was always a good place to start, and they weren't disappointed. They had their fill by the time the dog noticed them and set up such a howl that the homeowner ran outside in his pyjamas to discover what was going on.

By then, Booker and Fancy were back inside—if you could say you were inside a blown-out building—but there was that corner behind the upside-down chair that would have to be home for now. Until Liz came for them.

~

Rob slowly gained consciousness and looked around. He saw Liz and two strange women sitting nearby. His groan brought Liz running to his side.

"Rob, Rob, how are you feeling?"

"Horrible," he said. His voice raspy from having been intubated during the surgery. "Where am...What?" Still confused by the anaesthesia, he wasn't quite focused.

"Rob, I'll tell you all about it when you're a little more awake. Your father's wife, Mona, and her friend, Cora, are here to support us. So don't you worry about a thing."

But by now Rob had lapsed back into a low consciousness and soon he slept.

"How am I ever going to tell him about his leg, Mona?" Tears were running down Liz's face.

"You saved his life and he's going to get to see his child grow up. Just keep that in mind."

"And," Cora said, "you both have other problems to deal with,"

"Why, what do you mean?" Mona asked, her brow furrowed.

"Liz knows what I mean. Don't you, Liz?"

For the first time since they left the hotel and drove to the hospital, Liz let herself think about their situation. Okay, they had survived an explosion. *How many lives did she and Rob have?* she pondered. It was a good question, since it seemed the whole world was out to kill them both.

The more she ruminated about their situation and what she should tell Mona and Cora, the more certain she became that they needed to know the truth—or as much as Liz knew of it.

"There's stuff you should know," she said slowly, "and I want to tell you. But there's a thing I have to do first."

"What thing?" Cora asked.

"Our apartment. It's a wreck now. I have to get some things out of it." *Booker and Fancy!*

"Do you want us to come with you?"

Liz was already on her way to the door. "No, I'm okay. But if you could stay with Rob...he might wake up again at any time."

Mona nodded. "We aren't going anywhere."

Cora said, "Unless some other crazy thing happens. So hurry back."

The drive to Wolfville seemed endless, but finally Liz was able to park just down the street from the blasted building. There was yellow police tape strung around everywhere, but nobody actually standing guard who might want to stop her.

Liz climbed over blackened bricks and broken glass and furniture, and made her way to what had been the front door, and called, "Booker, Fancy!"

She almost sat down and cried when she heard their squeaks and their black eyes and whiskers appeared in the doorway. Climbing the rest of the way into the building, she sat down and let them clamber up onto her shoulders. They nuzzled her hair, squeaking excitedly.

Then they ran down her arm and over to their 'gifts' in the corner. Liz followed them and bent down to pick up the metal objects, as Booker and Fancy sat upright, hoping the objects would please her. She searched her pockets and found a few treats. That confirmed to the two that they had made the right decision.

Liz secreted them in the deep pockets of her hoodie for the trip back to the hospital. There was nothing else she could see that she wanted to take.

Back at the hospital, both women looked up as Liz came through the door.

"Rob's just waking up," Mona said. "Did you find what you were looking for?"

"How do you feel about rats?"

"What do you mean?" Cora said.

Liz pulled open her pockets and Mona peeked inside.

"Oh, you have pet rats! Wonderful! They'll come home with us as well."

Cora didn't share her friend's love for 'all creatures great and small', and the thought of driving home with rats as passengers made her shiver; but best not to upset Liz any more than she already was. So, Cora graciously kept silent.

~

Allison could hardly contain her glee as the poison from the concealed needle started to take effect. It had been a last-minute decision to poison The Old Man with a quicker method—less chance for things to go wrong. Mancini had hardly noticed the tiny pinprick.

Popa had arranged the meeting to have the legal paperwork completed needed to turn all Mancini's assets over to Rob, the new heir to the Mancini crime syndicate. As far as Allison knew, Popa didn't suspect this would be his last visit with Mancini.

But now, Mancini was beginning to feel uncomfortable. Odd sensations were coursing through his body. He looked briefly at the site of the pinprick and up at Allison, his eyes widening.

"You?" he said thickly.

She smiled at him and nodded in agreement. "It had to be somebody."

He collapsed sideways out of his chair and landed with a thud on the cement floor of the prison visiting room.

With that, Allison set all hell in motion in the lives of so many people.

She raised the alarm and stood to one side, wide-eyed and innocent, as the guards ran in. They called for a medic, but there was nothing to be done.

They seemed more interested in getting her out of the place than asking her any questions, so she was soon back in the prison parking lot with Popa.

She wondered what Rob would think when he heard. He was the heir apparent; then his mother, Robecca; then Alfredo the Rat Killer, his step-father; then that cousin of Rob's, Cindy.

But it doesn't matter what he or any of them think. I will be the final victor.

The autopsy wouldn't find anything, Allison was sure of that. She just had to be careful not to kill off her remaining competitors too quickly and raise suspicions. *No, all in due time.*

"Helicopter time," she said to Popa. "Let's be somewhere else before they think of any questions we don't want to answer."

"Where to?"

"We can wait in Wolfville until the time is right for the next step."

Popa shook his head. "My room there is a mess."

Allison shrugged. "You'll find a solution. It's what you do."

~

Rob was finally out of the anaesthetic and demanding to know what had happened to him. *No sense trying to soften the blow,* Liz thought. *Indeed, no way to soften the blow.*

"Rob, do you remember that you had red streaks forming from your sore ankle and going up your leg?"

"Oh, yeah. That was when you said you were going to take me to the hospital."

"That's right. And the doctor's diagnosed you with a flesh-eating disease."

"Oh, my God. That can be fatal."

"Absolutely, and that is why they had to amputate your leg just below the knee. To save your life."

There was a long silence as Rob struggled with the news. Liz took his hand, but he pulled it away.

"My leg is gone?"

"Just below the knee." Liz felt silly saying it, even if it was true.

He turned away from his visitors. He hadn't cried since he was a child; now he couldn't stop. Liz tried to comfort him by putting her hand on his shoulder, but he would have none of it and shrugged her hand away.

Mona said, "Give him some space, Liz. This is a terrible shock and he'll need time to come to terms with it. The word is grief. He will have to grieve this great loss, but in time he will adapt. He's young, healthy and has his whole life to look forward to."

Mona put her arm around Liz's shoulders and led her gently to the nearby chairs. They sat for hours, not wanting Rob to be alone.

Finally, he turned, his eyes red and swollen. "I need water," he whispered.

They brought him some food as well, which he didn't touch.

"We're going to give him a sedative, ladies," the nurse said, "so he'll sleep until morning. You all go and get some rest. You're going to need it."

Mona, Cora, Liz, and the rats drove back to Middleton mostly in silence.

~

The next day, Liz called her brother, Popa, to let him know that she was at the hospital.

"Your baby is okay?" was his first response.

"Yes, yes, it's Rob. He's had his leg amputated. I might lose him, Popa. I'm just so scared that he won't be here for me and the baby."

Popa realized his conundrum was indeed all about loyalty: to whom was he going to be loyal?

"Don't worry, Liz, I'll always be there to support you and the baby. But first, I have something to take care of."

"Where are you?"

He was in the Old Orchard Inn, in the room next to Allison's. It suddenly occurred to him that she might actually be able to hear his voice through the wall. "I'm nearby and safe, so don't worry about me."

"But where—?"

He disconnected the call.

Now he had to prepare carefully for his next meeting with Allison. Everything had to be perfect; nothing could go wrong.

~

"Popa," Allison said. "Sit down."

She was wearing that white pantsuit, with her beautiful blonde hair pulled back into a loose ponytail and perfect make-up. "I think it's time to talk about your future in the business. Glass of wine?"

"I can't believe they just let you walk out of the prison."

"Well, of course, they thought it was natural causes. But he knew, for about ten seconds. The best ten seconds of my life," she laughed. "Now, once the others are out of the picture, I'll be the boss and you'll be my trusty lieutenant. How does that sound?"

There was a loud rapping at the door.

Allison's look became wary, hard. "Is this some trick of yours?"

"Not mine."

There was more knocking. A voice said, "Police. Open up."

Allison shrugged and Popa went to open the door. There were three large men in the hall, two in uniform.

"Yes?" Popa said.

The guy in the suit said, "Sean Nickerson, RCMP. Let us in or we're coming in anyway."

"If it's a traffic ticket," Allison said, "Popa's your man."

"It's a bit more than that."

The room had seemed spacious until the three large newcomers crowded in.

"Care for a drink?" Allison said. "Or not while you're on duty, right?"

"There's been a death," Nickerson said. "We suspect it was a murder."

Allison turned to Popa. "Have you been up to your old tricks again?"

20: A shut mouth catches no flies

Ronan O'Driscoll

Fancy and Booker did an intricate dance, whiskers and tails twitching in unison, causing time to stand still. Their consciousnesses jumped from Mona's home and back to the indescribable swirling colours and sounds of the meta-astral plane.

As Blomijedorians, beings from the fifth dimension, they experienced time and space as a single continuum. However, this particular stretch of space and time, in the aftermath of the explosion, was becoming a little confusing.

"My head's spinning trying to follow it," Booker said.

"Oh, come on," Fancy insisted. "This is fun. We're going to love the way it ends."

"Sure," Booker said. "But why can't we have the jet packs? We have every three-letter secret agency you can think of running around, not to mention the M-O-B. Remember when you said Nova Scotia would be quiet and relaxing? The place names even reminded you of our species name. Perfect for this round of the game. *I* was worried it might be boring. Instead, look at how things are! These people are meant to be in lockdown and they're running around getting up to all kinds of mischief. So why can't we push things a little?"

"The rules are straightforward. We have to limit our involvement in the game. We only nudge and suggest. Plus, what would it do to Denali-Liz if we interfered too much?"

"What do you mean? Wouldn't it be better if we helped her out with something advanced? Maybe not a jet pack, but a cybernetic leg for Rob or something."

"No, no. That would be boring. She has all she needs. You know it's bad for pets when you spoil them."

"We're supposed to be the pets!"

"All part of the fun. Sure, we've always pointed her down the right path."

Before Booker and Fancy assumed their rodent forms, they were the IT consultant at the Casino where Liz had a summer job. They helped hone her hacker skills by showing her several gaping backdoors in the tribe's site. But they didn't make those go away. They let her figure out how to patch the vulnerabilities herself.

"Like when she set up the honeypot and tracked down the Nigerian gang that thought they had an easy target. Were they ever sorry!"

Fancy radiated a mixture of rueful humour and regret. Blomijedorean emotions were rarely straightforward. "Yes. Our girl is special. She's been through rough times. Always scraping to make ends meet. Every scrape stretches her and helps her improve. I'm not sure about Rob, though. He's always had it easy."

"Oh, stop being jealous. He just lost a leg, didn't he? That will stretch him! Fine. No pulling out any more sci-fi solutions. So what do we do?"

"We don't have to provide any new solutions. There's already one available. She just has to figure it out..."

"Yes, we led her to the neolithium. Pulled it from Alfredo's corpse. She thought she was training us to retrieve shiny objects. But she's not done anything with it. It's the correct alloy, not the unstable kind the others worked on—"

"Blowing up most of Eliot Hall—"

"I know. And student accommodation was already hard to come by. Neolithium will change the world. Alfredo—"

"The Rat Catcher—"

Fancy was briefly taken aback by this very un-Blomijedorean outburst. "Circle of life, Booker, circle of life. Anyway, he's gone now. He was going to make the proper alloy disappear. Out of mob loyalty."

"So, what do we do? Start tugging on the pocket she's hidden the alloy in?"

"Too obvious. Remember, Denali-Liz isn't the only one with a curious nature."

~

Cora set the martini down next to Mona. "Get that into you," she said. "It'll cure what ails ya, as my Mum used to say."

Mona put down a mangled tissue and looked up, her eyes raw. "Thanks, Cora. Don't know what I'd do without you.

"Don't mention it, dear! You've been through so much."

She patted her friend's shoulder, sitting beside her on the couch. "Do you remember when I moved here from Yorkshire? What's it, about thirty years ago?"

"You were a bit of a curiosity, all right. The town was pretty boring back then..."

"Not like now! So many goings on—"

Cora noticed Mona's lip start to tremble. So much for trying to distract her with tales of the past. "How's that martini?"

"It's good. What's your secret?"

"It's all in the zest. No olives for me. I find a little twist of lemon makes such a difference."

Mona nodded absent-mindedly, gulping back the drink.

"I took a mixology evening course at the university," said Cora. "You'll never believe the name of the lecturer. He was called Gin Buttons! I asked if he had a cocktail named after himself but he didn't like that too—"

Mona started sobbing. "Him! Doug knew that man. He's got something to do with this weird company Doug was involved with. It's like I never knew my real husband."

"There now, dear, try not to dwell on it so much." Mona reached over to pat her friend again. "Tell you what, why don't I make another drink? Maybe grab a few more tissues as well."

Cora grunted as she stood up. The little things about getting old, like grunting when you stood up, irritated her the most. She left her disconsolate friend and headed towards the kitchen.

On the way, she noticed the door to Doug's office was ajar. He had always kept it locked, something which made a lot more sense now. A quick movement caught Cora's eye.

"Ugh!" she said, at the sight of Liz's pets. "Get out of there!"

One of the rats scurried across the keyboard, awakening the login screen. The other tiny beast sat indolently on a filing cabinet, next to something shiny.

"I said clear out!" Cora said. "Or I'll tell Liz you met with an accident."

She waved her hands about until the rats got the message. Imagine having vermin as pets. What would her father back on their farm near Huddersfield have made of it?

She flopped herself down on Doug's rickety office chair. The cursor blinked back at her from the login screen.

"Doug Berenson," she said. "What would you use for a password?"

Cora was no computer expert but knew she only had a limited number of tries. She tried Mona's full name, only to get her first failure. She looked around the clutter of his tiny office. No sticky notes or obvious slips of paper anywhere.

Her eye settled on the top of the filing cabinet where the furry creature brazenly stared back at her. Was that the key to Doug's mysterious PO box? She pushed herself to her feet and looked at the number on the key.

They had another computer in the living room he had shared with Mona. Now it made sense: he kept everything private on this "work" computer.

Cora entered the digits and smiled as the aging computer wheezed, slowly pulling up the last windows Doug had opened.

~

"You hacked into Doug's computer!"

The surprise in Liz's voice had an edge of admiration to it.

"Shhh!" Cora hissed. "Mona might hear you. She may be half-sozzled on my last cocktail but you never know. Poor thing's been through so much."

"Fine. To be honest, I'm just a bit miffed you got it before I did. Look, I need your help putting all the pieces together. Do you mind if I get my laptop?"

"Not at all, sweetie. That's why I called you. I know you'll be better at this kind of thing. Besides, I think your...pets helped me figure out the password."

"Aw! Aren't they the best? Glad you're starting to like them. I'll leave them here, then."

Before Cora knew what was happening, both rats had scurried down Liz's arms and into Cora's ample lap. Cora, too terrified to move, stared down as they cosied against her.

"Here we are!" Liz announced brightly when she returned, placing a laptop next to Doug's old computer. "Although Popa took the memory card from the Raspberry PI, I always back up my files before working on them. I can run this through an emulator and show you. Are you okay?"

Cora had barely moved in Liz's absence. "Could you?" she said. "Take them back?"

"But they really like you! Okay. Come on, you two."

Fancy and Booker retreated to their usual perch and Cora found herself able to breathe again.

Liz busied herself scrolling through a document full of technical formulas and images. "You see! This file looks the same as the one on Doug's computer. Just a sec."

She poked a thumb-drive into the back of the PC. "I usually hate using these, but we need to hurry things along. So many attack surfaces with removable media."

Cora nodded. Although she sometimes missed what the girl was talking about, she was determined to follow along as best she could. "What are you doing now?"

"I want to compare the files. See how they have different byte sizes?"

"Whatever you say."

"I've got a pretty good File-Diff program. Even works on PDFs. Let me just... Oh!"

"What is it?"

"There. See! Different formulas."

Cora squinted at the side-by-side comparisons of both files. "There are different images underneath, too...some kind of metal. One's dull. Looks a bit like lead. The other's shiny."

"Look at the different captions..."

"That one's something called antilithium but the shiny stuff is labelled neolithium? Whatever does that mean? Does it have anything to do with how Doug got sick?"

Liz said nothing, mouth agape as she considered.

Cora watched her with amusement. "Liz, dear," she said, "'a shut mouth catches no flies' was a favourite saying of my mother's."

"What? Sorry. I was just remembering something."

She retrieved an Altoids tin from her laptop bag and opened it. Inside were some small shiny ingots. "B and F pulled these off that body. This must be the viable lithium. But that's not what I remembered."

Cora gave her a confused look.

"Look at the message."

Inside the tin was scrawled *Raspberry pie @ six?* Write! in red marker.

"At first, I thought it was just a hint on which files to decode. But what if it's also a server address?"

"Server address?"

"Sorry. I don't mean to race ahead. Think of it like an email address. After the @ symbol tells you the server and before is the username. I'm guessing "Write!" is the password. If I'm correct, this can give us access to some very incriminating files."

"Are you sure?" Cora said. "How could six be a server? I'm no expert but doesn't it need .com or something?"

"You're right. Unless it was on a private network. Wait a minute..."

Liz went back to the PI emulator software and clicked an icon on the toolbar. The dialog asked her to confirm access to a VPN. Face intense, she opened another window and typed the server's credentials.

"Oh wow!" she said. "We're in."

"In?" said Cora. "I don't understand."

"This desktop has access to a private network and the details there got me access to Mancini's private computer. Ooh! There's got to be some good stuff here. Look! I bet that's the original of the chart I was sent before."

She downloaded the mafia org-chart. Cora gave a surprised laugh.

"What's so funny?"

"Sorry. I didn't realize Organized Crime was so corporate."

"Everything's gone corporate," Liz muttered, studying the chart intensely. "That's the problem with the world. I think I have a way to sort this out."

She pointed at a name. "There! That's who we call..."

~

From the outside, to Robecca's eye, squat Soldier's Memorial Hospital stretched before her like an anaesthetized patient. At the entrance, she put on her medical grade mask and adjusted her fake doctor's badge.

Inside was frenzied chaos. Little need to worry about anybody checking credentials, she thought. Medical staff rushed about, shouting. Dazed patients lined the corridors, some in gurneys bearing wounds from the explosion in Wolfville. There were signs everywhere about COVID protocols. The desks to check visitors for infections went unstaffed.

Perfect, Robecca thought.

She hadn't lied to Cindy when she got her out of this hospital before. She was a doctor when she needed to be, even graduated from medical school in New York before marrying Alfredo and the mob. She hadn't kept her practice up, but was able to bluff her way into the Nova Scotia system as a locum. To be honest, they were grateful anybody was offering to help out in the pandemic-strapped hospital system.

Despite her usual calm, Robecca gasped audibly when she found Rob. It had taken a moment to recognize the sunken eyes staring at her. The thin hospital bed covers made clear what had happened to his leg.

"Oh Rob!" she gasped. "What have they done to you?"

"Mom?" Rob said. "Is that you?"

Robecca put her hand on the metal bed frame. She needed a moment to gather herself. He wasn't her biological son but she had raised him as her own. To see him in this state...

She shook her head, taking a deep breath. "This is my fault. I never wanted you to get caught up in this…in your father's life."

"My father?" His voice had an edge. "Which one do you mean?"

"I was going to tell you everything. There's no time now. I know it's a lot but we have to get you out of here."

"Out of here? I'm not exactly ready to leap out of bed…"

She stared at his chart, it was easier than looking at him. "It'll be fine. They've got you pumped full of antibiotics and pain meds and I can get more. I'm sure you're familiar with that viper, Allison? I've just got word your grandfather's dead and she's jockeying to take over. It means you can't stay here. There's a big target on your back."

He groaned and let his head fall back on the pillow. "Let her come. What have I got to live for? I'm done with it all. The lithium project just..." His mouth closed, he didn't want to finish that sentence. "Besides, I've just had half a leg removed. I'm stuck here."

He let out a frustrated groan.

"No, you're not," Robecca said. "They're desperate for beds and discharging anybody who isn't bleeding onto the floor. I can get you out. And I've got a connection with—"

"No, Mom. All my life you've been rushing about, lying to me. I've always known my family was dubious. The perks helped me look away, but I knew. Private schools in Canada. Holidays in Europe. I can't do that anymore. I won't do that anymore. Let Cindy or you or whoever take over. I'm staying put."

"What about when one of Allison's henchmen puts a bullet in your head?"

He looked away. She knew that look.

"Fine."

She pulled out her phone, gave it a few taps, then spoke tersely at it. "You were right. He won't budge. Here. You talk to him."

"It's Liz," she said, handing over the phone. "She'll talk sense into you"

"Liz!" Colour came to his cheeks. "You...you've met?"

"Nice girl," Robecca said. "Guess I'm not the only one keeping secrets. She called and filled me in. You talk to her while I do the discharge papers."

He took the phone from his mother as she whirled off. She was only a moment in the corridor before demanding to speak to someone in authority.

Rob shook his head and slowly put the phone to his ear. "Liz?"

"Hi, Rob. I had to call her. I figured she was the one person we could trust. I can't talk for too long. Don't know who's listening. Just trust us. There's a way out of this but we have to make sure you're safe."

"I don't know, Liz. Everything's falling apart: me, my family, the company and—"

"None of that matters now. I can't say anything but you've got to trust me. And..."

Silence. For a moment, Rob wondered if the connection was cut.

"What is it?"

"The... our baby," she said, voice wavering a little. "She'll need you."

It was Rob's turn to stay silent.

"That's what I mean," he finally said. "What good is a dad who can't walk?"

"At least she'll have a dad. Just get out of that hospital and get over here. I'll make it work. Trust me."

"She?" Rob asked, voice faint.

He was still staring at the silent phone when Robecca returned, a flustered orderly and wheelchair in tow.

~

It was dark by the time Popa pulled into the parking lot of the Old Orchard Inn. On top of Allison's jibe, Nickerson had pulled him in because he was Indigenous and tattooed. It had been a tedious day of answering questions about some kid named Natalie. Eventually the cops had to let him go.

The ease with which Allison offered him up stung the most. Sure he'd done bad stuff, but always because he needed money from her kind. And they generally dropped him in it, afterwards.

He sat in his car, listening to his sister's frenzied messages. She had called five times while he sweated it out at the Wolfville RCMP station.

Jaw set, he tucked the phone into his pocket and strode down the hotel's hall to bang on Allison's door.

Stepping back to let him in, she gave him an appraising sideways glance. "Had fun playing cops and robbers?"

The last straw.

"I'm done," he said. "Today showed me how you treat people who work for you. That's it."

Her smile was thin as a dagger. "I don't think you understand. Leaving isn't an option."

"I think it is. I got proof you set off the explosion in Wolfville."

He enjoyed watching her smile fade.

"What did you say?"

"You sure have been busy. Connections with the Bratva, as well as working your way through the ranks over here."

"I don't know what you're talking about."

"No? Just listen."

Allison stood statue-still as Popa pulled out his phone and played back the file Liz had sent him. He didn't fully understand how she got the crackly recording, but it was Allison's voice plain enough.

> I've done it. It's been sabotaged, there was an explosion and the apartment isn't even there anymore. The project is done, as you wished, and best of all—Rob is dead now, as well as a few others.

Popa whistled. "Imagine, the new head of the East coast family has Russian connections!"

"How'd you get that?"

Popa just chuckled. He wasn't going to tell her that Mancini hadn't trusted her an inch and had had her bugged.

"I'll see you dead for this," she said.

"Don't think so. If me or Liz get so much as a scratch, that file's going to a bunch of people. Starting with that Nickerson asshole you had me stuck with all day."

She stared. Popa slowly stretched his neck left and right, a satisfying crunch each time as vertebrae cracked. He could feel the weight of her lifting off his shoulders already.

"Do you really think you can take control of the family?" Allison finally said.

"Not what I want. You can keep pulling strings so long as I've got this string to pull you." He tapped the phone. "Just so you know, Rob's alive. You can keep him out of this too. We'll be setting up a new lithium company down the road in Glooscap. I'm sure to get some of the elders on board. Keep it in the community."

He relished the sight of her trying to maintain her composure. Although he wished he had a piece on him. Who knew what somebody like her was capable of when cornered?

Finally, she made a dismissive nod towards the door. "Get out."

It was the last order he took from her.

21: Hats aplenty

Rhoda C. Hill

The rope was so faded and dingy it blended perfectly into the riverbank. If you weren't looking for it, you could easily miss it.

Tony didn't need to look for it. He'd beaten a path to it daily, sometimes several times a day, and he was certain he could find it blindfolded if need be.

He'd chosen a spot where the trees were heavy, and he had to squat to reach the river's edge. Due to the eroding riverbank, most of the trees in that area had slipped down the side and were either twisted or lopsided. They still thrived, even with their roots exposed, but some of the branches stretched over the river, the tips of their leaves touched the water's surface and, during swells, were totally submerged.

They came out no worse for wear, their prolonged dunk seeming to revive them. It made Tony's lungs hitch each time he noticed the branches submerged. A human, such as himself, would not come out the same.

His last dunk in the water had changed him. He'd gone down a child and been reborn a man. He'd spent his whole life waiting for the moment he would step out from under the umbrella of childhood, but adulting wasn't all it was cracked up to be. Now he'd do anything to step back beneath that umbrella where he had been safe and happy.

He lay on his tummy, the rope trapped beneath him, and stared out over the river.

The last time he'd been here he'd watched as a woman floated an iceboat on the water. It had taken several seconds for the boat to disintegrate. The last shards of its stern fetched up in the branches just below where Tony was watching from, and he'd witnessed the water lick at the ice until it slowly disappeared. Most of the scattered bits of papier-mâché caught on the branches and began a slow ascent to safety, each lap driving then further and further up the branch.

"Five hours to shape. Five minutes to float. Better than most of my creations," the woman had declared importantly, like she wasn't a one-person judge of the world's most lonely race. A race where you walked away empty-handed regardless of your rank.

She'd been too generous; thirty seconds was more like it. But at least she'd shown up, and that was saying something.

She hadn't made much of the black t-shirt he'd been paid to put there. Just a cursory glance and a 'what the hell?' He was lying there in the chilled evening air, freezing with no t-shirt on, and that's all she had to offer.

The world was a weird place to be in. You worry about the whereabouts of missing clothes when you see a naked child, but never about the missing child when you see discarded clothing in peculiar places.

Maybe his brain worked differently than others'. How many times had his mother driven past a random shoe on the side of the road without so much as a glance? *What about the missing foot that the shoe belonged to? What if the foot was still in the shoe, and the person it belonged to was somewhere, footless?*

He sought out the rope and pried it from the ground the elements had helped embed it into. He worked his fingers down the rope all the way to the riverbank's edge, and freed it from the murky wall until it dangled all the way to the water below, and then he began to reel it in.

With each retrieved inch of the rope, his memories became more vivid.

~

"Shelly?" His father had a nasty laugh. "No son of mine will be called Shelly."

"He's barely your son, John. He's twelve years old and you've yet to lay eyes on him."

"He wasn't miraculously conceived either," his father had yelled at his mother, and Tony had stretched on his tiptoes to try to see inside the opened window. "You're no Virgin Mary."

"You're a sperm donor, that's it."

"I may not have contributed material things to him, but I'm still a better father than you'll ever be a mother."

"You're right."

Shelly heard the strong voice of his ever-present, ever-tough mother break and he wanted to run to her. He couldn't. He'd been pushed from the window in desperation and warned to stay put.

"My Shelly almost has it all. A quick mind and nimble fingers, a handsome face and lithe physique, but he lacks in the parentage department. His mother's a failure with nothing but bad decisions under her belt, and his father's a money-hungry louse who runs away when the going gets tough."

"You foul-mouthed little harlot."

From his spot under the window Shelly could hear the heavy boots of the man who fathered him as he crossed the room.

He heard grunts and huffs and his mothers strangled voice. "What are you going to do to me? Kill me? And what will happen to Shelly then?"

"Tony. He will be called Tony, and I will care for him. I will turn him into the man he ought to be and would never become under your pandering care."

Under the window, Shelly shivered as the rain pelted down.

"No boy should be left in the hands of a weak woman like you."

His mother's chokes and gags filled the air around him, and then a thud. Shelly could barely breathe. If his mother was not breathing then neither should he, so he let himself fall to the wet ground, all the air scared from his lungs as he forgot how to breathe. And there on the ground, as his lungs fought for the air that they so desperately craved, he felt the world spin around him, and blackness settle in.

It had seeped into his soul, this blackness he could feel but not see, and as it reached its long cold fingers to claim him, he had heard his mother's soft voice.

"The rope is yours now, Shelly."

As she had spoken to him, small slivers of light penetrated the darkness, and he had felt the air enter his lungs again.

~

He removed the waterproof bag from the end of the rope and pulled at its ties. The bag was still as heavy as the first time he'd lifted it.

The wads of money didn't seem to be depleting—if anything, they seemed to grow. *How?* He had no idea.

He had never questioned his mother, he just waited on the bank while she fished the bag from the river and took from it what she needed.

He was not going to be so polite. He needed to leave this town before John returned and demanded something crazier than leaving a simple t-shirt on the riverbank. He'd already seen what he was capable of.

~

Shelly had fled to the river. His peaceful place when things weren't calm, but the sound of his mother's chokes and gags screamed chaos in his head.

It hurt worse than anything. Worse than her death, even; this constant regret of taking her love and care for him so frivolously. He'd always taken it at face value, assuming she did it because she had to, when his very own father had chosen to abandon him. That guilt hurt worse than anything.

He had sat on the riverbank, down low so that his feet could dangle in the water. He wept shamelessly because he hurt, and momma had always told him that tears were the appropriate venue for pain.

"What's your name, boy?"

The voice halted his weeping in its tracks, and he looked up. He knew the voice. He would know it anywhere, even though he'd only heard it one other time, just minutes earlier while he sat cowering beneath the opened window of his family's little camp. This man had called his mother weak, as he snuffed the life out of her like the weak man he was.

"I'm Shelly," he said.

The man huffed. "What kind of a name is Shelly?"

"The good kind," he said, because he didn't know what else to say.

The man drew nearer. Shelly scrambled to his feet. "No, no, no." He said as he moved sideways along the riverbank, his feet right on the brink of falling in.

"Come here, boy," his father ordered, slapping his side as though Shelly were a dog.

Shelly did not heel. Instead he turned and leapt into the water. The current tried to grab him, but the water was shallow here and he caught his footing and stood.

"Come here, boy," his father bellowed.

Shelly picked up his pace, stepping through the water, going downstream rather than across. He had no idea where he was going; he just knew he had to go.

He hadn't expected the man to step into the water too, and when he did the shock of it halted Shelly for a moment. Then his fight or flight response kicked in and, suddenly, he wanted to do both. He weighed each option in his head as the man moved in closer to him.

"By God, when I get my hands on you, you're gonna wish you were dead." The man seemed more worried about his perfectly-pressed trousers as he stepped cautiously through the water, hitching up his pants legs as he went along.

If he ran, Shelly knew he could lose him. By the time the man picked his way across the rocky patch of shallows and then made peace with the swimming he'd have to do the rest of the way, at the pace he was currently going, Shelly could be long gone.

If Shelly could make it across uninterrupted, he'd run to Ridge

Road and hope that a taxi was nearby. He couldn't go back to Hellsgate, where their get-away camp was—that would be too risky. He'd figure that all out later, once he was in the clear; when the man who'd killed his mother, the sperm-donor, was no longer immediately behind him, still within his sight.

How many times had he crossed the river this way? Too many to count. He should have been able to do it without a hitch, but all those other times he'd been freewheeling through life. Now he was caught between a rock and a hard place, and his mind was spinning out scenarios a mile a minute. All this distraction was weighing him down. He felt his feet falter, and he slipped.

He felt the water roll over his head, and he waddled about, going through the motions of bringing himself to the surface. But the surface was no longer fluid, and his head bucked against a solid mass that seemed to push down on his head hard, the harder he tried to surface.

He had no choice. He breathed in, and a huge gush of water pulled into his lungs. He tried to cough, but his cough bubbled in the water before him.

Then suddenly he was topside, and his cough broke on the surface. Water shot from his mouth in a projectile stream, and he pounded at his own chest.

It took a moment to regain his composure enough to open his eyes, and it was only then that he realized what was happening.

He only had seconds to take it all in before he was immersed again and held there, trying not to breathe more water into his already-burning lungs.

Then he surfaced again.

"I am your father, boy. When I say come here, I mean come *here*. You hear me?"

He couldn't speak, but he tried to shake his head beneath the hand that held a fistful of his hair. He tried to blink the water from his eyes, but he saw himself descending back into the water, and he squeezed them shut and gulped a breath of air before he was deep beneath the cold water again.

"Your name, boy?" He heard when he resurfaced.

"Shelly," he croaked.

It was obviously the wrong answer because he was doused again and held there.

And again, the air hit his face and he gulped for air. His lungs were tired. They'd been so overworked that they threatened to buckle under pressure.

"Your name?"

For twelve years he'd been Shelly. *Were those twelve years a lie?*

He felt himself being shaken although the only hand touching him was the one in his hair.

Maybe I'm Tony, he thought as the water rolled over his head again and the river squeezed at his chest. Shelly had been pandered to, but he knew that without his mother to care for him, his soft days were over. Maybe he was Tony now, maybe that's how this life of growing up worked. Maybe the child was shaken out of you and drowned in Gaspereau River, or some other river that was handy. Yes, maybe he was Tony now.

"Your name, boy." It was no longer a question; it had turned into a command.

"Tony," For the first time his voice was not a sputter of water. "My name is Tony." He waited for the dunk, but it did not come.

"Ah, a much stronger name for a Bernetti," the man said with a smile. Even his smile was cold. "And when I call for you?"

"I'll come," he said.

He didn't feel like a man. The only difference he felt now was fear. He had never been scared as a child. That's what adulthood was, a whole new set of emotions. Mainly fear, he would guess. He looked at the man before him, and wondered what *he* feared, but he wouldn't ask him.

The man tossed him aside and began to walk back to the riverb-ank, Tony followed.

His mother had feared daily. As a man he realized that now. As he walked behind his sperm donor, he thought about his mother's fears. The dead-bolted doors. The reiterating of safety protocols. Her refusal to let him attend public school. The constant looking over her shoulders, and the gun she kept in her nightstand.

He wasn't sure he was going to like being a man, but short of dying, he had no choice but to be one.

The man reached the riverbank first and slapped the side of his leg. "Come here, Tony."

Tony skittered up the bank to his side.

"You stay here, in that rundown little camp, until I tell you otherwise, you hear me? And this," he pulled at the ratty black t-shirt Tony wore, "take it off, place it over there." He pointed to a rock a ways off.

"But what will I wear?"

He cuffed him on the side of the head. "This is not your shirt. It looks like an old Frenchy's rag. Better to be naked then wear an old rag no one wants."

He had plucked the shirt from Tony's torso and limbs as though he were a rag doll. "Do as I say, you hear me?"

"I hear you."

He had grabbed one of Tony's ears and tugged. "You got your mother's big ol' ears." There was his nasty laugh again.

He tugged at the ear some more, then tucked a rolled-up $10 bill behind the ear. He flicked his finger against the ear for added effect. "You look like a wing nut."

~

Tony emptied the rolls of money into the backpack he'd brought with him. He tossed the empty can into the river. He had no idea how much there was altogether. *Maybe ten thousand*?

He didn't understand his mother's mentality. They struggled to live while this can dangled down the riverbank waiting for her to claim it. He didn't understand why she only took from it when desperation set in. There was a lot he didn't understand, and a lot he probably never would.

He was desperate. He needed to leave this place. He needed to learn all he could about who he was now, who grown-up Tony was. He couldn't just go on living, oblivious to everything around him. He needed to take stock. He needed to pay attention to little things, mundane things.

The fun was all finished. He was grown, and nothing sucked the fun out of life like being a grown-up.

Right?

He really had no idea anymore. His whole life felt like a lie now. His mother had told him the future was his to do with as he wanted. She'd told him only he could choose the direction he took.

After that day on the riverbank when he had become Tony, he realized that was a lie. A bold-faced lie, the worse kind of lie there was. A life-altering lie, in which he went from the sole driver of his life's direction to being a bystander watching his life self-destruct.

He tucked a roll of bills behind his ear, held securely in place by the stickiness of the rubber band around the roll.

He would find a taxi and toss him just one of the bills with loose directions to drive until the money ran out, and then he'd crawl out of the taxi and figure out the next thing.

~

No, Cora had not moved in to Mona's. She had her own gardens to tend to and a substantial liquor collection that missed her if she was gone too long. She was helping out. She went where she was needed, and she was needed right here.

She had hats aplenty. She went from Miss Fisher to Mary Poppins, to Poppy Pomfrey, to Professor Sprout, to a liquor connoisseur as needed, and could still drop right back into a doting grandmother in two seconds flat if need be. This was her lot in life, and the older she got the higher her hats stacked up.

Right now, she was just Cora, whoever that might be. Sometimes her head spun with it all, and she had to take a moment to remind herself who she was exactly.

Everyone was sleeping, tucked away here and there in Mona's house; some with the aid of pain meds, some with the aid of sleeping pills, and others from sheer exhaustion. But they were sleeping nonetheless, and Cora was collecting all her proverbial hats into a neat little stack for tomorrow, or whenever she should need them again.

She just wanted tea. A bitter cup of organic Smooth Move, so she could have a restful day tomorrow without worrying about her bowel track.

Mona's home was not the same as her own. Mona didn't have Netflix, or Prime, or anything aside from basic cable, but she did have an unread collection of Agatha Christie novels. Cora had chosen one at random and was now sitting in a maroon wingback chair with a small rag quilt over her lap, and her heels resting on a footstool, reading *The Man in the Brown Suit.*

It was quite a fetching tale and one line really resonated with her:

> Girls are foolish things.

That was definitely true of Liz. Only a foolish girl would own rats. If she'd yet become a woman surely her senses would have come about her, and she would have discarded the pesky rodents as soon as she'd reached womanhood.

Cora sipped at the tea and resumed her reading.

> In the succeeding weeks I was a good deal bored. Mrs. Flemming and her friends seemed to—

She stopped. *What was that?* She focused on the sound. It wasn't coming from inside the house like she'd first suspected. She listened intently.

Quiet.

Probably those damn rats up to no good. She turned back to the book.

> —Mrs. Flemming and her friends seemed to me to be supremely uninteresting. They talked for hours of thems—

What the hell was that? Liz had taken the rats with her, to the bedroom at the back of the house. And if she remembered correctly, it was her intention to put the rats in a pail she'd found in the garage until she could purchase them a new cage-home.

She heard the thud again. It was most definitely coming from outside.

She took one more big swallow of her tea and sat the book on the table. The foyer was cast in darkness, and she would leave it that way. No need to alert whoever was outside the door if they meant them ill.

Within seconds her Miss Fisher hat was secured to her head, and her sleuth brain was activated.

She didn't need to pull back the curtain on the sidelight door windows, Mona had cinched its middle with a curtain tieback. *So much for hiding in the shadows.*

She tried to focus with what light she was afforded. The person on the step was slight and looked no more than ten. *What the hell?*

If she remembered correctly, even though the neighbourhood was block-parented, Mona was not a block-parent volunteer. Why had this child chosen a house with no sign, rather than the next house, which she knew constantly displayed their block-parent sign?

Now she stuttered between which hat to wear. *Is this child just a decoy for someone more sinister lurking nearby? Or is he really in need of help?*

His knock sounded again, and she wondered about the strength —or lack thereof—of the knock. She had known children in her life, and a child of half his age could have knocked much harder.

Keeping her hats at the ready, she slipped into doting grandmother as she opened the door. "Hello?"

"Hi, I'm Tony, and I don't know where I am or where I'm going."

"Oh," she said, slipping small spectacles onto the tip of her nose and sizing the boy up.

His tousled head of black hair looked dirty, and his ears were too big for his tiny head, but his eyes were a brilliant shade of baby blue.

Well," she said in as soothing a voice as she could muster. "That is a very peculiar predicament you find yourself in, isn't it?"

"I'm Tony," he said again.

"Yes, you said as much." She stepped aside. "Come inside, Tony, and I can tell you where you are and try to figure out where you're supposed to be going."

22: More than guilty

Jean-Michel Blais

Despite the cocktail of antibiotics, pain killers, and sleep aids, combined with utter exhaustion, rest eluded Rob. It wasn't the pain as much as it was the repetitive worry, a deep-rooted concern about his future—a future that was as close as the now.

The almost-rhythmic worries about his love for Liz and their yet-to-be-born child, his role as the heir-apparent to a mafia family, his lost leg and his work looking for a lithium replacement played and replayed continually in his head. All with the backdrop of a worldwide pandemic.

In his fatigued state, he began to think dark thoughts about himself, about who he was and what he had stood for. He started doubting all that he had done, seeing himself as being nothing but a fraud, a cripple who couldn't take care of himself, let alone a family and a business.

Just two weeks ago he had been running carelessly in the countryside, contemplating how he was going to change the world and his life with a new technology; now he couldn't even change his own pants without help.

He looked over at Liz, sleeping quietly beside him, Booker and Fancy curled up beside her head. He shook his head, thinking how odd the scene was. But then his anxieties came roaring back. *If anyone is odd here, it's me—I'm the one to blame for all this mess. Damn! I feel so guilty. More than guilty: it's all my stupid fault and I have to solve this, somehow, someway!*

Voices coming from the front room of the house interrupted Rob's pity-rave. Since he couldn't sleep anyways, he decided to get up. He grabbed his crutches and hobbled towards the door, where he could distinguish Cora's voice but didn't recognize what he thought was a young woman's voice.

~

"So, Tony, where are your folks?" Cora inquired gently. She was still wearing her Miss Fisher hat, ready to change it for her caring grandmother's hat at a moment's notice.

"They're both dead. And his name's not Tony. It's Shelly. Shelly Bernetti," Rob said as he suddenly appeared in the hallway, teetering back and forth on his crutches, he was so weak. "He's my cousin's son. Or rather, my second cousin who was his...sperminator. The only things he ever gave Shelly were some DNA and a lot of grief."

Looking at the boy, Rob's demeanour and vigour changed on a dime, becoming aggressive. "So who sent you? How did you conveniently happen to arrive here on our doorstep?" He reached out to grab Shelly.

Cora was stunned, initially because of Rob's drained and sudden appearance, then by his familial knowledge of her young surprise guest and finally by his aggressive questioning. She wasn't having it. She instantly switched to her momma bear hat.

"Robert, you will calm down this very instant!" she commanded. "I remind you that, like Tony, er Shelly, here, you're a guest in this home."

Both Rob and Cora quickly recovered their respective composures. On came the caring grandmother's hat. "Rob, dear, sit down before you fall down."

Wearily, Rob tumbled into a large chair, grimacing as his amputated leg flopped under the weight of his movement. He glanced around, noticing the side table with a cup of tea and an old novel, briefly smiling to himself as he remembered having read it in grade 8 English class. He recalled how it centred around the homicidal manipulations of someone known as 'the Colonel'. *I guess those types have always been part of the landscape*, Rob thought to himself.

"Now," Cora said. "I am confused. Can you explain to me what's happening here?"

Before Rob could speak, the front door banged open. A shadow grew in the hall as someone came toward the bedroom door, and then filled it.

It was Popa, dishevelled and clearly agitated, his good fist clenched. He looked at Rob. "You, me, we gotta talk!"

~

Cindy woke up in a darkened room. Through her drugged haze, she looked at her surroundings as they slowly came into focus.

The room was furnished with a single bed, a table, and a chair. Her backpack was on the table.

Cindy took stock of herself: she was fully dressed, her shoes still on, but her hands and legs were bound with duct tape to the bed frame.

She tried to reconstruct what she had been through. She remembered driving up to the cottage, being shot at, her car stopping dead, the car door opening and some powerful hulk-like man hauling her up to the house. And seeing Professor Gin's lifeless body behind some strange woman. *And then they found my identification badge!* Her last memories were of being placed in the back of a car.

Somewhere outside her room, she could hear sounds: a floor creaking, followed by a not-so-subtle thud and then a... struggle. The sounds approached her door, then suddenly ceased. Cindy tugged in vain against her bonds.

The door opened, and Cindy recognized the woman standing there. "You're that doctor, or pretend doctor, or whoever who got me out of the hospital!"

"Yes," Robecca said in hushed tones. "This is becoming a bit of a habit for us, isn't it? We must be quiet. I was able to get rid of the two watching over you, but I don't know where Katenka is."

"What or *who* is Katenka?" Cindy stammered.

"Come now..." Robecca whispered as she undid Cindy's restraints, "you can't tell me that, as a CIA agent, you've never heard of the Bratva, the Russian Mafia? They control most of the liquid natural gas market on the North American east coast through a series of legitimate enterprises. You met their boss yesterday. *That* was Katenka."

"Ohhhh, *that's* Katenka." Cindy remembered having read something about her in a recent intelligence brief.

Suddenly, breaking out of her reverie, she blurted, "Wait, how the hell do you know who I am and why are you helping me again?"

"I'll explain later. Right now, we must get out of here. Bring your stuff." Robecca finished undoing Cindy's taped legs and guided her out the room into a short passage, where they gingerly walked over the bodies of the two hulks—now just bulks—she had run into at Professor Gin's cottage.

They left the small home and headed quickly on foot for about ten minutes; ten long gruelling minutes for Cindy as the effects of the knock-out drug were slowly wearing off. When they came into a clearing, Robecca pulled out a key fob and pressed the button to unlock a red SUV that was parked just off a dirt road. "Get in. Once we're on our way, I'll explain everything."

~

"Let me get this right. You're saying that I gotta make a choice between being the next family Don or being dead? That's not much of a choice, really," Rob deadpanned.

"Actually, you don't have a choice. It's either kill or be killed. This isn't some role-playing online game you're in. You only have one life, and yours is hanging in the balance," Popa retorted, becoming somewhat flustered himself.

He continued, "You see this arm? This lifeless limb. I used to play football at Acadia. And I was good. I was a power lifter who could bench press 350 for reps, a grunt who could take on anyone and anything. Then I started working for Allison. She appreciated my... talents. One day, I didn't quite finish a job. Allison didn't want me to forget my failure and had two thugs break my arm in two places. My arm never healed. And I learned my lesson: That I'll never trust Allison. She's capable of anything. What she wants, she gets. She wants to run the family. And she wants you dead! And me probably, as well."

Popa looked exhausted from the explanation, a lifetime of pain and disappointment wrapped up in his face at that moment, looking forlornly at what could have been. His head down, he slowly, methodically, raised his eyes to look at Rob. "I feel useless, just like a cripple and I don't want my sister and her kid to suffer because of me, or because of you."

These last words struck a chord deep inside Rob. His mind began to race as he put everything together. He knew what he had to do. But first, they both had calls to make.

~

Cindy was feeling better the further they got away from wherever she had been held. She noticed the name of the route they were travelling on: Virginia Road. She saw a sign that indicated some small place almost no buildings called Princedale. She had no idea where either of these places were; she was just relieved that she was alive and maybe moving away from danger. *But who is this faux doctor who's driving*?

She checked her backpack. No ID badge, no wallet, no gun. *Dammit!* But her cell phone was there, albeit with the battery ripped out. *The hulks must have done that, not wanting me to be traced*.

After a few minutes of trying, she was able to put the battery back in solidly enough to make the phone start up.

Immediately there was a call. It was Rob!

"Boy, am I ever glad to hear your voice, Rob!" Cindy gleefully sang into the phone.

Robecca momentary swerved as she reacted to hearing her son's name.

Ignoring Cindy's greeting, Rob said, "We have to talk. I've got a plan and I need your help."

~

Allison was not overly happy to see Popa's number on her phone. Their last time together hadn't been very cordial, and she didn't take kindly to threats from underlings. A subordinate who was threatening was no longer loyal but dangerous. Such a threat needed to be eliminated.

"Well, what do you want?" Allison's tone was laced with enmity.

Popa began, "I wanted to call and say that I was wrong. I shouldn't have, well, tried to go over your head like that. I want to make a deal."

"I'm listening..." Allison said.

"You leave Liz and Rob alone, let them live their lives quietly without any interference from you."

"And what do I get in return?" she asked dryly.

"You become the undisputed head of the family and all my recordings get deleted. And I continue working for you."

It was the last concession that pleased Allison the most. She appreciated loyalty from her underlings, but what she really wanted was total subservience; especially from Popa. This would be yet another opportunity to teach him a lesson.

"Agreed. But you have to get them out of my sight for good. And if Rob ever tries to lay claim to any advantage from the family, I'll kill him. Then I'll kill you."

"Understood. Meet us at the Halls Harbour Wharf at 7 tonight. I have a lobster boat ready to take them across the Bay of Fundy to Maine. I'll take them personally. Then I'll come back, and I'll erase all my recordings in front of you." Popa sounded servile.

Allison approved of his change in attitude. "That's acceptable. But I won't be alone."

Allison ended the call and immediately dialed another number.

~

"Rob, what's happening? Where are you?" Cindy asked.

"I'm fine. We're all fine. But we're leaving Nova Scotia for good. We can't stay here, and I won't become the next family Don."

"Then you're abdicating to Allison?" Cindy couldn't believe what she was hearing.

"No. I'm leaving that to you."

A long pause ensued. Cindy didn't know what to say. Finally, she stammered, "I, I don't want that!"

"Frankly, I don't care what you want. I have to think of myself and my new family first. Either you become the next head of the family or..."—here Rob weighed his words—"I disclose to the world exactly who you are."

"What? That I work for the CIA and that I was tasked with watching your back and protecting Tidal Bay Solutions? Old news!" Cindy shot back. "It seems everyone knows that around here." She glanced at Robecca, who was intently driving, pretending not to listen.

"I'm not talking about the CIA. I'm talking about your other affiliations and allegiances. You're not as innocent or as righteous as you pretend to be. And I have the evidence to prove it, thanks to my father's deathbed confession, his *recorded* deathbed confession. I don't care if you don't want to become the next head of the family. Your choice is simple: live as the family head with all its advantages and trappings, or live your life on the run."

Cindy's mind was racing. Her past had finally caught up to her.

It was a long moment before she said, "OK, Rob, what do I need to do?"

"Listen very carefully..."

~

The Halls Harbour wharf was dead quiet. Normally, at this time of year when the tide was high, it would be full of people fishing for mackerel and pollock along its 150-foot length. However, since COVID, people didn't go out at all, even if their chances of infection were minimal on such a wet, late September evening.

Allison pulled into the wharf's parking lot to find three vehicles already there. She noticed a man standing beside a large, black SUV. *No doubt Katenka's bodyguard,* Allison noted to herself.

She scanned the area for friend and foe. She recognized Rob, standing with his crutches and half leg. She also saw Liz and Popa. There was an old lady and a young boy she didn't recognize. *Shit, he brought the whole damn family for the last goodbye.*

Allison then noticed Katenka. They had never met in person, although they had communicated by phone regularly, as recently as that afternoon. *Finally, the infamous Katenka! This should be fun.*

She parked her car and got out, walking straight up to Rob. "You know what this means. Safe passage guaranteed, provided you stay underground forever, just like your father. If you dare speak to anyone, the cops, media types or any politicos, I promise you I'll personally hunt you down like an animal. The same goes for grandma and junior here," she added, pointing to Cora and Shelly. "Now get going!"

Katenka nodded. "*Da*, say your goodbyes. Make it *qvick*, it's getting dark."

Rob looked briefly at the calm ocean in front of them, barely catching a glimpse of a small vessel in the distance. He knew he had to stall a bit and buy some time. He slowly took a deep breath and hobbled painfully towards Shelly.

Rob took an Altoids tin from his jacket pocket and gave it to the boy. In a hushed tone that only Shelly, Cora and Liz could hear, he said, "Take this and go with Cora. She'll take care of you. She knows some important things that'll help you use what's here. With her knowledge and your energy, you're going to change the world. One day you'll understand all this. But that day's not today."

He gave Shelly a long hug, patted him on the head and turned the boy around, gently guiding him towards Cora, who had tears in her eyes. Cora took Shelly's hand and led him to her car.

Liz looked longingly on the touching scene, convinced now more than ever that despite their predicament, the future for her, Rob and their child looked very bright, indeed.

Allison impatiently looked over at Popa. "Come on, let's get this show on the road. And remember, as soon as you get him over to the other side, come right back. We've got some business to do."

With Cora's car out of sight, Popa helped Rob move along the wharf to where he could climb into the lone fishing vessel. The other boat was drawing closer slowly, but maybe too slowly.

Even though the tide was high, going down the ladder seemed to be a particularly painful process for Rob. He got slower with each step.

Liz followed with Booker and Fancy securely in her backpack, their curious faces visible in the unzipped top, intently watching the events unfold. Popa started the engine and cast off the boat. It lumbered towards open water, leaving the two women standing on the edge of the wharf.

The vessel was soon enveloped in darkness. Katenka flipped her wrist, illuminating her smartwatch. "Is time."

Allison grunted. "Yes, it finally is."

She pulled out her smartphone, punched in her password and accessed an app. She looked up at the water, at first frowning, then smiling wryly as she touched the app's red button.

A massive explosion ripped through the night out around where the vessel had been embraced by the darkness. A fireball surged above the water. Anyone and anything on board the vessel must have been instantly killed.

With her phone still in hand and as the thunder of the explosion subsided, Allison called a New York number and said, "It's done. The three of them are gone. This time for good. Let's get on with the...*coronation*." She liked the sound of that word.

Katenka, who was looking at the fiery scene without emotion, saw the total absence of feeling in Allison's face. She was impressed. *We are very much alike*, she thought. *Business is, after all, business.*

"So, *ve* are good, no? This lithium idea dies with them. *Ve* stay in our own areas, cause no trouble for each other now that there's no more competition. *Ve* must be ready for what is coming. The world is change *qvickly*."

Allison nodded. "Agreed, just as we negotiated. You Russians can keep on controlling the natural gas sector, while my family, of which I am now the head, controls all the oil on the Eastern seaboard. All free from any new meddling technology that could put us both out of business."

Katenka looked at Allison with a certain admiration. "*Ve* are one of a kind, us two. *Ve* could have been friends. Almost. I go now."

She walked towards the parking area and the rear passenger door of the SUV that her bodyguard was holding open, and got in.

Allison watched the Russian leave. She looked around, first at the smouldering wreck still visible on the water, then at her 'new' car that she had claimed from John Bernetti after she had him killed by that sucker cop.

She gloated at the irony of having eliminated both the car's former owner and her former driver. She was more than capable of driving herself for now until she got a new driver. *At least I have the use of both my arms and both my legs*, she chuckled to herself.

Content with her work for the day, Allison walked towards the driver's side of the black sedan. As she opened the door, she heard something rustle behind her.

Turning, she was stunned by the impact of the bullet as it struck the right side of her rib cage just below the armpit.

She looked up beseechingly at her assailant as her right lung began to collapse and her knees buckled. It took everything in her to blurt out the words before the second bullet hit her square in the forehead: "You bitch!"

23: One branch on the tree

MJ Foulks

July 9, 2021

They pursued me...killing my daughter Amie...

Of all you stupid kids, she was the only innocent one...the rest of you, you're all less than innocent...

Rob awoke just before the crack of dawn, still contemplating the swirling words in his mind. From the side of the room, he could hear scurrying of Booker and Fancy, rustling around slightly in their ever-open cage. His heart sank, as Booker and Fancy always had this strange ability to remind him of what he had seen, what he had done, what he had lost...

He pushed the dark thoughts away, pulled himself out of bed, buckled on his new prosthetic, and dressed for a run.

The pale light of early morning had begun to overtake the dark of night. He stretched and began his run, hearing all-too-familiar sounds of someone keeping pace just behind him. Rob didn't even bother to look back. *No such thing as privacy anymore*, he thought.

Just like every morning since the explosion, his mind tried its best to process everything, his family, the Muihtil...Liz...

Everything had changed the day Popa tried to blackmail Allison.

His early morning run was the only thing that helped clear his thoughts, and while his shoe and prosthetic took turns hitting the pavement, it was his family that occupied his mind.

I'd give anything...for more time...with you...

The father that he never knew, who tried with his dying breath to make right a wrong that wasn't his to right.

This is my fault...I never wanted you to get caught up in this...

The mother that he'd known all his life but never *really* knew, all for his own protection...a mother he had been enjoying getting to know better.

As Rob ran with relative ease, despite his lack of a leg, he thought of how she sacrificed everything to save him and his friends, to get them out of the family she never wanted to be part of. It certainly wasn't her fault, the ones she couldn't save...the ones *they* couldn't save...

He glanced down at the trail and caught sight of his sleek metal leg. It was brand new and top of the line, a giant spring bent back in the perfect position for running. His heart swelled at the sight of it, as it had been a gift from his dear mother.

"I'll have no son of mine give up over something as silly as a lost limb," she had said as he unwrapped it. "You're made of tougher stuff than that."

He remembered his mother taking him into her arms as he sobbed, feeling so out of control. "No matter what happens, you'll always have me," she had whispered. "Nothing in this world will take me from you again."

And she had been there, like a proper mother *and* doctor, to help him learn to use his sleek new blade that has replaced his lower leg. Rob knew that, without her expertise and guidance, he could never have run again. Yet here he was at his normal speed, taking an exhilarating breath as he felt the chilly air hit his face.

The footsteps tailing him, however, seemed to have slowed. Rob looked back to the familiar sight of a large man in a black suit with a dark pony tail, doubled over and heaving for breath.

Rob stopped, trotted back to the man and tugged on the pony tail. "Still can't keep up, eh? What's it been now, Jake, ten months since you were assigned here?"

Jake heaved for breath and swatted at Rob as if he were an annoying fly, but Rob started running literal circles around him.

"No wonder the other guys hate keeping an eye on you," Jake said as he elbowed Rob in the arm.

"Adam happens to be in tip-top shape," Rob said with a playful smile. "He should be on the morning shift for me, eh? Not much of a bodyguard if you can't keep up with a guy with one leg."

Jake laughed sarcastically, clapping Rob hard on the shoulder. "That joke never gets old. Really. I could hear it every morning for ten months and still—"

He held up one hand in a gesture of pause, and held the other to his clear earpiece. "Received loud and clear."

"What was that?"

"One of the perimeter guards," Jake said. "You have a visitor waiting for you in the boathouse. Care to take a golf cart?"

"No thanks," Rob said with a teasing smile. "I think I'll run."

He started for the boathouse, hearing Jake groan furiously before his footsteps could be heard in reluctant pursuit.

The boathouse was Rob's favourite part of their new property on Big Tancook Island, on account of its huge outdoor deck that looked on to the endless ocean before them. It was here, under the pale dawn light, that he found his visitor.

"Hey," he said lamely as he approached.

"Hey?" Cindy grinned as she pulled him into a hug. "That's all I get?"

"You were here just last month, so—"

"Yeah, but I didn't get to stay as long as I wanted."

"CIA keeping you busy?"

Cindy chuckled. "You know it."

They sat in comfortable silence for a moment, a rare moment of peace in their tumultuous lives.

"You know...I thought *you* shot Allison."

Cindy turned to look at him, but gave no response.

"Mom and I talked about it a few days ago. I'd always wanted to know, but looking back was just too--" his voice faded, as if his words were stuck in his throat.

He took a second to compose himself. "But Mom says she's the one who actually shot her."

Cindy blinked.

"You had your gun out and you guys were waiting in the shadows, but it was actually my mother that pulled the trigger."

Cindy smiled.

"Why?" Rob asked finally.

With a sigh, Cindy answered. "I think Robecca—"

"Maria," Rob corrected.

"What?"

"She.. wants to go by Maria again. You know..."

"Oh, right," Cindy lightly smacked herself in the forehead. "It's so hard to get into the habit. You told me I didn't have a choice. I needed to take over the family. But after I thought about it...I found another way out. If I took out Allison, Robecc—I mean *Maria*, would become head of the family, and I had her literally in the car next to me. She and I talked about it right after you and I hung up. I would kill Allison and Maria would—"

"Take the money and run?" Rob couldn't help but make the reference, since this is exactly what Maria had done.

Cindy laughed. "Exactly. So all that was left was to find Allison, which was made easy by a phone call from Popa. God, it was serendipity. He had called Maria shortly after she and I'd had a chance to come up with the plan. He told us *exactly* where to go to find Allison, and Robec—*Maria*—trusted him.

"Once we got there, I had my gun pulled and was ready to go. But right after the explosion, I think Maria just saw red. She grabbed my gun and just...shot Allison. She didn't even look to see if it was a fatal wound. I walked out of the bushes to find Allison with a hole in her chest, and Maria looked...almost sinister. Allison called her a bitch, then Maria shot her in the forehead."

"Go, Mom," Rob muttered, and Cindy chuckled.

"It's interesting, you know," she said with audible restraint. "I went back to headquarters after everything happened, to give a briefing on the Muihtil. When I did, people seemed to think that I'd personally brought down the Mancini Crime Family."

"And did you bother to correct their misunderstanding?"

"Well, there were so many of them at that point...it would've been impolite."

Rob snorted, then smiled. "Glad it's worked out for you, then."

Cindy sighed heavily. "They gave me a promotion. I'm supposed to lead the effort to 'solidify the dissolution of the Mancini family.' People report to me now. I have my own team."

"It feels like there's a 'but' coming."

"But we've hit a dead end," Cindy confided in a sober tone. "We've done everything we can. We've arrested a few people, but most of them have gone into hiding."

"Sucks," he shrugged.

"I need your help." Her voice was strong and steady, as if she were in the midst of a business transaction. "I didn't grow up on the inside like you did. You spent time with the Old Man, you know how he thought, how he ran his—"

"Your point?" Rob did not want to think about the Mancinis.

"The CIA wants to hire you for your expertise. We can't bring down the family without insider information."

Rob was about to mention that he and his mother weren't in the family anymore, but a realization suddenly hit him. "This is about Natalie."

"Not just her," Cindy said with flushed cheeks, "for everyone we've lost. Think about it, Rob. How many people have died because of this family? I'll admit, for me...this is for Natalie. But what about for you? So many people died...aren't any of them worth justice? Real justice?"

Rob's heart stung, and he felt so wounded he couldn't speak.

Cindy sighed with frustration and looked out to the ocean before them. After fidgeting impatiently for a second, she grabbed her phone from her pocket.

"I don't know if you remember Nickerson..."

"The RCMP guy? The one covering Nat's case?"

Cindy nodded. Tears began to well up in her eyes as she made swiping motions on the screen before handing it to Rob. It showed a lengthy text:

> *I wanted to thank you for you help with the Natasha Mayne case and give you an update. After the discovery of the bodies of John Mayne and Darcy Mayne, who was my partner, the investigation became more complicated and required more time. I can now confirm that Natasha was killed by her brother, John. John was then murdered by his father, Darcy, who killed himself immediately after, according to the coroner's report. Messy business with no clear motive, but with Natasha's murderer already dead, there's nothing more for us. Though it pains me to do so because of Darcy, we will be closing the case. I offer, again, my condolences.*

Silently, Rob handed back her phone. She took it, set it on the table, and watched with glazed eyes as the screen faded to black.

"It took him ten months to come up with that?" Rob finally said in a light voice, trying to cheer her up. "I could've told him that back in September!"

Even if he hadn't succeeded in cheering her up, he managed to force out a laugh.

"He's not the quickest Mountie, is he?" she retorted, but the gravity of what had happened seemed to pull her back down with lightning speed.

"There will be no justice for Natalie," she declared. "At least...not without your help."

Rob let out a deep sigh. "Cindy, John was killed by Nat's Dad because John killed Nat. Is that not enough justice for you?"

"No!" Cindy shouted. "It's not enough! *Why* was she killed? How did innocent Nat end up in that position? It all goes back to the family, and you know it. Can *you* tell me why Natalie? Can your Mom?"

"Come on, Cindy—"

"Do you even know your family?"

"...What?"

"Just...think about it." She tried to reclaim her cool. "You seem to think everyone in the family who had power is now dead."

"They are."

"But who else is out there? They weren't exactly open about family ties, were they? How many uncles or cousins or grand-uncles were kept away from us for some nefarious reason?"

Rob let out a mirthless laugh. "I'm assuming you know *exactly* how many."

"We have an idea. Our grandfather, Old Man Mancini...he wasn't an only child."

Rob's eyes grew wide.

"So far we've found seven other branches of the family, all descendants of our great-grandfather. Each one of these branches is headed by a brother, like our grandfather, each with a different last name."

"Like Bernetti," Rob said. "Or Mancini."

"Exactly. And get this: each one of these brothers is heading their own shady business empire. Drugs, insider trading, trafficking—"

"Trafficking?!" Rob rasped, though he could hardly say he felt disbelief.

Cindy nodded. "And each of these branches are seemingly blind to all the others. Whether that's by choice or manipulation...we don't know."

"Even though my mother dissolved our branch of the family—"

"You were merely one branch on the tree," Cindy concluded.

Her phone buzzed, and she looked at the message with a smile. "It's Maria. She saw my car and says she'll kill me if I don't come see her."

"Might wanna go visit, then, knowing her record," Rob joked.

Cindy pocketed her phone, then looked at Rob with a hint of pleading in her eyes. "Listen, you're all still in danger. Even if the other branches of the family never find you, Katenka is still out there and is still desperate to stop the Muihtil from becoming a viable product. You have enemies all around these fancy walls, and your mother's private security won't hold forever."

She gave him a kiss on the cheek. "Just think about it and get back to me, yeah?"

With that, she turned to the trail that led to the main house, patting Jake on the back as she passed.

Before Rob had much of a chance to process the conversation, Popa lumbered down the trail toward him.

"You're up early," Rob observed. He gestured for Popa to have a seat beside him, but Popa didn't move.

"What's the matter, Dom? Too tough to relax?"

"You call me 'Popa,' not 'Dom' or 'Dominic,'" he grunted. Rob was starting to think that everyone was going to abandon their 'family' names.

"The Mancini family takes good people, *desperate* people...They hire them, chew them up and spit them out. And if they survive the encounter, those good people turn into monsters."

Popa's words, especially without any sort of pretext, thickened the already tense air. "I heard what Cindy—"

"How the hell did—? Were you hiding in the boathouse?"

"Take the job, Rob," Popa said. "Stop the suffering. No more deaths. No more monsters."

Rob and Popa stared at each other in tense silence, until the buzzing sound of Rob's phone jarred them both.

He dug it out and saw the banner message from "her." With a smile, he unlocked his phone as Popa leaned in uncomfortably to look.

IT ONLY WORKS IF YOU TURN IT ON, ROB.

Rob grinned from ear to ear, then pulled a white monitor from his pocket and turned the dial. With a click, the sweet cries of a baby floated from the monitor, followed by a soothing voice.

"There there, Henry. Mommy's here..."

"Liz is with him," Rob stated needlessly.

"Getting salty since having the baby, isn't she?" Popa said with a little smile.

"Either that or surviving an explosion."

"Two of them," Popa said.

"Yeah," Rob laughed. "Good thing you were onto Allison with the second one."

"She got desperate. Sloppy. Even Liz's rats could have figured out her plan."

"To be fair, they're pretty smart rats," Rob chuckled, then grinned foolishly at a resurfacing memory. "I'll never forget the look on Liz's face when I yeeted her into the water that day."

"I'm glad that humours you, my baby sister nearly dying..."

"Ah, she was never in any real danger with you on the case and my backup boat closing in," he said. "And lighten up, Uncle Popa. We made it, didn't we?"

~

Rob made his way into the main living space, where nearly everyone gathered most of the time.

And "everyone" was no small number of people.

Cora sat in a squashy recliner making a sweet jacket for the baby, a sage colour with little blue buttons. To Rob's surprise, Booker the rat kept handing the buttons to Cora, and Cora was actually thanking him with each button that she received.

Shelly sat in the floor with puffy headphones over his ears, a set of joy cons in his hands, and his favourite video game, one of the Zeldas, displaying on the big TV in front of him.

At this rate, he's going to get the master sword before me, Rob thought. He felt a pang of guilt when he looked at Shelly, and vowed to spend more time with the poor kid, even if it were just over Zelda.

Fancy the rat, for no discernible reason, was making a ruckus in the liquor cabinet.

Maria was sitting on the couch, happily watching Link fight the bad guys on the big screen. Cindy sat beside her, their arms intertwined. The sight of them together made Rob's heart swell. *They deserve family,* he thought. *We all do.*

Mona sat at a nearby table reading *The Berenson Bulletin,* the delivery of which was something Cindy had arranged to help with her loneliness after Doug's passing.

But what had helped more than anything was the tiny human

being Liz was carrying around, the one named after both of her husband's lives: the life he had that begat Rob, and the life he shared with her.

"Henry Douglas Williams," Rob said aloud as Liz gently passed the fussy baby into his arms while Mona looked on with pure love. "Did you miss me?"

"He needs a bottle," Liz murmured before making her way to the open kitchen just off the living space. As she passed, Fancy fell out of the liquor cabinet along with their half-consumed bottle of gin.

"You silly thing," she said. She put the bottle back in the cabinet, scooped up Fancy and placed her on her shoulder while she fiddled with a bottle.

As she waited for the bottle to warm, Fancy kept trying to get down.

"Alright, alright," she finally conceded and put Fancy back on the floor. The rat immediately went for the liquor cabinet again.

Liz looked to the closed cabinet, then at Booker, who was still helping Cora. "Hey Rob," she said as she handed him the bottle and sat beside him on the couch. "Do you think we could change the name of the lithium replacement? Muihtil is such a clumsy name."

"If you'd like," he said in a baby voice while positioning Henry for his bottle. "What did you have in mind?"

"Dimitrium," she said without thinking about it. "In honour of Professor Buttons."

Henry's tiny cries stopped, replaced with the soft sound of him sucking on his bottle.

Rob took the opportunity to look at his beautiful Liz. How grateful he was for her...how lucky he was that she was alive...how he would do anything for her...

Out of the corner of his eye, he saw Cindy look at him with an air of defeat, as if she had sensed an answer to her earlier offer.

Taking a note from Cora, he put on his 'CEO of Tidal Bay Solutions' hat before grinning at Liz.

"Dimitrium it is."

The end

The making of the book

In early 2022, I was casting about for a project that would help Moose House authors, isolated under the necessary restrictions related to the COVID-19 epidemic, feel more connected. I wanted something that would engage a group of writers in *writing*, which, d'oh, is what we do. We already had a short-story anthology in the works, but I was looking for something with a different sizzle.

This problem was rattling around in my mind while I should have been paying attention to the conversation in an online meeting at my other job with the Apache Software Foundation. We were discussing a problem that turned out to be less serious than we had first thought.

Andrew Wetmore 9:54 AM
that sounds a lot less toxic

gstein 9:54 AM
yeup. I don't even put that into the "innocent mistake" column.

it's somewhere over near collateral damage

Andrew Wetmore 9:55 AM
"Less Than Innocent": coming to a theater near you

gstein 9:55 AM

And the idea for this book appeared in my head. I therefore consider Greg Stein, the head of the Foundation's Infrastructure team, as its literary godparent.

Now I had the title, at least. I wrote to the forty writers whom Moose House had published to that point, to invite them to join me in writing a 'progressive novel' (like a progressive supper):

- The first writer would create chapter 1 and then pass it to the second writer.
- The second writer would write chapter 2 and send chapters 1 and 2 to the third writer.
- ...and so on until we reached the end of the book.
- There would be no story outline prepared in advance. Each writer would use the 'yes, and' principle of improvisation theatre, accepting everything already written and trying to build on that. We would let the story tell us where it wanted to go.

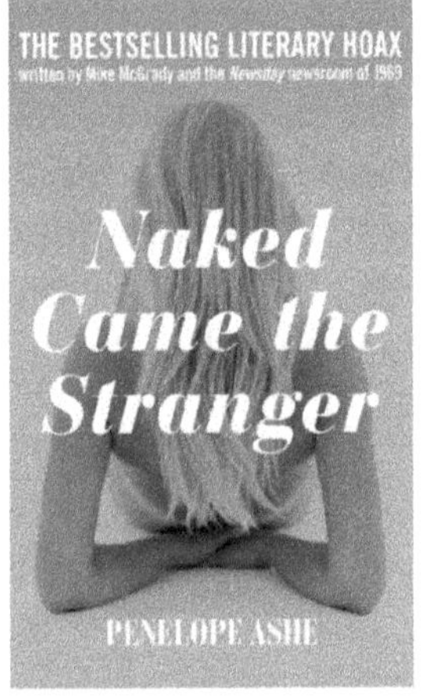

Crazy idea, but not without precedent. In the 1930s in England, a group of prominent mystery writers used the same plan to create several novels, including *The Floating Admiral*. In the 1960s in the United States, a team of journalists co-wrote the spoof erotic novel, *Naked Came the Stranger*, that was a bestseller and the basis for a movie.

Twenty of our writers indicated they would like to take part in this adventure. I set a very few additional guidelines (the story takes place during the COVID lockdown in 2020, each chapter should be about 3,000 words, each writer would have one week to write their chapter, and so on), and then I wrote the first chapter.

We created a 'story bible' to track details ranging from characters' hair colour to who was related to whom, and highlighting what interesting threads were dangling in the text that the next writer might want to use. I updated the story bible as each new chapter came in.

I started writing chapter 1 on January 31, 2022. MJ Foulks turned in the final chapter on July 17. A couple of authors had to leave the project due to other commitments, so MJ, Rhoda Hill, and

I ended up writing two chapters each.

I believe that for most of us the experience was a combination of a fun parlour game and a terrifying, blindfolded ride on a toboggan down a forested hill. We hope you, gentle reader, find it more of the former and less of the latter.

We rooted for our favourite characters, experienced shock or delight when they turned out to be not as we had thought, and grieved when some of them became terminally unavailable. There is even talk of spin-off stories about the earlier adventures of Gin Buttons and some of the other characters.

When I wrote chapter 1, I had a certain type of adventure in mind. Almost nothing of what I had thought would happen came to pass. All in all, though, I think the book you hold in your hands is better, wilder, and more fun than the one I would have come up with, writing all by myself.

I also cannot think of a smarter, braver, more engaged crew of co-authors than the 'innocents', as we came to call ourselves.

Andrew Wetmore
Moose House Publications
November, 2022

The authors

Jean-Michel Blais spent 31 years in policing as a senior executive with the Royal Canadian Mounted Police and the United Nations, and as chief of Halifax Regional Police. He has worked throughout Canada and was posted in four different provinces. He spent almost two years in Haiti, working as a frontline police officer and senior executive.

Moose House published his first book, *Working the Blue Lines: Lessons in Leadership from Hockey and Policing*, in 2022.

Carol Ann Cole is a best selling author and a member of The Order of Canada. She is the founder of the Comfort Heart Initiative that has raised more than $1.5 million for the Canadian Cancer Society.

In the summer of 2022 Carol Ann introduced *Paradise d'Entremont Private Investigator*, her fourth fiction in *The Paradise Series*, and available from Moose House. Carol Ann is making revisions to books one and two (*Paradise* & *Paradise 548*) as well as the fifth instalment in the Paradise Series, due for release in the summer of 2023.

Carol Ann is also working on her fifth non-fiction book: *The Cole Connection and Moving Home*, due for publication by Moose House in 2023.

Wayne Currie is a retired naval officer living in the Annapolis Royal area. Upon retirement, he took to acting in live theatre, directing live theatre and playwriting. As well, he is involved in the music scene as a percussionist, and as a singer in a sea shanty *a capella* group. He also does forced labour for his wife in their extensive gardens and, when time permits, he golfs.

Moose House published Wayne's *A Dash of Currie*, a collection of 17 of his ten-minute plays.

Angel Flanagan lives beside Saint Mary's Bay, Nova Scotia with her husband, two sons, and three cats.

Flanagan's work has been published in T*he Chronicle Herald, Le Courrier de la Nouvelle Ecosse, Xalt Magazine, Coastal Life Magazine, The Lobster Bay Shopper* and *The Clare Shopper.* One of her short stories appears in *Moose House Stories Volume 1.*

Moose House published her first novel, *Lost and Found*, in 2021.

Flanagan's author website is **angelflanagan.com**.

From Hampton Roads, VA in the United States, **MJ Foulks** lives immersed in ideas: ideas about the world, the power of stories, and the magic that can only be found in your imagination. Her heart and passion belong to her fantasy series, *Legends of Akelian*, a world she has been weaving for over 20 years. Beyond the stories, she is a mother, a wife, and a beloved friend.

Rhoda C. Hill writes a broad array of fiction that spans several genres. Her writing has appeared in *The First Line*, and she was a finalist in Harlequin's Killer Voice contest in 2014. Two of her short stories appear in *Moose House Stories, Volume 1*, and Moose House published her first novel in the *Love Shack* series, *Loving Number Seven*. She is hard at work on the next books in the series.

Rhoda lives in Doucetteville, Nova Scotia with her husband, three children, and five furbabies. She is on Facebook (rhodaswritingpage) and Twitter (@Creaeh).

Grace Keating grew up in the small university town of Antigonish, smack at the tail end of a large family and a long line of story-tellers. She has spent most of her adult life on the west coast, working in the costume department for film and television. Recently retired, she hopes to devote more of her time to writing.

Grace's short stories have won several awards and have been published across North America and in the UK. Her work appears in Volumes 1 and 2 of *Moose House Stories.*

Garry Leeson is an award-winning author, playwright, auctioneer, and by times, logger and farmer. His works have appeared in periodicals in Canada and USA; his plays have had productions in Kentville and Lunenburg and CBC Radio has showcased his short stories. He was long-listed for CBC Writes in the Creative Nonfiction category in 2012. He was a recipient of an Arts Nova Scotia grant and in 2020 received the The Margaret and John Savage First Book Award for Non-Fiction for his book, *The Dome Chronicles.*

Moose House published his first novel, *The Secret of the Spring,* in 2021, and will release the sequel, *Dan Johnson's Ashes,* in 2022 Garry lives with his wife, Andrea, and a menagerie of animals, in the community of Harmony in the Annapolis Valley.

Kerri Leier is a teacher and theatre creator from the Annapolis Valley, where she lives with her two children, her partner, and her cat familiars.

She is currently working on a novel, *Life Lessons from a Fashionably Feral Female,* inspired by her late grandmother, and shopping around for a songwriter to pen the music of her latest musical.

Pam Calabrese MacLean's writing for the stage includes *Her Father's Barn,* 'Is it Wednesday?' and 'Awake', all included in her collection *Sofa: plays for strong, older, female actors who want to get off the couch!* MacLean is also the author of two poetry books and two children's books. This is her very first novel. She lives in Nova Scotia.

Author and journalist **Carol Moreira** can't stay in one place but is currently based in beautiful Nova Scotia. She is the author of the YA novel *Riptides* (Moose House Publications 2021), the YA fantasy *Membrane* (Fierce Ink Press, 2013) and the YA contemporary novel Charged (James Lorimer 2008). She is a contributor to the immigration anthology *Coming Here, Being Here* (Guernica Editions, 2016) and is a partner in both entrevestor.com, an innovation news site, and the soon-to-be-launched BlueTechToday, an oceans-themed publication.

Moose House will re-publish *Membrane*, and will publish Carol's adult fantasy, *Glow*, both in 2023.

Marie Mossman grasped the *Less Than Innocent* pandemic writing adventure at first call-out because the cooperative project offered socially-distanced interaction with human beings. She is the author of *A Rebel for Her Time*, a novel about the experiences of Della, an independent Nova Scotian who nursed in Europe during World War I, which Moose House published. Mossman's "Wormhole", appears in Moose House's second short-story anthology, *Blink and You'll Miss It*.

Mossman's second novel will explore the challenges and romances of Maud after she returns to Nova Scotia, set free of Della's guidance.

Carolyn Jean Nicholson worked in the health care field, teaching in post-secondary education, and ministry in The United Church of Canada. She followed in her mother's footsteps in researching her Nova Scotia ancestors, resulting in her first book, *William Forsyth: Land of Hopes and Dreams.* Moose House will be publishing her second book, *Traitors, Cannibals, Highlanders, and Vikings*, in 2023. One of her short stories appears in *Blink and You'll Miss It*.

Ronan O'Driscoll, originally from the West of Ireland, lived in Chicago, Dublin and Japan before settling in Dartmouth, Nova Scotia with his wife and children. A software developer and educator, he has always enjoyed writing. His first novel, *Chief O'Neill*, pays homage to his love of history and traditional Irish music.

His casual discovery of unmarked graves from a 19th-century "Poor Farm for the Harmlessly Insane" in Cole Harbour sparked his interest and research for the novel *Poor Farm*, which Moose House published in 2021.

After graduating high school, **Thibault Jacquot-Paratte** left his native Annapolis Valley, first to do a work term in translations in Cameroon, then to live in a van all around North America, then to do a Bachelor's and Master's of Nordic Studies at the Sorbonne before returning to Nova Scotia and the valley in 2018.

His first three plays came out in 2016-2017, followed by his collected verse, *Cries of somewhere's soil* (2020); a miscellany, *Souvenirs et fragments;* and the novel *A dream is a notion of* (2022).

Dozens of his short stories and poems have appeared in journals and anthologies, including *Moose House Stories*, Volumes 1 and 2.

He recently co-edited a charity anthology for Ukraine, *Il y a des bombes qui tombent sur Kyiv* (2022). He writes in both English and French, plays music, tells jokes both good and bad, and likes to spend time with his wife and their daughter.

A native Haligonian and King's Bachelor of Journalism graduate, **Mark Shupe** gave up a career as a sports writer to write edgy and tightly worded audit reports for a gi-normous corporation. Temporarily living in Calgary, he has walked some 9000 km of Cowtown's streets. When he has walked the final Calgary street, it will be time to settle the oceanfront land he owns in Shelburne with the famous writer Lana Shupe. Mark owns 29,481 comic books, has run 17 marathons and is shorter than his three children.

Moose House will publish his novel *The Wish Doctor* in 2023. His blog, adventuresofshuperman.com, is live now.

P. E. R. Sprague was raised in New Brunswick and now lives in Nova Scotia. He has loved stories for as long as he can remember. Ever since he was able to put pen to paper he has tried to come up with characters and settings to immerse himself in. This is P.E.R. Sprague's second published work (the other appears in *Moose House Stories Volume 1*). He intends to continue writing and honing his craft.

Kate Tompkins lived in the Northwest Territories for 35 years before shifting her allegiances to Nova Scotia. Her career has focused mostly on crisis intervention, trauma therapy, adult education, workshops in leadership, management and communication skills, and program evaluation research.

Kate's writing before adopting the Maritimes had been mostly stuffy business reports. After creating a children's novel about the north for practice, she wrote her first non-fiction book, *The Non-Therapist: how to help as if you were a pro (or even more so!)*. Moose House is publishing it in the fall of 2022.

Kate directs the Guysborough Players, a musical theatre troupe, and enjoys sailing, renovating her 165 year-old house and murdering the gout weed colony in her garden.

Andrew Wetmore is Editor at Moose House Publications and at The Apache Software Foundation. Three of his collections of short plays are available from Moose House. He coordinated the *Less Than Innocent* project.

Given that **Gordon Wetmore** and *Ellery Queen's Mystery Magazine* both came into existence in October of 1941, it's no wonder that writing a chapter for *Less Than Innocent*, with its murders, mayhem and malice, was a dream come true.

Born and raised in Annapolis Royal, he began a teaching career there that took him to Nunavut, British Columbia and Quebec, where he has lived with his wife Carol (Kemp) since the early '70s. Besides teaching, he has had stints on several newspapers and is the education editor and senior writer with *Community Connections*, a bi-monthly magazine written and published by volunteers.

One of Gordon's short stories appeared in *Moose House Stories, Volume 1*.

CPSIA information can be obtained
at www.ICGtesting.com
Printed in the USA
BVHW050233231222
654878BV00006B/72